MURRIETA GOLD

BY WILLIAM NIKKEL

SUSPENSE PUBLISHING

OTHER BOOKS BY WILLIAM NIKKEL

Jack Ferrell Series
NIGHT MARCHERS
CAVE DWELLER
GLIMMER OF GOLD

Max Traver Series
DEVIL WIND

MURRIETA GOLD
By
William Nikkel

PAPERBACK EDITION

* * * * *

PUBLISHED BY:
Suspense Publishing

Copyright 2012 by William Nikkel

Cover Design: Shannon Raab
Cover Photographer: iStockphoto.com/gmutlu

PUBLISHING HISTORY:
JMS Books, LLC., Print and Digital Copy, 2012
Suspense Publishing, Print and Digital Copy, August, 2014

ISBN-13: 978-0692275825 (Suspense Publishing)
ISBN-10: 0692275827

*For my brother Ray and his wonderful quirky
contributions to this story.
And to the memory of our brother Robert,
who would have been there with Jack had it been
possible. But then maybe he was.
And as always, for my wife Karen who has stuck by
me,
and my mother Shirley for her unconditional love.*

PRAISE FOR WILLIAM NIKKEL

"Nikkel's solid character development and strong storyline keep the book moving at a fast clip. His law enforcement background in patrol, SWAT and homicide add grit to his tales. Throw in some local history, a love interest and lots of action, and you have a winner in "Murrieta Gold.""

—Michael Russo, co-owner of Russo's Books at
The Marketplace

"Part mystery, part ghost story, and all high-seas adventure, William Nikkel's "Night Marchers" is a thrilling novel that mixes modern piracy with Hawaiian history and mysticism. A debut not to be missed!"

—James Rollins, *New York Times* bestselling
author of "Blood Line"

"I must say that William Nikkel knows how to draw you into his story and hold you there.... In many ways Nikkel is like a latter-day Jules Verne, having written a thoroughly enjoyable adventure tale that follows a band of scientists from sunlit coral reefs to the subterranean depths of remote coastal mountains to remarkable discoveries fraught with high danger.... And above all that, this is a thriller with a message—and one as old as the cave-dwellers."

—Gary Braver, bestselling author of "Tunnel
Vision"

MURRIETA GOLD

BY WILLIAM NIKKEL

CHAPTER 1

"Killing someone is easy," the man said. "And there are ways to do it and not get caught."

"What's one of the ways?" Hector asked. He exchanged an anxious glance with his brother.

"Yeah," Kyle agreed. "I ain't never wanted to go to no jail for killing someone and end up some tattooed gorilla's girlfriend."

"The surest way," the man said, "is to keep your mouth shut."

He wasn't surprised Hector asked the question. The idiot considered himself to be smarter than his brother Kyle. But they both had the same dumb look. And an all too annoying propensity for foolishness.

The stupid sonofabitches.

They were lucky they grew the best dope.

The man fought back the urge to shoot them dead and be done with it.

Still, if something did go wrong, it'd be because of these jokers.

And that thought galled him. No one jeopardized even a dollar of his money and stayed alive, let alone a couple million.

Still, the twins were an acceptable risk, for now. The crop they had growing showed to be prime bud. That was the bottom line.

But they'd better do what they were told.

"What would another way be?" Hector asked.

The man's eyes narrowed to an icy glare.

"You bury the body deep," he said. "And you bury the damned thing somewhere it's going to stay buried."

Hector slapped Kyle on the back and laughed.

The man failed to see the humor.

"You remember the guy's body that old lady's dog dug up in that vacant lot over in Stockton?" Hector said to Kyle. "Carried the head into her house through the doggie door and started chewing on it right there in front of the woman's church group."

Kyle's lips spread into a grin that showed his half-dozen missing teeth. He chuckled and added, "I bet the lady shit her pants, too."

The man scowled at the twins. "It doesn't matter what that old woman did. What's important is that if someone stumbles into this field of dope, they don't live to talk about it."

"You mean you want us to kill anybody who comes snooping around here?" Again, it was Hector asking the question.

Jesus.

The man wanted to reach out and strangle them both. He might yet.

"Kill 'em!" he said. "Bury the body deep, and keep your God-damned mouths shut tight." He reached out his massive hands, grabbed each brother by the meat above the collarbone, and squeezed.

He watched their knees buckle. A small satisfaction.

He said, "Now don't screw up."

Hector's face twisted into a knot of pain. But he hadn't quite yet gone to the ground on his knees.

With obvious difficulty, he peered up at the man and said, "Don't worry about the dope. We'll take care of anyone who comes sniffin' around here sticking their big nose where they shouldn't."

"You'd better," the man said. He tightened his grip, forcing Hector onto his knees next to his brother. And then he gave their pinched skin a twist, adding an extra dose of pain to make sure they remembered.

He released his grasp.

Hector and Kyle might have qualms about killing. He didn't.

* * * *

Deacon stood peering into a narrow canyon—maybe two or three hundred feet wide at the mouth with steep sides perhaps half that high. So far, he was no closer to finding the gold than he was when he started.

The clues he had to guide him were slight. He knew that going in. But he hadn't realized how slight until now. Still, three hundred pounds of gold was worth the effort. Close to five million dollars worth by his reckoning—he couldn't imagine what it would be like to have all that money.

For a few minutes, he surveyed the trees, rocks, and grass. Rain, wind, and even snow—the granite boulders would be right where they were, but trees grow and trees die and fall to the ground, grasses and wildflowers come and go with the seasons, brush grows high where there wasn't any, soil erodes and is washed away. There was evidence of it everywhere he looked.

Twenty yards ahead of him a pine tree lay rotting, returning nutrients to the soil it had taken away. Gullies gouged the walls of the canyon; a stream took a slice out of the middle.

No doubt the hills around him had changed a lot in the last hundred and fifty years. Even if he knew what to look for, markers that had been there a century and a half ago might not exist today.

It made sense he wasn't going to just stroll into the woods and find a great big "X" marking the spot and a sign saying "dig here." But then he hadn't expected it to be such a monumental task, either.

The problem was he had a solid starting point and little else. It turned out the information Al had given him made for an interesting story, but it hadn't put him any closer to the gold.

Unless Al wasn't telling him everything.

He started up the narrow canyon, his eyes searching for anything that looked like a good quick place for a bandit on the run to stash three hundred pounds of gold bars. He truly doubted Al was holding out on him. It wouldn't make sense. If Al had held back crucial clues to the location of the treasure, the man would've followed up on the information long ago. The old codger simply did not know more.

But he wasn't going to let that dampen his spirit.

It was easy—he knew—for a person to get discouraged in times where things did not go as planned. He'd experienced it salmon fishing. More than once he'd gone long hours without a hookup. And then, just when he was ready to throw in the towel, the fish struck with such ferocity he couldn't get one off the line before another hit, and another, and another. Searching for gold was not salmon fishing, but he had learned to be patient.

And that was not all. In the end—on the ocean with the setting sun warming his back—he'd found a peacefulness few people experience. Walking in the forest was much the same.

Being at one with nature was normally reward enough, but finding Murrieta's gold was the payoff he was after here.

Keeping close to the creek, he gave some thought to what he knew. Joaquin Murrieta or Snake-Eye Carlos Sanchez or both of them were wounded in a shootout with a posse at Robbers Roost. Their trail was lost a few miles north of there in a creek at the mouth of a small canyon. By the time the posse picked up the bandit's tracks again, Murrieta and Sanchez were long gone. Neither of them were seen again, the gold either.

Two men—he reasoned—can't make a fast getaway lugging a hundred and fifty pounds of gold each on the back of their horse in rough country, knowing they needed to move fast. The men hide the yellow stuff hoping to come back for it. Only Joaquin Murrieta and Snake-Eye Carlos Sanchez didn't make it back.

Murrieta's gold was hidden there someplace, Deacon was confident of that. If not in this canyon, the next.

He'd find that gold.

After a few minutes more of searching, the trees in front of him opened up on a meadow of sorts. Only he wasn't looking at a vast field of lush green grass and brightly-colored wildflowers.

Marijuana, a lot of it—somebody's dope crop. He needed to get his ass out of there, and fast.

He turned to hurry down the canyon the way he'd come. But a man's voice from behind stopped him in his tracks.

"Should I shoot him, Hector?" the man behind the voice said.

"What you think, mister?" said another voice not all that unlike the first one. "Should Kyle shoot you?"

There were two men. Deacon figured it reasonable to assume the second voice had come from Hector.

"I was just leaving," Deacon said. He slowly raised his hands and flashed a friendly smile even though the men behind him couldn't see it.

"Sorry, can't let you do that." It was Hector talking. "Now turn around and don't you go doin' nothin' stupid."

Deacon did as he was told and found himself looking at two of the ugliest red-haired men he'd ever seen—twins to boot—and into the gaping bores of two sawed-off 12 gauge double barreled shotguns.

CHAPTER 2

A flash of lightening cracked the night sky, drawing Jack's attention away from the copy of the e-mail clutched in his hand. Thunder shook the walls. A blast of wind rattled the rain-streaked glass in front of him.

He silently cursed the storm. And he cursed himself.

The last time he saw his brother Deacon, there had been an obvious, clumsy and ridiculously unwarranted tension between them. He wished their time together had been different, the way people do when events in a loved one's life suddenly go terribly wrong.

Another blast of wind buffeted the glass.

He peered through the window at the enraged inky-black water of Kaneohe Bay and anxiously watched his sixty-foot catamaran *Pono* bob and jerk against its nylon mooring lines.

The e-mail he received from his brother a week and a half earlier and the phone call he received from his father an hour before the storm hit late that morning, put his pending marine research project in the Northwest Hawaiian Islands on hold. A single objective remained.

Find his missing brother.

Or so he'd sworn the moment he received the news Deacon had gone missing. But now he stared into the raging tempest that stood in the way of him catching a flight to the mainland.

By far this was the worst downpour Oahu had seen this year. Rain dumped from the sky in a deluge that flooded the gutters and drains. The wind peaked at forty miles per hour.

And the power had just gone out.

Mother Nature had turned against him it seemed, doing her best to keep him from his vow and make sure his younger brother's fate remained a mystery. But the torrent wouldn't last forever. And the moment the storm let up, he'd be on a plane to California.

The authorities might be reluctant to begin a search. He wasn't. He'd find Deacon at any cost.

And Deacon would be all right.

That was the only way he could see the nightmare playing out.

Accepting the fact that Deacon was missing was difficult enough. To think of him lying dead in a muddy ditch somewhere was beyond comprehension. He just wouldn't go there.

Couldn't.

But something had happened to him.

Deacon captained the family's forty-foot salmon boat. That's how he made his living. This year's moratorium on commercial salmon fishing had sent him job hunting along with a hundred other people in town. He'd taken a job at the nearby boat yard. And with so many people out of work and so few jobs available to him, he'd been lucky to get hired.

Now he'd failed to show up for his first day of work—September fifteenth—two days ago.

That was not Deacon's style. For any reason. Still, none of the family or any of his friends had seen or heard from him since the 7th of September when he called home to say he'd be back in a week. And that he looked forward to starting his new job.

Jack swallowed. The same day Deacon sent him the e-mail.

Ten days missing.

A lump rose and lodged in his throat. Too long if Deacon lay seriously hurt somewhere.

And all the more reason the authorities should have begun a search for him twenty-four hours ago when their father reported him missing. But that he failed to return home as planned was not enough for the Sheriff's Department to open a missing person's case and launch an expensive search and rescue operation. Not without an indication of foul play or special circumstance. They simply believed Deacon had run off somewhere and would return home or contact family when he was ready to.

Jack sighed. He wasn't so easily convinced.

He flipped open his cell phone and to his surprise, saw bars. At least he could call. He punched in his father's number and pushed send. He was glad they were able to set aside their differences, at least for now.

After the third ring, Jack heard his father's voice say hello. He sounded old and frail and tired.

"Any word from Deacon?" Jack knew his father would have called if there had been. Still, he had to ask.

"None."

"And he didn't tell you where he was going?"

"Only that he was heading up into the gold country to strike it rich."

Jack could hear the concern in the tone of his father's voice. "I'll be on the first plane out of here."

"Jack—Son—please hurry. I'm afraid your brother's gone and gotten himself seriously hurt."

Jack had never known Hugh Ferrell to say please to anyone. And the man hadn't called him *Son* in ten years. The old man's hardheaded holier-than-thou attitude had cleaved a chasm between them. And now a father's need for a son's forgiveness was bringing them back together.

It was time they bury the hatchet for good.

"I'm on my way," he said. "The moment this damned storm lets up."

He lowered his cellular, ready to snap it closed. Reconsidered. Raised the phone to his ear and added, "Dad, try not to worry. I'll find Deacon."

* * * *

Eighteen hours later, Jack leaned against the portside window next to his seat in the tail section of Hawaiian Airlines Boeing 767 to

Sacramento and settled into his five-hour flight. Unfolding the copy of the e-mail he'd received from Deacon days earlier, he read it for the hundredth time:

I can't believe I'm actually doing something I've only dreamed of. Treasure hunting, can you believe it? There's gold buried in those hills and I'm going to find it—and I don't mean hard-rock mining or panning it, either. You found your treasure. It's time for me to find mine. The answer came to me in Angel's hand. Al holds the secret.

Deacon

Deacon in search of lost gold . . . Jack struggled with the concept. His brother was a fisherman, not a treasure hunter, or even a serious prospector. Now that he thought about it, the e-mail he'd received from Deacon on the seventh was the first communication he'd had with him in several months. Regrettable. It seemed there was much about Deacon's adult life he didn't know: like Deacon's sudden interest in buried treasure.

But was it all that difficult to believe?

Deacon envied his adventures, especially last year's expedition off Kauai's Na Pali coast. He'd said so. It was clear; jealousy had wedged unfortunate tension between them. Still, Deacon never mentioned heading off into the hills treasure hunting.

So why now?

And that line: The answer came to me in Angel's Hand . . .

What did he mean by that?

Had he meant to say in *an* angel's hand?

If so, why was Angel capitalized as though it was someone's name?

Was it?

And the other line: Al holds the secret.

What did that mean?

And who the hell was Al?

Jack couldn't recall having ever heard his brother mention anyone by that name.

The answer came to me in Angel's Hand.
Al holds the secret.
Definitely clues.
Eleven days missing.

CHAPTER 3

It was after midnight when Jack pulled to a stop in front of his family home in Fields Landing, California. The air off the bay had a chill to it that made Jack glad he'd brought a jacket, and happy for the rental Jeep's heater.

The porch light was on. A single bare bulb blazed from a socket on the wall next to the front door. Not much had changed in the two years since his last visit—since childhood actually. A new roof and a new coat of paint—both gifts from him—otherwise it was the same small wood-sided two-bedroom house, the same weathered wood-slat fence, the same tattered lawn, the same clumps of weeds that always seemed to grow six inches taller than the patches of grass around them.

The warmth inside the Jeep made it easy for him to sit there a minute longer and ponder the nostalgia of his childhood home. Good memories and bad, some real bad. Mostly good memories, he decided. When he saw his father open the front door, and wave him up, he shelved his thoughts and grabbed his duffle bag from behind the passenger's seat.

He climbed out of the Jeep. The night chill crept in on him. He asked, "How are ya holding up, Pop?"

"Not good, Son. I'm glad you're here."

Jack stepped close, put his arm around his dad's broad shoulders, and gave him a firm squeeze. It felt good. And long overdue. Even frail from the lingering effects of the broken back he suffered a decade and a half earlier and showing his age, his father remained hard muscled, more so than most men half his age.

"Got the coffee on?" Jack asked.

His father seemed to brighten a little. "A fresh pot."

They stepped inside, walked into the kitchen, and took a seat at the scarred 50's vintage metal and Formica table where most of the family talking had taken place over the years.

Hugh Ferrell reached for the coffee pot and poured them each a steaming mug full. "I've been waiting for you to arrive so we could go through Deacon's room together. Don't really know why. Guess I just didn't want to be in there alone going through his stuff."

This was a sensitive side to his father Jack hadn't seen, or taken notice of before. Thinking back, he recalled the day his mother passed away after having finally succumbed to skin cancer. He was twenty at the time—eighteen years ago. His father was a pillar of strength through it all. It wasn't until two years later that the old man's strength began failing him.

That's when the guilt settled in.

It still ripped at Jack's guts to think he'd left college after barely two years when he had a full four-year scholarship paying his way. But what choice did he have? His father had broken his back. His mother was dead. Deacon was in his first year of high school. Bills needed to be paid. Was he supposed to stay at the University and let his family starve while the bank took the boat, the house, and what little else they had? Not as long as he had two strong hands and a strong back. So he'd done what any good son would do. And because of it, he'd spent six years doing the very thing he was trying hard to get away from. If it weren't for Deacon's willingness to take responsibility for the family business two years out of high school, he would still be up to his elbows in salmon guts.

But all that was behind him. And even though he'd lost his scholarship, he'd gone back and finished school, received his bachelor's degree, a master's degree, and finally a PhD in Marine Science. His focus of study: the destruction of the world's reefs and its effect on apex predators—specifically the shark. Plus, he lived the swashbuckling life he'd dreamed of as a kid.

Now his brother had gone in search of gold and turned up missing. As far as Jack was concerned, he'd trade all he had achieved, the adventures, his sixty-foot catamaran *Pono*, every cent he had just to know Deacon was all right.

A small price to pay to know his little brother was safe.

He took a sip of coffee and stared into the heavy mug. No one, from what he'd been told, saw this coming. That might be a place to start, one of Deacon's friends. They might know something they'd been reluctant to tell the old man. His father had that effect on people.

"You mentioned on the phone," Jack began, "that you talked to Deacon's friends."

"The ones that count, anyways."

Jack noticed his dad peer deep into his eyes. The focused, almost-blank look of a person gazing into the past. His dad said, "The last year or so Deacon's been spending a lot of time with Willie Langford. You remember him."

Jack remembered Willie Langford all right. He was two years older than Langford but knew the jerk off well. Langford was a rotten kid. He doubted the juvenile delinquent had grown into much of a man.

Jack said, "How'd he get hooked up with him?"

"Gold panning and the like. Willie's into that kind of stuff, and he's been teaching Deacon."

"You don't think he's holding back do you?"

"I know what you're getting at. Trust me, I've mellowed. He'd have told me if he knew something."

"Then we're back to searching his room."

"Let's get to it."

Jack stepped through the doorway ahead of his dad and stopped a couple of steps inside. The bedroom he and Deacon shared growing up didn't seem all that different to him. The twin beds had been replaced with a double bed and the pictures on the wall updated, that was about it. The same old dresser and the same old desk sat against the wall with the same old wallpaper. Only now, a new HP flat screen PC and high-speed printer sat atop the desk instead of the clunker Royal typewriter that sat there when they were growing up.

His gaze fixed on the computer. If the hard drive wasn't password protected, he might be in luck.

Jack switched on the CPU and once it powered up, he checked to see which sites Deacon had recently accessed: gold panning, gold prospecting, gold mining, legends of lost gold, Joaquin Murrieta, Joaquin Murrieta and the California gold fields, Captain Love and Joaquin Murrieta.

Deacon was definitely interested in the infamous Mexican bandit Joaquin Murrieta. Was it *his* gold that Deacon was after? Jack wished he had access to Deacon's e-mail.

But without a password, he wasn't getting in.

Resuming his search of Deacon's room, he found a stack of gold prospecting magazines sitting on top of the bedside table. Inside the drawer he found last month's issue of *Playboy* magazine and a small glass vile containing a few flakes of placer gold. He resisted an urge to check out the centerfold and eyed the gold instead.

A few dollars at most.

He slid the drawer closed, straightened, and scanned the room. They were coming up empty, and he wondered if he was missing the obvious . . . or the not so obvious. The bed, he remembered. When he was a teenager, he hid his nudie magazines between the mattress and the box spring.

It was worth a look.

He lifted the mattress.

Nothing.

He hefted it a few more inches and that's when he saw something: a spiral notebook sticking out just enough for him to recognize it for what it was.

"Bingo!"

"You found something?" A shred of hope showed in the old man's tired voice.

"Deacon's notebook," Jack said.

He sat on the edge of the bed and silently read what had been written inside. Deacon kept meticulous notes on locations, dates, river water levels, and even the time of day he'd panned for gold. He'd sketched detailed maps. His brother had been busy. The empty hours of a man accustomed to working long days, or those of a man in search of a dream. But according to his notes, his efforts hadn't netted him enough gold to pay for his gas.

He kept reading, and it was the last two entries that struck him. The first note read:

August 31st:
I spoke to Albert Brink in Angels Camp today. It was by chance that we met. Nice old guy, a prospector, he's been around the area a long time. And for the price of a couple of drinks, he told me a story that piqued my hope of finally finding a cache of gold stolen by Joaquin Murrieta. It has always been my belief that the tales we heard as kids are true. I've dreamed of finding Murrieta gold and feel my time has come. But it's not here quite yet. It's unbelievably frustrating to leave town when I'm so close, but landing the job at the boat yard is far too important. I need that job.

Jack reread the last sentence: *I need that job.* If Deacon were able, he'd have returned home in time to start work. No doubt about that.

He read on and had his thoughts confirmed. The second entry read:

September 5th:
I talked to Fred this morning. Will start work on the 15th. I feel lucky to have gotten the job with so many unemployed fishermen after the work. The failing economy is turning friend against friend and I fear I may lose a couple because of it. I'm going back to Angels Camp today. And I'm finding that gold.

Jack closed the notebook and peered up at his dad. "Did Deacon mention anything to you about going to Angels Camp?"

"No, why?"

Jack held up the notebook so his dad could read the final entry.

"That little shit." Hugh tapped the page with the tip of his calloused index finger. "He's been keeping it a secret from me for

God knows how long."

"What can I say?" Jack took another glance at the entries. "He should have trusted you."

"He sure should have," Hugh said, his gaze still locked on the notebook.

Jack heard his dad's words, but his mind was already working on the e-mail he'd received from Deacon. *Angel's hand* was Angels Camp. *Al* was Al Brink. Clues, just as he thought.

A simple internet security precaution.

Or a premonition something would go wrong.

CHAPTER 4

Main Street in Old Town Angels Camp took Jack a step back in time a hundred and fifty years. A dozen one and two story wood and brick buildings with high facades common to the Old West lined each side of a two-lane road. Some were in obvious need of restoration, but most appeared solid in construction.

According to the sign posted on the edge of town, the official population was 3,150. That, and the quaintness of the century-and-a-half-old buildings, brought a sigh of relief to his lips.

Crowds and big cites made him feel uneasy. He could get along fine in the masses when it was necessary, but he preferred a small group of friends and the open ocean to a throng of empty faces, tall buildings, concrete, and blacktop. That wasn't the case with Deacon. Deacon was amiable, outgoing, and just plain nice. His good looks and pleasant manner made him easy to notice and easy to remember.

Between the two of them, Jack had always thought of his brother as being the more handsome man. He had the same wavy black hair, the same angular face, the same broad chest, the same hard muscles. And even though Deacon was six years younger and a full inch taller, Jack was pretty sure he could still take him in arm wrestling.

Or maybe not.

That made him grin.

Now that he thought about their looks, he and Deacon were the same in so many ways it was difficult for him to say exactly why he thought of Deacon as being the better looking. Deacon just was, and women flocked to him.

Knowing his brother, he couldn't help believe that if Deacon was in trouble, quite possibly a woman was involved. Because of his good looks, genuine kind nature, and generous smile, Deacon sort of expected the ladies to like him, and it was no secret they did. From the way he talked, he was never without a pretty girl hanging on his arm or trailing after him. Several of which had tried real hard to tie him down . . . an exercise in futility it turned out.

Handsome, a hard worker, a ladies' man—and now by every indication an adventurer as well. He and his brother were alike in so many ways he wondered why they hadn't spent more time together.

That was going to change.

Nestled among the century-and-a-half-old brick buildings was a three-story hotel named Gold Trail Inn. A newer building designed to look old. He parked in front and walked inside.

The man standing behind the counter looked and dressed the part of an old-west businessman. He wore his dark hair parted in the middle and slicked down. He sported a thick handlebar mustache, jeans, a white on white striped shirt, and two-inch-wide red suspenders.

Jack flashed his best smile at the man. "Don't suppose you have a room?"

"Depends on how long you'll need it."

"Not more than a couple of days." Jack stifled a yawn. "Three tops."

"Looks like you're in need of it, too."

"About three hours sleep in the last twenty-four, yeah I need it."

"Well, you're in luck. We've got one that faces the street if you don't mind the traffic noise. Sign the register." The clerk opened a large leather-bound book and handed him a pen.

"A little old fashioned, isn't it?" Jack took the pen and signed his name.

"The register is here for the benefit of tourists. The computer's in back." He handed Jack a 3X5 index card and said, "Fill this out, and I'll need a credit card number on file."

Jack handed over his Hawaiian Miles VISA and said, "I'm looking for my brother Deacon Ferrell. It's possible he had a room here sometime in the last couple of weeks?"

Mustache squinted at the card and gave a little nod, apparently satisfied the last names matched. "Don't normally do that, but I'll make an exception. Let me check the computer."

The clerk returned from the back room a couple of minutes later and handed Jack his credit card and room key. "I remember your brother now. Nice smile, pleasant sort of fella. He stayed here one night, the seventh. Checked out the next day."

Jack gave some thought to that and said, "One other question, do you have a computer for guest use?"

"Over there. Two-bits a minute for the internet."

Jack peered at the computer, thinking the pieces were starting to fall into place. His brother had most likely sent him the e-mail from that computer the day he checked out.

"Anything else I can do for you?" the clerk asked.

Jack rubbed the stubble on his chin. "Just direct me to my room."

"Number 16," the clerk said, pointing up. "Top of the stairs and straight ahead."

Jack retrieved his duffle from the rear floorboard of the Jeep and carried the bag upstairs. The room—he discovered—had a double bed with a lace bedspread, an antique oak dresser with a big flowered bowl and pitcher sitting on it, a round lamp table next to the window, a wingback chair, and an old-fashioned bathroom complete with a claw-foot bathtub and a big round showerhead. He was thankful the owner hadn't gone overboard with nostalgia.

He dropped his bag on the floor next to the bed and sat down on the edge of the mattress. Deacon had only stayed in the hotel one night. If he came to town in search of gold stolen by Joaquin Murrieta, he would surely have needed to stay more than that one night. So why had he checked out?

More questions without answers.

He could only think of two reasons Deacon would have checked out. Either he was passing through on his way somewhere else or he planned to camp out. Either way, Deacon could be anywhere.

Jack checked his watch: five after one. Plenty of daylight left.

Sleep—he'd decided—was not an option. Every minute counted. He didn't plan to waste even one.

But he did need to eat.

And that's what he'd do; after a shower and a shave. Then he'd find Al Brink.

Al holds the secret.

CHAPTER 5

It was 1:30 in the afternoon when Jack plopped into a chair at a rear table in Nel's Diner. He patiently waited for the one waitress on duty to work her way over to him. Early twenties, perhaps twenty-five, black shoulder length hair, long lashes, big dark brown eyes, full lips glossed a deep red, large breasts, and skin the color of milk chocolate that suggested Mexican or American Indian ancestry— she was quite pretty. Plus she had a flirtatious manner about her.

Deacon's type if there ever was one.

Jack caught her looking at him, not sexually, but quizzically. He held up his cup and waved her over. She poured coffee, and he showed her the photo of Deacon he'd brought with him.

"I'm looking for my brother." He did his best to sound sincere. The sight of her breasts spilling over the bodice of her blouse made it difficult for him to look her in the face. "Have you by chance seen him?"

Her eyes widened, and he knew at once that she had, even though she still hadn't said so.

"Hard to resist, isn't he?" Jack smiled, knowingly. "When was it that you last saw my brother?"

"You look like him," she stammered.

"He's the better looking one." Again, Jack smiled. "But I have the brains in the family." A lie of course. Deacon was by no stretch of the imagination lacking in intelligence, but it seemed like the

31

thing to say to keep her talking.

She appeared to relax.

"A couple of weeks ago," she said. "We had dinner together. He told me he was going hiking, and that he'd be gone a few days. Your brother promised me we'd get together when he got back."

"Did he say where he was going?"

"The mountains around here, I guess. He was kind of secretive about it."

It fit that Deacon hadn't told her where he was headed. With a fortune in gold at stake, he'd have been careful. Still, he could have let something slip. A pretty girl could do that to him.

Especially a dark-haired, brown-eyed, large-breasted woman with a friendly disposition.

"Not even a hint?" he asked.

She hesitated a moment and said, "I kind of got the feeling he was married and didn't want to say so."

"He's not." Jack watched her full red lips curl into a hint of a smile. "There's something you're not telling me."

Her gaze dropped to the coffee pot in her hand. "After—well, when he didn't come back like he promised I kind of felt like he was playing me. I'm not exactly sure why, but I thought he was different from the other men I've known. It hurt to think—"

"He didn't come back because something's happened to him," Jack snapped before she said more. "That's why I'm here . . . to find him."

Her eyes fixed on his. And it seemed to him she hadn't understood the reason behind his questions. She did now.

The bell above the door tinkled, making her look. She stiffened.

Jack saw a tall powerfully built man with a face that looked like it had been carved from a granite boulder step inside. Clean shaven with neatly trimmed dark brown hair, he looked to be about forty. And even from across the room, Jack could see the flinty coldness in the man's dark eyes.

The big man held Jack solidly in his gaze as he stepped to the register.

Jack returned the look. A real hard case if he ever saw one. He was being sized up.

For what?

There was nothing he needed to prove to Hard Case today, tomorrow, or the next day. He wasn't in town to pick a fight with the local cock-of-the-walk or get into a pissing match over a woman. His only interest in the dark-haired waitress was what she could tell him about Deacon.

He dismissed the big man's taunts and focused on the woman. She was still watching the asshole as if she half expected him to walk over, pick her up by the hair, and drag her back to the register.

Maybe he would. But not today.

Jack glanced at her nametag. "Della," he said, drawing her attention. "You were saying?"

She swallowed and refocused on Jack. "Your brother's truck is at the Texaco station at the other end of town. Henry towed it in. Talk to him."

Jack saw her eyes dart to Hard Case who now stood glaring at her from the counter next to the cash register. It was obvious she was visibly shaken by the big man's presence there.

"Know the man?" Jack asked, realizing full well she did.

"Elliot Marsh," she managed to say. The name spilled from her lips as if the mention of it made her sick to her stomach. Without asking Jack if he wanted something to eat, she scribbled his tab, laid it on the table, and hurried off in the direction of Marsh who stood there eyeing her.

Jack calmly sipped his coffee and watched her and the big man speak to each other in hushed tones, with an occasional glance his direction. Good or bad—he figured it was the latter—there was history between the Della and Marsh. Maybe *he* was the reason she hoped Deacon was different.

When he'd swallowed the last sip from his cup, he dug five dollars out of his wallet, dropped the money on the table, and set his empty cup on the bill to hold it down. Then, making a point to wave and smile at the big man hovering over Della, he slid his chair back, got up, and walked outside without even as much as a glance back.

Letting the front door to the restaurant clang solidly closed behind him, Jack stepped onto the concrete sidewalk fronting Nel's diner and stood there. His brother was in serious trouble. He was sure about that.

But what kind of trouble?

Getting beat up, robbed, stabbed, shot, or all four was easy, especially with the nation's economy in the crapper. Even a small tourist town like Angels Camp had its unsavory characters.

Was that what Della and Marsh were whispering about, and the cautious looks they cast his direction? Had Deacon somehow managed to stumble into a den of snakes—the two-legged kind? Had he been shot or stabbed and his body dumped into a ditch someplace?

The Deacon Ferrell Jack knew wasn't a man who backed down from a fight when diplomacy failed. But he wasn't the sort to go looking for trouble either. His temperament was such that he would go out of his way to avoid unpleasant confrontations.

So what happened to him?

The question he still couldn't answer.

His only lead was the young woman in the restaurant. She'd spent at least one night with Deacon and knew his truck had been towed and stored.

He'd talk to Henry at the Texaco station. And he'd check the pickup.

Then it was time he found Al Brink.

CHAPTER 6

By Jack's reckoning, a person could walk from one end of Old Town to the other in fifteen minutes tops. He made it to the Texaco station in five.

The caffeine, the growling in his stomach from having his lunch interrupted, and the few minutes of exercise he got walking to the Texaco was enough to keep him awake and moving for at least a little while longer.

Deacon's ford pickup and several junkers sat in a lot on the far side of the gas station. He walked straight to it.

"Can I help you?" a round-bellied fiftyish-looking man in oil-stained coveralls asked when he saw Jack eyeballing his brother's truck.

"This belongs to my brother," Jack said. "I was wondering what you're doing with it?"

"Towed it here myself a little over a week ago." The man wiped his hands on a greasy rag and walked to where Jack stood. "Sixty a day to store it. You might want to tell your brother to get in here and take it off my hands or he'll owe more than it's worth."

"You the owner?" Jack figured he was.

"Henry Bastion." He stuck out a calloused paw.

Jack took the man's hand in his and shook it. "Jack Ferrell. You say you towed my brother's truck here?"

"That's right. Sheriff himself called it in. Found it abandoned up the road a ways."

"Mind if I take a look inside. I assume you jimmied the lock."

"Had to." Henry smiled. "But I'm as honest a soul as you'll find. Everything is there what was there."

Jack saw sincerity in Henry's eyes. He believed the man.

"So tell me, how far up the road is *a ways?*" Jack opened the passenger's door and leaned inside the cab of the truck.

"Four or five miles up Murphy's Grade. Your brother's pickup was parked on an old fire road that ends about a mile below Robbers Roost. Some history there, I tell you. Used to be a popular area for hikers. Not so much anymore."

"Any idea why he parked his truck where he did?"

"Going hiking, I suppose."

Jack nodded to himself. What the old-timer said about Deacon being parked on the fire road made sense. Deacon was looking for lost gold. He'd be on the trail of the yellow stuff.

"You said the area is popular with hikers. There's no reason for the Sheriff to have his truck towed, is there?"

"No reason that I can think of, unless there was a problem. With him . . . no telling. Now I wished I'd asked."

Henry's answer tightened the knot already gripping Jack's gut. He'd come to Angels Camp fearing the worst and hoping for the best. Finding Deacon's pickup stored at the Texaco station only worsened his fears.

But there was still hope.

He took his time going through the interior of the cab. He found a tattered copy of *Guide to the California Gold Fields* lying on the passenger's seat, an empty plastic water bottle on the passenger's side floorboard, a California state map along with the trucks registration and insurance card in the glove box, and a dime and three pennies in the center consol. Behind the seat, he found a jack, a folding army-surplus shovel, and a plastic gold pan. About what he expected to find.

He checked the open bed in the rear and came up with a couple of bottle caps and a handful of dry oak leaves, otherwise nothing.

If Deacon brought camping gear along, he had it with him.

Jack closed the door, dug a crisp Franklin out of his wallet, and handed the hundred to the man. "Thanks old-timer. My brother and I will be back for his truck." He jabbed his index finger at the bill in Henry's hand. "In the meantime, see that nothing happens to it."

Henry's eyes lit up at the sight of the hundred-dollar bill. "Hell, son, for another one of these, I'll wash and wax the thing."

Jack chuckled and started walking in the direction he'd come from. After a couple of steps, he paused and faced Henry. "By chance, would you happen to know where I can find a man named Al Brink? It's possible he might be able to shed some light on where my brother might have gone."

Henry scratched the graying stubble of beard covering his cheeks. "Likely as not you'll find him most anyplace this time of day."

Jack smiled. He liked this guy. "And if you had to guess?"

Henry stared in the direction of town. "Try the Nugget Saloon. If Al has a thirst on, he'll be there."

"Take 'er easy," Jack said and took off walking back up the street.

"These days I'll take it any way I can," Henry called after him.

Jack chuckled and waved farewell without breaking stride.

Five minutes later, he came to a building with a large wooden sign suspended from the overhang out front proclaiming the place Ben's Dry Goods and General Store. He hadn't yet found the Nugget Saloon.

When he passed by the large window fronting the walkway, he glanced inside and saw Marsh talking to a middle-aged man standing behind a long check-out counter sitting off to the right of the front door. The two men appeared to know each other quite well.

Jack couldn't resist.

He opened the door and walked directly to the register. Liquor bottles lined shelves on the wall behind the counter. "Don Julio tequila," he said to the skinny weak-chinned clerk.

Standing this close to Marsh, Jack got a good look at just how big the man was. NFL linebacker big. The behemoth towered over him by a good six inches: six-six, maybe six-seven. And he was far broader in the chest and all of sixty or seventy pounds heavier—two hundred and fifty pounds or more of solid muscle. He was big boned and brutal looking. His angular face was the size of a dinner plate.

The flinty coldness in the man's eyes was still there.

Jack shot a glance at the empty countertop in front of Marsh. Whatever the big man's reason was for being there, it wasn't to make a purchase.

At least it didn't appear so.

"The good stuff," Marsh said, nodding at the bottle of Don Julio in the clerk's hand. He settled his butt against the edge of the countertop, folded his muscled arms across his massive chest, planted the heel of a fancy cowboy boot against the baseboard, and looked squarely at Jack. "You in town long?"

"I'm here to find my brother." Jack reached into his shirt pocket, removed the photograph of Deacon, and held it up in front of him where Marsh could get a good clear look at it. "I don't suppose you've seen him?"

Marsh snatched the snapshot from Jack's fingers, glanced at it, and handed the photo back to him. "You two look alike."

This was the second time he'd heard that. "He's the better looking one of the two of us. Seen him?"

"Nope, can't say I have."

"Figured that'd be the case," Jack said and handed the photo to the man behind the counter. "How about you?"

"Nope." Chinless handed the photograph right back.

Jack tucked the snapshot into his shirt pocket and said, "Right."

"Tell me," Marsh's thin lips spread into a nasty grin. "Your brother shacked up with a whore someplace here in town or what?"

Jack could tell right off that Marsh considered himself to be the he-bull in town. The big man was pushing hard and it was difficult for Jack to keep from doing his best to make the guy's dentist a rich man. But he'd learned to not let anger get in the way of common sense.

He'd let Hard Case play his game.

"Either of you men know a man named Al Brink?" he asked, keeping his eyes focused on Marsh.

"Sure do." Again, it was Marsh talking. "What do you want with that useless old drunk?"

Jack bit back his frustration. He'd seen Marsh twice and talked to him just this one time. Already he didn't like the man. "I take it you don't think much of the guy?"

Marsh narrowed his eyes at Jack. "Al Brink is nothing but a crazy old drunk full of outlandish stories conjured up to get people to buy him drinks. My advice is don't waste your time talking to the likes of him."

Jack noticed Chinless grin. He turned his attention on him. "I suppose you agree?"

Chinless chuckled and said, "Nobody in town pays any particular attention to that drunken old fool. Like Mr. Marsh said, don't waste your time or your money buying that crazy old coot drinks."

"I'll keep that in mind," Jack said.

He took the bottle from Chinless, paid for it, walked out onto the sidewalk, and stood there a moment looking in the direction of his hotel a few doors down. He didn't like either man. But they could very well be right about Al Brink.

Al holds the secret.

He sighed inwardly.

It appeared the man he hoped held answers to Deacon's whereabouts was quite possibly nothing more than the town drunk.

Twelve days missing.

He had to trust that Al Brink was not the crazy old coot Marsh and Chinless made him out to be.

CHAPTER 7

Jack spied the sign to the Nugget Saloon attached to the front of a building two doors down from his hotel. He hadn't noticed it on his way into town. Odd, he thought, especially with it being a bar. But then he had more pressing issues than a drink on his mind. Three old sots sat on a bench out front. Any of them could have been Al Brink.

His search for Deacon would most likely begin or end with what the man had to tell him.

Not a comforting thought.

But whatever direction his search took from here, Jack wanted to take his time talking with Al. He doubted the guy was quite the crazy old drunk Marsh made him out to be.

He hoped, anyway.

Before heading up the street to the bar, he made a quick stop at his room to drop off the bottle of Don Julio. Five minutes later, he walked up to the three men sitting on the bench. He had a mental image of what he imagined the old prospector would look like. He made his choice.

"Are any of you men Al Brink?" he asked in a calm even voice. "I'm looking for information about my brother."

An elderly man that Jack guessed to be pushing eighty, wearing faded denim bib overalls and a red and green plaid shirt, narrowed his eyes at him in obvious speculation. He was a portly fellow, maybe five foot seven, two hundred pounds, short gray hair—what little there was of it—wire-rimmed bifocal glasses perched on a small bulbous nose, and round red cheeks from years of heavy drinking.

Exactly how Jack pictured Al to look. He waited.

"How about we go inside, young fellow," the old guy in the overalls said. He stood up. "Talkin' is thirsty work."

With the two other men watching them from the bench, Jack and Al stepped inside the Nugget Saloon and took seats at the bar. Jack ordered a couple of draft beers. The bartender filled their glasses, and Jack reached into his shirt pocket for the photo of Deacon.

"Like I said, I'm looking for my brother." Jack slid the photograph along the bar-top and angled it toward Al to make it easy for the man's tired eyes to focus on the smiling face in the picture. "This is a photo of him taken two years ago. I understand he's been talking to you."

"You look a lot alike," Al said with a squint of appraisal.

Jack felt a quiver of excitement. Not at what Al said—nothing new there—but that he said it without so much as a slur. The man was sober—or at the very least handled his drink well.

And he didn't sound crazy.

He tapped the snapshot with the tip of his index finger. "So you remember talking to him?"

Al nodded almost imperceptibly, his gaze fixed on Jack. "Are you familiar with Joaquin Murrieta?"

Jack peered deep into the man's eyes. Deacon had come to town looking for Murrieta gold. His dream. *Al holds the secret.*

He said, "I know he was a Mexican bandit who plagued the California Mother Lode after the gold rush of 1849. And I'm finding out my brother had taken an interest in him. Beyond that, about all I know is he was shot and killed and his head put on display."

"That's the official version."

Jack saw the glint of skepticism in the old man's hazel eyes. "You don't agree?"

"With some of it, so did your brother."

Jack smiled. "I'm listening."

41

Al took a sip of beer, returned the glass to the cardboard coaster in front of him and said, "Some Californians romanticized Joaquin Murrieta as a Mexican Patriot—a Zorro or Robin Hood of sorts. Supposedly, some called him the Robin Hood of El Dorado. Most claimed the self-made hero of the Mexican people was nothing more than a common desperado."

"And you?" Jack asked. He needed to know right off exactly where Al stood on the issue. It would say a lot about the man's credibility.

Al narrowed his eyes at Jack. "I prefer to call coldblooded thieving scum like Murrieta what they are: rabid dogs that should be put down like any other. You can believe whatever you want. It's of no importance to what I'm going to tell you."

Jack got the answer he wanted. Al wasn't just a romantic old fool fascinated with spinning outlandish yarns of the old west. But the man had only just gotten started.

He shrugged. "I say call a spade a spade."

Al flashed a nod of approval. "Like I said, our opinion of Joaquin Murrieta is of no importance. To be honest, not much is known about the man. It's believed he was born in Sonora, Mexico in 1829 or 30. And that some twenty years later, he traveled with his older brother Carlos and his wife Rosita, to the gold fields of California where they began working a claim near Placerville—Hangtown as it was called in those days.

"As the story goes, their white neighbors did their damnedest to run Joaquin and his brother off of their diggings by telling them it was illegal for Mexicans to hold a claim in California. It wasn't true of course. But that same year, California legislators did impose a Foreign Miners Tax in the state.

"Now mind you, history's a bit sketchy on why Joaquin Murrieta turned to crime. The most popular account is that a group of white miners murdered his brother, raped his wife, and horsewhipped Joaquin almost to death."

"Sounds reasonable," Jack said.

Al peered directly into Jack's eyes, settled onto his thick forearms resting on the bar, and leaned in close. Jack felt himself being drawn in like a child listening to a late-night campfire story.

He listened.

"One legend," Al continued, "has it that Murrieta left his claim and opened a saloon in Hangtown; where one by one, miners bodies—all who were said to have been part of the killings at the Murrieta claim—turned up with their ears cut off. After fourteen miners had been found dead, a settler in town identified Murrieta as being responsible for the killings, and once again, he was on the run. It wasn't long before he formed his gang of outlaws and continued his vendetta against the white settlers through robbery and mayhem."

Al paused for a swig of beer. He set his glass down and said, "That's one legend. I'm sure there're others. One thing is for certain, Murrieta no doubt felt the same sense of injury from Anglo bigotry that many of his countrymen did at the time."

"And still do," Jack pointed out.

Al looked at him. "I'm sure we don't need to go there."

"We don't," Jack agreed.

Al continued, "No one can say for sure Joaquin Murrieta was responsible for all the reprehensible deeds blamed on him. Robberies and other violent crimes were epidemic in and around the mining camps where men at times carried what was considered to be small fortunes in gold. Joaquin Murrieta simply provided a convenient name to hang the crimes on.

"What *is* known is that Joaquin Murrieta quickly became the leader of a band of murderous trash suitably named *The Five Joaquins*. As well as a real badass known as *Three-Fingered Jack*— Murrieta's right hand man. Between 1850 and 1853 they supposedly stole over one hundred horses, made off with more than a hundred thousand dollars in gold, and killed nineteen men."

Jack said, "And in the end Murrieta lost his head."

"That's what they claimed." Doubt showed in Al's voice. "Murrieta managed to avoid the law for several years, killing three lawmen in the process. Then in May of 1853—having had enough of *The Five Joaquins'* and the out-of-control lawlessness in California—Governor John Bigler created the *California Rangers* and put a thousand dollar reward on Murrieta's head."

Al paused and took another sip of beer.

Jack felt he knew where the story was headed. He said, "And that thousand dollar bounty did it?"

Al nodded. "For the rangers. Under the command of former Texas Ranger Harry Love, their first assignment was to hunt down *The Five Joaquins* including *Three Fingered Jack*. On July 25, 1853, having chased Murrieta's gang across the Mother Lode and west into the foothills of the coastal mountains, Love and his men confronted a group of Mexicans with a heard of horses near Panoche Pass. There was no avoiding a gunfight and they had at it right there. When the smoke cleared, two Mexicans lay dead in the dirt: one believed to be Murrieta, the other his right-hand man Manual Garcia—*Three Fingered Jack.*"

He took a breath and said, "July—a hundred degrees or more— the bandit's bodies would never last the trip to the state capital. So to claim the bounty, Love cut off Murrieta's head and Three Fingered Jack's hand and preserved them in jars of brandy for the ride back. Eventually seventeen people, including a priest, signed affidavits identifying the head as Murrieta's. Convinced Murrieta was dead, Bigler and the state legislature paid the Rangers involved the thousand dollar reward along with a five thousand dollar bonus.

"Not long after that, Murrieta's head was put on display in San Francisco, Stockton, and the mining camps where curious spectators willing to pay a buck could see the bandit's grisly remains."

Jack watched Al gulp down the remainder of his beer. The account was a history lesson and an interesting tale, but surely not the story Deacon sought when he went looking for Al Brink. There had to be something Al wasn't telling him.

He waved to the bartender for another round. Then he settled his forearms on the countertop and focused his gaze on Al. "Now tell me the story you told my brother Deacon."

Al's lips spread into a broad grin. And in the smile, Jack caught a hint of certitude. Enough to know the two of them connected with a measure of trust that made the talking easier. No doubt, the same connection Al shared with Deacon.

"In 1862," Al began, "five armed Mexicans robbed a stagecoach a couple of miles up the road from here. The bandits made off with one hundred thousand dollars in gold. At roughly twenty dollars an ounce—market value back in those days—that would make it right around three hundred pounds of the yellow stuff. At today's price, it'd be worth fifty times that much. And that's not taking into account the collector value of the ingots."

Jack furrowed his brow. "Collector value?"

"You bet your ass. What you've gotta understand is that back then each assay office had its own smelter. They'd melt down the gold dust and nuggets brought in by the miners and pour it into bars stamped with a unique identifying mark. It's that smelter's mark that makes the gold bars so valuable—way beyond mere gold value—to collectors today."

Jack nodded. "I take it the gold was never recovered."

Al shook his head. "And three hundred pounds of bullion is a lot for one man or even two men to carry moving fast at night in rough country."

Jack mumbled to himself in understanding. "Buried?"

"At the very least, stashed in a hole or in some crack in a rock."

Jack met Al's gaze and said, "So those gold bars lured Deacon into these mountains."

"That's right." Al's eyes cleared as though he'd suddenly sobered. "Just as they did my great, great Uncle Donald."

A furrow creased Jack's brow. "Your great, great Uncle Donald?"

CHAPTER 8

October 10, 1862

Donald Brink watched the two men strain to lift the metal reinforced wooden box onto the stage. The coach sagged under the weight. Ten feet in front of him, a brown-skinned man in his mid thirties wearing a gray *sombrero*, dusty clothes, a week's growth of black beard, and a hard look took a step closer. His steel-eyed gaze focused on the strongbox.

Donald thought he'd seen the man before, in Sonora possibly or a saloon in Stockton: Snake-Eye Carlos Sanchez—a vicious sonofabitch if there ever was one. The predawn light made it hard to tell for sure.

He thumbed back both hammers on the double-barreled shotgun in his hands and slid his right index finger onto the front trigger. An hour before, he'd tamped an extra quarter measure of powder and another half ounce of buckshot into each barrel. He'd cut the Mexican in half if he stepped closer.

The *desperado* turned and strode off into the morning gloom, spurs jangling with each step.

Donald eased off on his trigger finger. But he maintained a firm grip on his 10-gauge shotgun. Caution wouldn't let him relax. Not until the gold was safely locked in the safe inside the Wells Fargo office in Sacramento.

He kept his gaze focused on the Mexican until the man swung himself up onto his saddle and spurred his horse into a gallop up the street leading north out of town.

The last he would see of that *hombre*, Donald hoped. Snake-Eye Carlos Sanchez or not, he knew the type. He had a bad feeling they'd see each other again, and that it would be in the sights of his double barrel.

Two hours later, Donald stood with his shotgun at the ready. The stage had moved as far as the blacksmith's shop on the edge of town. A busted spoke on a rear wheel delayed the coach's departure. Now the blacksmith was saying it'd be another hour before they could roll.

Not a good omen.

He scanned the buildings across the street: a saddle shop and a feed store. A whiskered man in shabby clothing stood with his back against the wall of saddle shop, smoking a cigarette. From the looks of him, a miner. His thoughts did not appear to be focused on the stage or its cargo.

Donald stepped to the rear of the stage and peered at the man keeping watch from the side of the coach with the missing wheel. He'd ridden guard with Joe Slade on two other occasions. A sandy-haired, hard-muscled, determined lad of about twenty-five, the young man was vigilant and committed to his work. And he could shoot fast and straight. A good person to have along if it came down to a fight.

"Anything?" Donald asked.

Joe used the double bores of his shotgun for a pointer. "Just that old guy across the street."

"No sight of that Mexican we saw early this morning?" Donald nervously scanned the street in front of him as he talked. He'd be glad when they were rolling.

"Not since the Mex road out."

"Well, keep your eyes open."

Donald paced to the front of the coach and checked with Bodie Chapin, the grizzled guard posted there. A man in his mid thirties and range hard, he had narrow eyes and a square jaw. This was the first time they worked together. But he'd ridden with enough men to know character. Bodie showed the steadfast dedication to duty of a man worth his salt. And from the way he held his gun up and ready, the man knew how to use it.

"Anything?" Donald repeated to Bodie.

"That guy standing in front of the saddle shop," Bodie answered. "And a coyote that crossed the road up a ways. Nothing much else movin."

"Where's Frank?"

"Checking on the smitty."

"Any idea how long?"

Bodie glanced over his shoulder in the direction of the blacksmith shop. "They're rolling out the wheel now."

Donald turned at the sound of the approaching men and grunted approval. "Keep an eye out for that Mexican. I didn't like the look of him."

"Me either." Bodie adjusted the grip on his gun. "I've got a double load of buckshot for the man if he comes looking for it."

"Let's hope he doesn't," Donald said. "I'd just as soon make this trip without any shooting."

* * * *

Two miles north of town, Donald rode atop his saddle, back straight, eyes focused on the uphill slope of rutted road ahead of them and the brush and trees to both sides. The Mexican continued to worry him. Not the one man by himself, but the *desperados* who rode with a *hombre* like that: bad murderous men, the lot. And Snake-Eye Carlos Sanchez was as bad as they come.

Knowing bandits could make a play for the strongbox at any moment, he held the butt of his large-bore shotgun braced against his thigh, the yawning twin barrels pointed at the clouds, his trigger finger poised, his thumb resting on the double hammers ready to cock them back. On a horse next to him, Bodie rode much the same way.

He too was ready for trouble.

Donald twisted in his saddle and checked behind him. The stage creaked and shook, wheels crunched on gravel, the hooves of the six horses pulling the coach pounded the dry trail north, dust billowed. Edger worked the reins. Behind the stage, Frank and Joe rode rear guard. He could see Joe, his shotgun at the ready. Frank was out of sight, riding next to Joe. He'd have his shotgun poised as well. The men knew their jobs.

Donald brought his gaze back around. A couple hundred feet ahead of them, a blue jay fluttered to a tree across the road.

Spooked . . .

His horse's head came up, nostrils flared.

The stallion sniffed, then snorted—shook his head.

Donald thumbed back the hammers on his big-bore shotgun and leveled the barrels, searching.

Nothing.

Then he saw movement next to the trunk of a massive oak tree twenty yards up the slope to his right. A man with a rifle, the gun raised and pointed at them. And more movement, a man's head rising up from behind a boulder ten feet below the tree: a *sombrero.*

Snake-Eye Carlos Sanchez.

"Bandits," he yelled. In the next instant, gunshots thundered, white smoke billowed onto the roadway. He swung his shotgun in the direction of the man by the rock, ready to fire.

His horse reared. And at the same time, a lead ball struck him in the head, knocking him from his saddle. On the edge of unconsciousness, he felt himself falling and squeezed the tandem triggers, unleashing the furry of both barrels.

Too late. The shot peppered the treetops.

Lying flat on his left side on the ground, now, Donald struggled to raise his head. He managed an agonizing couple of inches amid a searing pain that tilted the hazy world in front of him. He squeezed his eyes shut tight and blinked them open, bringing the confusion into focus. Syrupy warmth streaked his cheek. He slowly maneuvered his right hand to the side of his heard and probed a grove in his scalp; examined his fingers and saw blood.

More gunshots, a thousand miles away.

His mind struggled to pull together what was happening. Bandits, the strongbox, he was remembering.

Snake-Eye Carlos Sanchez and his men were after the gold.

A horse whinnied and reared, front hooves clawing the air. A man slammed to the ground in a puff of dust. Bodie Chapin, the top of his head a bloody mass of grey-matter and shattered bone. His eyes stared wide open and glazed.

Donald rolled onto his stomach, reached out with both arms, and clawed the ground in desperation to drag himself forward. He needed to get behind cover. He had to get his hands on a gun.

Fifteen feet in front of him, a Mexican wearing a black sombrero stepped into view: Snake-Eye Carlos Sanchez.

No, not Snake-Eye Carlos Sanchez.

A black sombrero . . .

He strained to see the bandit through a red blur.

It couldn't be.

But it was . . . or was it?

He rubbed the blood from his right eye and looked again.

Joaquin Murrieta!

CHAPTER 9

Jack shook his head at the codger's yarn. The adrenaline rush of urgency to find Deacon kept him alert, but did nothing to ease the dread hollowing his stomach. The story was entertaining. But had Al told him a tall tale dredged from the old guy's overactive imagination. Historical accounts—though vague on the subject of Joaquin Murrieta—were clear on one thing: the legendary bandit was long dead by the time of the gold heist in 1862.

He wasn't sure what he expected Al to tell him. That Deacon was staying with a woman in town somewhere? That he was alive and safe? He'd taken a liking to the old coot, but had a nagging feeling the man wasn't proving to be the lead he'd hoped for.

Or was he?

"I'm not sure I buy that," he said.

Al chuckled and said, "Your brother was a mite skeptical at first, too. But he sure got over that in a hurry."

Jack remembered how Deacon had been as a kid growing up. And even into his adult life. And this.

"Deacon's a bit more impetuous than I am," he said.

"I'll have to take your word on that." Al lifted his glass to his mouth, took a gulp of beer, and added, "But I don't think so."

Jack flashed his even white teeth in a broad grin. "Appears we might be a bit more alike than I want to admit."

"Been disappointed if you weren't," Al said. He continued, "As I was saying, seventeen people who knew Joaquin Murrieta by sight identified the head pickled in that jar of brandy as his. But there were as many people or more—people who knew Murrieta —who said the head in the jar was not that of the famed bandit. But Bigler so wanted to believe in Love's success, his own pride wouldn't let him consider the possibility of a mistake."

"But that doesn't make sense," Jack said. "The robberies and killings stopped after Murrieta's death in 1853, right?"

"The ones pinned on him did. Or maybe the authorities just quit blaming him."

Jack could see the logic behind the old guy's reasoning. If Murrieta was blamed for most every crime in the gold fields, and people believed he was dead, then it was possible many of the ongoing robberies and even some of the killings lacked the sensationalism that had been there before, making them more of a problem for local authorities and less of a nuisance for good old Governor Bigler. Besides, there was a steady supply of horse thieves, robbers, and killers stepping out of the woodwork to take Murrieta's place.

For a moment, he wrapped his mind around the thought.

Had there been a mistake?

He couldn't keep from wondering. Was there a cover-up . . . a ruse of sorts perpetrated by Love to collect the sizable bounty Governor Bigler placed on Murrieta's head?

Maybe . . . then again.

He saw Al watching him and knew the old guy waited for him to get his head right.

Had Deacon reacted the same way when he heard the story?

Had Al sat back and waited on him to sort everything out in his mind?

He'd bet money on it.

"You were saying?" Jack said.

Al gave him a satisfied nod. "You got her worked out?"

"I'm ready to hear more, if that's what you mean?"

Al winked. "Thought you might." He settled his bulk onto his thick forearms and leaned close, drawing Jack in. He said, "This is the part that got your brother all worked up."

CHAPTER 10

October 10, 1862

Donald sagged against the stage, probing the blood-soaked handkerchief covering the groove in his scalp. His head throbbed, and his left shoulder ached where it had slammed against the ground when he fell from his horse.

"I tell you Joaquin Murrieta did this." He jabbed a thumb at his head when he spoke and locked gazes with the dozen miners crowded in front of him. "He stood as close to me as I am to you. I've seen the murderous scum more than once. It was him, I tell you."

"Murrieta's dead," scoffed a raw-boned miner wearing a tattered red shirt and a wide-brimmed hat stiffened by dried sweat.

"I saw Murrieta's head myself—on display at the Stockton House, pickled in a jar of brandy," added a gangly, spectacled man standing at the back of the group. "So was the hand of Three Fingered Jack; cost me a buck to see 'em."

"Alright, alright," Donald commanded. Adam and Duncan had made their point. It didn't change things. But the comments had gotten the men muttering among themselves.

Donald raised his bloody hand in front of him to quiet the talking. "Joaquin Murrieta is alive or dead, doesn't much matter which. But I say the man shot me, or one of his men did; killed Bodie and Joe. Frank and Edger will be lucky to live through the night."

"And you'd a been lying next to them if we hadn't heard the shooting and come checkin'," Adam was quick to point out.

Again, Donald probed the bloody bandage tied around his head. "And I'm a thanking you for that. Now I'm asking you men to join up with me. No matter what it takes, I'm going to hunt down those thieving murderous bastards, each and every one of them. Murrieta isn't getting away this time."

"I'll help hunt down those rotten sonsabitches," Duncan said from the rear of the cluster of miners. "If Murrieta ain't dead, the thievin' son-of-a-whore owes me a dollar."

"You can count on me," Adam added. He tugged his sweat-stiffened hat down on his head. "Joe was a friend of mine. And I want the back-shootin' bastard what killed him."

Other miners nodded and muttered agreement.

"Good." Donald straightened and glanced around, searching for his shotgun. He saw a stocky redheaded man in front of him holding it: Rollie, a reliable sort. He took the gun from Rollie's hands and said, "A couple of you men drive the stage and the bodies and what's left of my men back to town. Do what you can for Frank and Edgar. The rest of you load up and follow me."

Donald remembered firing his gun. Before doing anything else, he lifted the powder flask and poured a heavy charge into the right barrel. That done, he slid the metal ramrod from the guides affixed to the bottom of the barrels and used the wide blunt end to tamp down a robin-egg-sized lead ball. He repeated the process with the second barrel. But in that one, he loaded a palm-full of pea-sized buckshot. When that was tamped into place, he thumbed the two hammers to half-cock, and replaced the primer caps on both nipples.

He was ready. And his injuries were not going to keep him from doing what he needed to do.

Men who had horses or mules, climbed into their saddles, gun in hand. The few without mounts followed on foot. Donald had every reason to believe Murrieta was long dead. Only he wasn't. Captain Love had collected the bounty for killing the wrong man. The mutilated hand put on display in the jar of brandy had been cut from Three Fingered Jack's dead body. But the head was not that of Joaquin Murrieta. The notorious Mexican bandit was alive, and he and his gang of cutthroats had just killed two men and stolen three hundred pounds of gold bars.

The hoof tracks left by the bandits' horses led a hundred yards up the road before turning east up the mountainside—five riders from the looks of it. Donald figured Murrieta had wanted to get off the open road and into the high country where it would be difficult for men to give chase without exposing themselves to ambush.

Donald remained determined to catch up with Murrieta, but he wasn't in a hurry to walk into another bullet. One ambush had been enough for him. The rough country gave him even more reason to go slow. And he did. The men on foot had no problem keeping up.

Moving at this pace, the posse pursued the band of outlaws higher into the mountains. Each man proceeded quietly, meandering around brush instead of busting through it, even if it meant momentarily diverting from the bandits' trail. They'd been at it for an hour when Donald raised his hand in a signal for the men behind him to stop. He was sure he'd heard someone cough: not one of his men, someone up ahead.

Murrieta . . .

The thought running through his mind was that the bandits were holed up for the night. But that didn't make sense because there was two hours or more of good sunlight left. Still, it might if Bodie had shot one of the bandits before they blew the top of his head off. Perhaps Joe or Frank put some buckshot into one or two of them before going down, or even Edger before he was shot. Then again, Murrieta may have thought they'd put enough distance behind them for the day and brought out the tequila bottle to celebrate.

Donald slid from his saddle and motioned his hand for the men behind him to wait there. Satisfied they understood what was happening, he tied his horse's reins to a bush and crept up the slope. Twenty-five or thirty yards up, he ducked between two rocks large enough for him to take cover behind. Fifty yards ahead and a hundred yards up the slope from him loomed a massive outcropping of granite boulders: a natural stone fortress put there by nature.

He heard talking, now—low tones not meant to be heard beyond the men in the stronghold. The clink of glass. And he saw a man with a rifle raise his head above one of the boulders and scan the slope.

Donald slid from sight of the lookout. He waited a minute then raised his head just high enough to peek over the rock he hid behind. The man with the rifle had ducked back down.

Taking advantage of the moment to make his move, Donald scurried from his hiding place and returned to where the rest of the posse waited. It was time for them to make their move.

"The bastards are up there on the ridge in some rocks," he whispered to the men hunkered down in front of him. "The place is a damned fortress. And I have to tell you, it's going to be hell rooting them out of there. But if we go slow and have at them from the front and sides, we just might get the drop on them before they know we're there."

"What about lookouts?" Adam questioned. "Surely one or two of the bastards will be keeping an eye on their back-trail."

"I saw one, there might be more." Donald scanned the group to make sure their eyes were fixed on him. He wanted everyone to understand. "Fan out, go slow, and stick to cover. And keep your eyes peeled."

"And if any of them shows his face?" Duncan questioned.

It was obvious to Donald that Adam and Duncan were the talkers of the group. Again, he scanned the men in the posse to make sure they were listening. Their eyes focused on him.

His expression hardened. "Kill them."

"I'll take Quentin and Charlie with me," Adam said. "We'll work our way up on the north side."

Donald nodded, turned to Duncan, and said, "You, me, Morgan, and Rollie will have at them from this side."

It was late afternoon when the men fanned out along the hillside. Overhead the sky was dark blue with only a few puffy white clouds floating about. The air was cool; a light breeze ruffled the leaves. Donald couldn't help thinking it was perfect weather for the dirty business facing them.

They'd all be sweating soon enough.

Hunkered low, he watched Adam lead Quentin and Charlie fifty yards to the north. Adam would take the point. Once Adam, Quentin, and Charlie had filed off, he waved Rollie to a tree twenty feet north of him. At the same time, Duncan moved to take the point twenty yards to the south with Morgan filling the gap. Good capable men, all of them. They knew what to do.

As the men took their positions, Donald noticed they seemed anxious to have a go at the bandits. He wasn't all that fired up to kill. But if that's what it took to bring Murrieta and his band of thieving murderers to justice, he wanted to get the killing over with.

With a wave of his hand, Donald signaled the men forward. Each man picked his way up the slope, sticking to the brush and trees and rocks for concealment and cover as they advanced on the bandits' position. Donald slowed the men on each side of him to give Adam and Duncan at the ends of the line time to work their way up the hill so that the group moved in a formation shaped like the horns of a bull.

Each step took them closer to the bandits—bad, dangerous men who would not go down easy. Peering through the brush at the natural granite fortress, Donald hoped he wasn't relying too much on getting the drop on Murrieta and his gang. They were killers, all of them. And they made their living at it.

Donald glanced to the left and right of him. He and his men were close now. He couldn't see Adam and Duncan, but he knew they were nearing the ridge. The tips of the horn would make the difference; they'd catch the bastards in a deadly crossfire.

Donald crept to the two boulders he'd taken cover behind earlier. No sign of the guard he'd seen. Careful to stay low, he narrowed his eyes at the rocks where he'd seen the man raise his head and look around. That's where the bandits were hold up. A long shot for his smoothbore shotgun, even the barrel loaded with the patched ball.

He needed to get closer.

He swept his gaze over the hillside in front of him. Twenty yards away a single oak tree with a fat trunk looked promising. But he'd have to cover some open ground to get there.

Not impossible if the bandit lookout kept his head down.

He checked. So far so good, then he saw the outlaw's head rise up.

Shit!

In the next instant, a shot thundered with a cloud of smoke. It came from his far left: Quentin, Charlie. The bandit's head jerked backwards.

Dead or wounded, the lookout disappeared behind the rocks. Donald made his move. A bullet notched the bark an inch above his head the second he ducked behind the tree.

A shot boomed to his left—Rollie—followed by two to his right. He peered in that direction and saw Morgan crouched behind a log, tamping another shot into his rifle. A few yards beyond Morgan, Duncan stood behind a tree, working his ramrod up and down in the barrel of his rifle.

More shots shattered the forest quietude, from above and to the north of.

At almost the same instant, he saw Morgan take a ball to the face and fall over backwards.

Donald leveled his shotgun against the side of the oak, took aim, and let loose the ball in the right-hand barrel. The bandit in his sights collapsed face-first onto the boulder in front of him.

A thunderclap and a cloud of smoke erupted from the far end of the granite fortress. Donald heard a man cry out. Not Rollie, farther away. Adam, Quentin, or Charlie had been hit.

Donald poured a healthy charge of black powder down the empty barrel, positioned a patch and ball over the muzzle, and rammed the projectile home. Then he thumbed back the hammer to half-cock, used his fingernail to remove the expended primer from the nipple, and shoved on a fresh one.

He wanted the shot to count.

Leveling his gun against the trunk of the tree, he scanned the rocks for a bandit to focus his sights on.

Nothing . . .

He kept his shotgun aimed, waiting for a target. After a minute he lowered the double barrel, but stayed ready should a bandit show himself. Thick, gray black-powder smoke hung like a morning haze on the hillside, but the shooting had stopped.

Donald took stock of the situation. To his right, Morgan lay exactly as he had fallen: dead. Beyond him, Duncan huddled behind a tree. In the granite fortress above, one bandit laid sprawled face-first on a bloodstained boulder: dead. Two, maybe more, bandits had gone down with wounds. To the north, Rollie crouched behind a rock, his gun at the ready. On the hillside beyond him Adam, Quentin, or Charlie had been shot and maybe killed.

How many more would die before the day was over?

* * * *

Donald tugged his coat tight around him. Night brought a thirty-degree drop in temperature. In the rocks above, the glow of a campfire told him the bandits were still there. A few gunshots had been fired back and forth after the first volley, but none since dark. Now Murrieta and what remained of his outlaws, enjoyed coffee and a hot meal.

It would be their last.

Watching the glow of the bandits' campfire dance on the rocks, Donald felt the first stirrings of a plan tug at the recesses of his mind. He dug a piece of dried venison from his possibles bag, bit off a chunk, and chewed. To the desperados peering into the blaze, the darkness beyond the reach of the fire's light would be black as molasses. There was a lookout posted, but only he would be able to see movement in the gloom beyond the granite fortress. And even his vision would be limited to what was visible in the feeble light of the stars.

The fire had been a fool's choice, and for a moment, Donald considered the advantage that provided. For them, darkness was a shroud to maneuver behind. For the bandits holed up in the rocks, darkness was their enemy.

He decided it was time they make a move.

His eyes had long grown used to the feeble light of night in the forest. He couldn't see Morgan's body, or Duncan huddled behind the tree beyond. But he could see the ground around him clear enough to avoid stepping on deadfalls or tumbling loose rocks that would betray his movement to a bandit looking for something to shoot at.

Drawing in a deep calming breath, he let it out and sidled along the hillside in the direction of where he knew Morgan's body lay. He'd seen enough dead men to know Morgan was beyond help, but he owed it to the man to check. Too many men—good and bad—had died.

Not just today, he thought.

And for what?

In his mind, no amount of gold was worth a man's life. Still, for thousands of years man had killed for riches. And the killing would continue. And he would for sure be part of that killing.

Donald narrowed his eyes with resolve at the glow in the rocks. Murrieta would die. But not for gold or silver.

To stop the killing.

CHAPTER 11

Al finished his story, and Jack stared into his beer quietly listening. He'd pretty much guessed how the gunfight in the rocks played out even before Al relayed the final accounts. And he could imagine Deacon's mind whirling with visions of all that Murrieta gold.

He said, "So that stronghold of rocks where your uncle and the rest of the posse shot it out with Murrieta and his gang is this Robbers Roost place I was told about?"

"Got the name after that robbery," Al said.

No surprise. Jack said, "It figures Murrieta managed to sneak his thieving ass out of those rocks that night. Don't see how he managed to pull it off though. Not with that posse of men keeping watch."

"That's the story, Son. My Uncle Donald wrote it all down in a journal; got the book at home, or what's left of it. The darn thing burnt in a fire when I was a lad about half your age. But not before I'd read it enough times to know what was written there."

Jack doubted existence of the journal, but could see no good reason to ask the old guy to produce a bunch of charred pages as proof. He kept quiet and watched Al stare wistfully out the door at the mountains on the edge of town.

"They made off with the gold alright," Al said. "Murrieta and Snake-Eye Carlos Sanchez."

"That's where it ends," Jack said, a statement not a question. "No one knows what became of Murrieta, Snake-Eye Carlos Sanchez, or the gold bars they made off with?"

"Like I told you, the blood trail leading north suggested at least one of them had been shot. Uncle Donald followed the bandit's trail a couple of miles or so before losing it in a stream at the mouth of a small canyon. And by the time they found the bandit's tracks again, Murrieta and Sanchez were long gone. The way Donald wrote it down, they just up and disappeared."

Jack couldn't see how the two bandits managed to disappear without a trace. It just didn't pan out, especially not with one or both of them shot.

He narrowed his eyes at Al. There had to be more. "Murrieta's trail had to lead someplace?"

Al didn't flinch. "It did, to the north. Just like before. But a storm came up sudden like and drove Uncle Donald and his men out of the mountains. A few days later, he and a couple of men went looking but the rain had left them with nothing to follow."

Jack leaned heavily on the bar, his tanned angular face intense with thought beneath his wavy black hair. He couldn't blame his brother for going after those lost gold bars. The thought of getting one's hands on three hundred pounds of gold was enough to make a man's mind race with lust.

Any man's . . .

For a full minute, he stared out the open double doors of the Nugget Saloon at the century-and-a-half-old buildings lining the street. His mind replayed Al's story like a slide show in a penny arcade.

One or both of them shot and bleeding, Murrieta and his murderous sidekick fled north from Robbers Roost carrying the gold with them. Slim information at best. But he was sure that's where his brother had gone.

He blew an exasperated breath out through his nose. The bandits were long dead. Deacon might be, too. He had to hurry and find him. And sitting there wasn't getting it done.

He raked his fingers through his hair. What he needed to do was to think.

And he needed to plan.

He stood and offered his hand to Al. "You believe Deacon went after that gold, don't you?"

Al took Jack's hand in his and gave it a firm shake. "Now that I know your brother's missing, I do."

Jack nodded. He'd come looking for Al because of the e-mail Deacon sent. Al repeated the story he'd told Deacon. Deacon believed Al. Al believed his long dead uncle Donald. And it was quite possible the robbery went down exactly as described.

One man believing in another.

"Well, he said. "I appreciate your candidness. Believe me, I'll find Deacon."

Al went back to his beer. "You do that," he said. "And let's hope nothing bad has happened to your brother."

Jack laid a twenty on the bar, walked out of the Nugget Saloon, and stood in the late afternoon sun. He was a step closer to finding his brother, but only a step—an enigma for certain. With the intention of returning to the quiet of his room, he strode in the direction of the Gold Trail Hotel, and then on past the building. When he realized what he'd done, he found himself standing across the street from Chinless' general store.

Useless, that's what Marsh called Al; a crazy old drunk full of outlandish stories he'd conjured up to get people to buy him drinks.

That wasn't the Al Brink he just talked to.

Al was a drunk maybe, full of outlandish stories probably.

The story he just told wasn't one of them.

Jack turned to walk back to the hotel. A few feet in front of him, a woman stepped off the walkway with the obvious intent to cross the street. She had her purse raised in front of her and her hand thrust inside. He could tell at once that she was oblivious to the BMW speeding toward her.

There was no way she'd make it.

He hurried and grabbed her arm, pulling her back just in time to keep her from being run down by the inattentive driver.

The woman let out a screech of surprise and took a couple of deep, calming breaths as she watched the white BMW convertible speed away. When the car was several buildings farther down the street, she smiled at Jack and said, "Thank you. I don't know where my mind was at."

The woman had raven hair, cinnamon skin, was pretty, and about his age. He winked. "The driver of that Beamer should've been paying attention to what was in front of him instead of talking on his cell phone. The important thing is you weren't hurt."

"Thanks to you."

Jack would have tipped his Stetson had he wore one. Instead, he grinned. And with that he said, "Be sure and watch out for cars."

"I will," she said to his back when he turned and walked off in the direction of the Gold Trail Hotel.

The sound of her voice caused him turn his head and peer over his shoulder at her. She was indeed lovely, and for a moment, he considered going back and striking up a conversation with the lady. He resisted the urge and kept walking, knowing he needed to stay focused on finding his brother.

Jack managed to put all thoughts of the woman out of his mind, and a few minutes later settled into his room bone weary and ready to drop. Robbers Roost and Murrieta's desperate trail north from there appeared to be the key to finding Deacon.

But that was a lot of wild country to search.

He poured himself a half-inch of tequila in the bottom of a water glass he found sitting on the counter next to the bathroom sink and collapsed in the wingback chair by the window. He took a sip, set the glass next to the lamp on the small side table, and slid the window open to let the street sounds drift in on the fresh mountain breeze.

One more day, Deacon.

He retrieved his drink, tossed back the tequila, returned the empty glass to the table, and sunk into the chair. There was much for him to consider. And much to work out.

Deacon had gone into the hills looking for a century-and-a-half-old stolen gold shipment. He hadn't returned. His pickup truck had been towed and stored at Henry's Texaco. Deacon was not a man to stick his nose where it didn't belong. But something bad had happened. That was obvious.

He sighed and settled his head against the backrest.

Twelve days missing.

CHAPTER 12

Jack bolted upright in the chair and scanned his room. A gentle rap on the door had awakened him. Only then did he realize he'd dozed off in the chair he'd sat down in. And now it was dark outside.

Rubbing the grit from his eyes, he brought the room into focus and looked around. He still wasn't completely sure he'd heard someone knock. He'd been listening to creaking wagon wheels, the clip clop of horses' hooves on the street below, drunken barroom laughter, and the occasional boom of a gun shot in the distance. But that was the dream he'd been awakened from.

A second knock on the door to his room, cautious, not too loud—this time he was positive he heard it.

Stifling a yawn with the back of his hand he stepped to the door, curious who it could be. He sure wasn't expecting visitors.

Another knock, louder this time.

Impatient.

He pulled open the door and was immediately brushed aside by Della who rushed in half out of breath.

"Close the door," she said, stepping to the side of the doorway as if to not be seen by someone passing by in the hallway outside the room.

So a woman *was* involved. Jack closed the door and stood facing her in the dim light filtering its way into the room through the open window. "Mind telling me what's going on?"

Della sat down on the edge of his bed without being asked. She still hadn't answered his question but it was obvious to him she had something to say. He retook his seat in the chair and leaned forward to switch on the table lamp.

"Leave it off," she snapped. "He might see us."

Jack didn't need to be told who she was talking about. He closed the window, pulled down the shade, and switched on the table lamp. The instant he looked at her in the light, he saw the bruise under her left eye.

He cringed. "Marsh do that to you?"

She glanced at the floor as though embarrassed. "It's not important."

"It is to me." He leaned closer, resting his elbows on his knees. "And the law if he's assaulting you."

"That's not why I'm here. I want to help you find Deacon."

"Is that why he hit you?"

"He doesn't like that you and I talked in the diner this afternoon."

"So he remembers seeing my brother?"

"Your brother's not an easy man to forget." The corners of her lips curled into a thin shaky smile. "Marsh was jealous. He still is."

"Does he know what happened to Deacon?"

"I don't think so. He just doesn't like guys getting friendly with me."

"Like Deacon."

She glanced at the floor. "And you."

Della was pretty, but well used. He didn't want to play. "It's time to stop cutting bait and put your line in the water, Della. You said you wanted to help. What is it you think you can do?"

"Town's small." She looked directly at him. "People have ears. I know you talked to Al Brink about your brother, and that he told you about a shipment of gold that he says was stolen by Joaquin Murrieta after he was supposed to be dead. And I know Deacon told me he was going hiking and would be gone a few days. It's not hard to figure out he went looking for that gold."

There was only one person who could have overheard his conversation with Al Brink: The bartender. So he'd blabbed to Della. That pissed Jack off.

"Tell me," he said, "the bartender at the Nugget Saloon, is he a friend of yours, or Marsh's?"

"He's my brother," she said. "I think he liked Deacon."

Jack calmed. He hadn't paid enough attention to the bartender to notice a resemblance. Now he wished he had.

"I'm listening." He snagged his empty glass from the lamp table, stood, retrieved the other empty glass from the bathroom, and poured them each a slug of tequila.

She took the glass from his hand, put it to her lips, and tossed back the amber liquor. She held the glass out for another shot.

He poured it and retook his seat in the chair. "You were saying?"

She peered into the glass without taking a drink. After a couple of beats she said, "Al has told that outlandish yarn a hundred times. Claims to be related to one of the men in the posse that went after the bandits who ripped off those gold bars: his great, great uncle, or something. Even says his uncle wrote everything down in a journal that accidently burnt in a fire. Quite honestly, no one has really paid much attention to his stories. I guess Deacon believed him and figured the gold is buried in the hills around here someplace."

Jack settled into his seat. "It sounds like you're one of those people who don't believe Al's story."

She brought her gaze up and met his. "I was born and raised in Sonora just south of here. The legend of Joaquin Murrieta is no secret. I grew up with it. So it's well known Murrieta and his right-hand man Three Fingered Jack were shot and killed by Captain Love and his men in 1853. And that his head was preserved in a jar of brandy and put on display for anyone with a dollar to see."

Jack was confused as to where she was headed with her story. She'd said she wanted to help. Obviously, she believed she could. But she wasn't telling him anything he didn't already know.

"Della, you came here to tell me something you believe will help me find Deacon. Just tell me what it is."

She looked at him for a long second and said, "As you've probably noticed, I'm Mexican-American. Joaquin Murrieta was thought of as a Robin Hood for the Mexican citizens living in California at the time, especially those trying to work claims in the gold fields."

She paused and took a sip of her tequila.

WILLIAM NIKKEL

"And?" Jack said. She was slow getting to the point.

The look she gave him suggested she was having second thoughts. Perhaps she felt she was betraying her countrymen. He realized he shouldn't press her. She needed to tell him in her own way.

"Excuse me for pushing," he said. "But I 'm sure you understand why I'm anxious to hear what you have to say."

She peered into his eyes a couple of seconds longer. Finally, she sighed and said, "There's a woman my mother knows: Theresa Montero. She claims to be related to Joaquin Murrieta—his great, great, great, granddaughter, or something like that. Anyway, according mom, Ms. Montero believes Murrieta wasn't killed in that shootout with Captain Love. And that it wasn't Murrieta's head in that jar. She claims she has proof he died ten years later in Mexico."

She had his attention, though he still didn't know how the information would help him find Deacon.

He asked, "What kind of proof?"

"I haven't seen it," she said. "But my mother says it's an old family bible."

He thought about what Della was telling him. This Theresa Montero woman corroborated Al Brink's story. At least that Joaquin Murrieta was alive to commit the robbery. What else was she getting at?

Did she think Theresa Montero might be able to help him in some way?

Did the woman's family bible hold information that would point him to the treasure Deacon sought?

He couldn't be sure, but figured that's where she was headed.

"I think I see where you're going with this," he said. "Since Deacon went off in search of the gold shipment Murrieta ripped off years after he was supposed to be dead, you think Theresa Montero has information that will help me figure out where to look?"

"I'm telling you what I know because I want to help."

"Did you tell Deacon about Murrieta's great, great, great, granddaughter?"

"I would have." She stiffened and raised her free hand in front of her face as though she expected a backhand from him. She quickly added, "But I swear I didn't know what he had planned except what he told me: that he was going hiking and would be gone a few days. He never told me he was looking for that lost gold shipment."

"How about other people? Marsh for instance? You said Al Brink has told that story a hundred times."

"I might be a lot of things, but I keep my promises. Ms. Montero likes her privacy. Mom made me swear not to tell anyone about Ms. Montero's family bible or her relationship to Joaquin Murrieta. I've kept that promise until tonight." She narrowed her eyes at him. "Look, it might do some good to talk to her and it might not. I think it might. But you won't know until you go see her and hear what she has to say."

"And she lives in Sonora?"

Della shook her head no. "She lives about a mile and a half down the road from here: a big house that sits on a hill in the middle of a grape vineyard; about a quarter of a mile off the main highway. I can draw you a map."

Jack arched a brow. "Sounds like the woman's rich."

Della shot him a strained look that told him he'd guessed right.

"Like I said," she cautioned, "Ms. Montero likes her privacy. Keep that in mind when you talk to her."

CHAPTER 13

Jack checked his watch: Almost nine. If he left right now, it'd be close to nine thirty by the time he got to Ms. Montero's house. Too late to show up without a call ahead to let her know he was coming.

Especially if she likes her privacy.

He rubbed the last dregs of sleep from his eyes. Deacon needed his help now if not sooner. He wanted to be on the trail early in the morning. He didn't want to wait until then to talk to Ms. Montero.

He asked, "You wouldn't happen to have her phone number, would you?"

Della said, "I got it from my mother before I came over."

He watched her dig her fingers into the right hip pocket of her skin-tight blue jeans. He didn't exactly have an uneasy feeling about her showing up at his room the way she did, but he couldn't help wonder how her mother knew Ms. Montero. And how her mother knew about the woman's family bible and her relationship to Joaquin Murrieta.

Did her mother work at the Montero household as a trusted servant?

Or were she and Ms. Montero old friends from a time before lavish holiday balls and extravagant cocktail parties became part of Ms. Montero's opulent lifestyle?

"I'm wondering," he said, trying not to sound guarded. "How is it that your mother knows Ms. Montero so well?"

Della paused and glared at him.

He knew at once that he'd offended her. And he was sorry for that. But in his mind, it was important the question be answered.

He waited. It only took a second.

She jerked her fingers from her pants pocket and thrust her open hand down rigidly at her side. "Are you insinuating me and my mom aren't good enough to associate with someone as rich as Ms. Montero?"

Seeing the flat of her hand and the fire in her eyes, he'd have sworn she was going to take a swing at his face. He quickly raised the flat of his palm between them. "Whoa, Della. Don't get upset. I wasn't implying a thing."

"It sounded like you were to me."

He couldn't tell her he was just being cautious. That was like telling her he didn't trust her.

"Please," he said. "Forget I asked."

She huffed a drawn-out sigh, dug a folded piece of paper from her hip pocket, and slapped it into the palm of his hand.

Jack glanced at the number, snagged a small pad of paper and a pen from the lamp-table next to the chair, and held it out to her. "I really am sorry I hurt your feelings. Please, draw the map. I'll call Ms. Montero to see if it's all right for me to drop by."

Della held him firmly in her gaze. A long silent moment later, she took the pad and pen from his hand and went to work on the map.

A minute was all it took for her to scribble directions. When she was done, she handed the paper and pen back to him and said, "You shouldn't have any problem. Just look for the sign advertising the Annual Frog Jumping Jubilee. That's your turn."

He glanced at the map. Simple, easy to follow.

She added, "Deacon was nice to me. I hope you find him."

Jack peered deep into her eyes. She held his stare a second then lowered her gaze as though she could not look him in the eye. He got the feeling she hadn't known many nice men. Deacon had been an exception. A turning point for her, hopefully.

He said, "Let me walk you to your car; or home if you're on foot. I'd hate for you to be hurt."

"Please," she said. "If he sees you and me leave the hotel together it'll only make things worse."

"Men aren't supposed to hit, you know?"

"Find Deacon," she said. "I'll slip out the back door."

"You're sure. It's no trouble for me to walk you."

"I'll be fine." She opened the door to his room, stepped into the hallway, and closed the door with a soft click.

Jack didn't feel right letting her walk away from there alone. But she had a point. He punched Theresa Montero's number into his cell phone and hit send.

* * * *

Ten minutes after hanging up with Theresa Montero, Jack climbed into his rental Jeep Wrangler and drove south on Highway 49. She'd been less than receptive to him dropping by for a chat. He could understand why. A visit from a strange man at nine thirty at night was something few women warmed to, especially those who enjoy their privacy.

Under normal circumstances, he would have called back in the morning and tried to reason with her.

Not this time.

Finding Deacon alive was infinitely more important than ruffling a few well-manicured feathers. Now he just hoped he could show up at Theresa Montero's front door and convince her to talk to him.

The map Della had drawn him was easy to follow. The side road to Theresa Montero's house was more like two miles south of town, but the sign advertising the Annual Frog Jumping Jubilee and Calaveras County Fair was on the corner of the turnoff making it easy for him to spot.

He turned right and followed a single lane of asphalt through a wide expanse of well-tended vineyard. Just under a half mile in, the roadway ended at a gated drive. The house—more of a walled hacienda than a house—sat atop a rise fifty yards in. He noticed a callbox set into the stone wall to the left of the gate and glanced up. A security camera stood sentry from above.

He pressed the call button and waited. A dog barked from somewhere inside the courtyard—a large, very alert dog by the sound of it.

"Ms. Montero is not accepting visitors tonight," a man's firm voice said over the speaker.

Jack peered up at the camera and saw the lens hone in on him. "My name is Jack Ferrell. I called about a half hour ago. I assure you, it's imperative I speak to Ms. Montero, tonight."

Long seconds ticked by: five, six, seven. He silently counted each one.

"Please drive on up." There was a tone of surprise to the man's voice, that wasn't there the moment before.

Without another second's delay, the massive iron gate isolating the hacienda from the rest of the world, rolled aside. No more polite refusals or demands from the person at the other end of the callbox—no lengthy explanations or prolonged pleading on his part—it seemed almost too easy. Jack doubted his pretty face or his irresistible charm had anything to do with it. That made him wonder what it was Ms. Montero hoped to gain from meeting with him.

Perhaps she was just being accommodating.

And then maybe not.

"Thank you," Jack said with equal surprise and drove on through.

He wanted to throw caution and concern to the wind for once and believe in a common good in people, but he knew that was not going to happen. Some people were just inherently bad. Marsh, it appeared, was one of them. The jury was still out on Della, though it seemed she was a good kid. He'd reserve judgment on Ms. Montero until they'd had a chance to talk.

Beyond the gate, the paved roadway turned to crushed rock. He followed the graveled drive into a walled courtyard and on to where it circled around at the ornately carved front door to the southwest-style mansion. There, he stopped the Jeep and peered through his side window at the courtyard. It was almost exactly as he had pictured it.

Spotlights in the center of the circle drive lit up the immense trunk and limbs of a huge oak tree that sat as a hundred-year-old bastion to nature. Flowers and decorative plants accented by similarly strategically placed ground-lights lined both sides of the driveway. Ivy tentacles crept up the walls.

Impressive and as well maintained as the vineyard he'd driven through to get there. He hadn't expected less.

Swinging the driver's door open, he started to climb out. But immediately reconsidered his move when he saw a very large and visibly protective German Sheppard trot up and sit at alert five feet away.

He eased the door closed, hoping to not startle the vigilant beast. The click of the door latch made him cringe.

The dog growled and bared its teeth.

He glanced at the front door to the villa. The tiled porch was well lit in bright white light as though it invited him there to knock. No way was he going to open the door to the Jeep with that hairy mass of muscle and teeth glaring at him, let alone step one foot in the direction of that porch.

Again, he glanced at the ornately carved front door, hoping Ms. Montero or the man whose voice he heard on the callbox was watching for him. To his relief, the front door opened and a woman stepped onto the tiled deck.

"Quiet, Max." Her command silenced the dog.

The instant her elegantly sculptured features came into view, Jack recognized her as the raven-haired woman he saved from the speeding car.

The sight of her caught him off guard.

She had on a gray jogging suit with dark blue accents, the top zipped up half way, a white pullover blouse underneath. Nothing pretentious or fancy, but she had a presence about her that made him suck in a breath and hold it.

There was no doubt at all in his mind. She was the lady of the house; and the woman he'd come to see.

CHAPTER 14

Jack allowed himself to breathe. This was the second time he would have tipped his hat to her had he been wearing one. He combed back his windblown wavy black locks with his fingers, took a calming breath, climbed out, and stepped into the light so she could get a better look at him.

"Ms. Montero, I'm Jack Ferrell. I called a little while ago." He smiled. "And if I'm not mistaken, you and I met briefly this afternoon."

"Indeed we did." She stepped off the porch and walked to her ever-vigilant German Sheppard. She patted the dog's head. "If we hadn't, you'd never have gotten past the gate."

"In that case, I'm glad for two reasons. I saved a beautiful woman from being run down by an idiot in a speeding BMW and doing so got me past the gate to talk to you."

"Please call me Theresa."

He noticed a man in his mid to late fifties with graying hair and a hard look standing in the doorway. The voice on the callbox. It seemed a bit odd he hadn't stepped outside with her.

"Theresa, it is." He stepped toward her, keeping a cautious eye on the dog. "The man standing in the doorway"—Jack nodded in that direction—"he's your husband?"

"Leandro was killed when his plane went down in the mountains near Napa three years ago." She squatted and hugged the dog. "It's just Max and I now . . . and Carlos there." She smiled in the direction of the man standing in the doorway. "He and Max make sure I'm not bothered."

Pretty, widowed, and wealthy; now he had a better idea why she desired her privacy. A necessity for a woman in her position. He could have kicked Della in the butt for not telling him her husband was dead.

"I hope you can excuse my boldness," he said. "I shouldn't have pried."

"You didn't." She smiled. "Let's go into the house where we can talk more comfortably."

Jack followed her to the front door and politely stood back while she talked in low tones with Carlos. He noticed Carlos cast him a wary eye before turning and walking away leaving him and Theresa standing there alone.

The man obviously had doubts about the late-night visit. Or, Jack thought, it wasn't him or the time of night. He doubted many visitors found their way past that ornately carved front door regardless of the time or day.

He felt a bit privileged when Theresa smiled, motioned her hand toward a room off to her left, and said, "Please, come in."

He stepped inside and found her to be as charming a hostess as he could have imagined. He relaxed into an overstuffed chair in the spacious living room while she excused herself into the kitchen to get them coffee. Strong and black—a heavy dose of caffeine was definitely something he could use. The piece of berry pie she offered, he didn't need.

He rose politely from his seat and took his mug of coffee from her when she walked back into the room. He remained standing while she settled onto the sofa across from him. She was prettier than he remembered—slender, voluptuous, exotically beautiful.

"Please sit," she said.

"As I explained on the phone," he began as he retook his seat. "I'm trying to find my brother Deacon."

Her brow furrowed. "How long has your brother been missing?"

"Twelve days." From the look on her face and the tone of her voice, he could tell she was genuinely concerned. He was sure the lines creasing his face and his tired eyes betrayed his own worry.

After a moment, she asked, "And just what is it you think I can do to help?"

"Straight up," Jack said, "I don't know. Deacon went looking for a cache of gold supposedly stolen by Joaquin Murrieta and hidden in the mountains around here in 1862. Della told me you're related to Murrieta and that you have proof he wasn't killed by Captain Love in 1853."

"And you think my being related to him can help you find your brother?" Her tone took on a slightly suspicious quality.

He wasn't the only person in the room suffering from a case of paranoia. He sighed. "It was Della who thought I should talk to you."

"Her mother *is* a dear friend."

"I'm sure she is." Jack leaned forward, planted his elbows on his knees, and cradled his cup in his big hands. He wanted to get to business. "Ms. Montero, it's like this. Deacon came to Angels Camp in search of a shipment of gold bars Joaquin Murrieta stole in 1862, nine years after he was reportedly killed. I know he hiked into the hills near Robbers Roost and it seems, never walked out. Henry Bastion towed in Deacon's pickup when it was found abandoned and has it stored at the Texaco station on the edge of town. The trail of that stolen gold is the only clue I've got: follow the gold, find my brother."

She gazed at him a long moment without saying anything.

He waited.

"I asked you to call me Theresa," she finally said. "Having saved my life this afternoon vouches for your character. That's why you're sitting here talking to me tonight. Still, I think you understand why I'm a little cautious."

"Trust me," he said. "I'm not here to judge anything you have to tell me. And I'm not here to take anything from you. I just want to find my brother."

Again, she held him in her gaze several long seconds, not saying a word. Finally, she stood and said, "Wait here."

She walked from the room without saying more, and he watched her go. He wondered what she was up to.

Five minutes later, she returned with a book-sized wooden box cradled in her hands. She retook her seat on the sofa and set the box on the coffee table in front of her. "This is my family's bible." She lifted a book from the box. The brown leather cover was scuffed, the edges frayed. "It was handed down to me by my mother, to my mother by her mother, and to *her* mother by her mother's mother when she lived in Sonora, Mexico. I'm not sure how long the bible has been in the family, but it's well over a hundred and fifty years old. The first date noted inside is 1839."

Jack had wondered what a century-and-a-half-old bible would look like. It appeared to be in amazingly good shape for its age. "I'm surprised the pages aren't falling out of it."

She pointed to the wooden box. "Sixty years ago my grandmother placed it in this box for safe keeping. It has been kept in there ever since."

She set the bible face down on the tabletop in front of her and carefully lifted the back cover. "Unless you read Spanish, you'll have to trust me as to what's written here."

His knowledge of Spanish—written or spoken—was limited. He nodded for her to begin and said, "I trust you."

She used her index finger for a pointer as she translated. "The notation is dated September 13, 1863. It says: Joaquin died today of complications from a gunshot wound he received in California nearly a year ago. Before joining God in the kingdom that is heaven, he asked me, his loving wife Carmella, to write his dying words. Even as he speaks them, I do not know the importance of what he says. But I write the words to make his passing easier."

"So he *was* alive to pull that robbery in 1862," Jack said, thinking aloud.

"Yes," she agreed. "But there are many who want only to believe he was killed by Captain Love in 1853."

"But the bible proves—"

"There's more," she said, cutting him off. "Let me finish."

She placed the tip of her index finger on the page and continued to translate the inscription. "All that I have sought and dreamed of, lies in California. What should have been mine rests with the bones of my friend. My only regret is that I could not return with my beautiful wife to live out my final years as they should have been."

She stopped translating and looked at Jack. "My family believes—as do my close friends—Joaquin referred to his love for California."

"But it could also refer to that stolen gold shipment."

"That's been my belief all along."

Jack sucked in a breath. "Let's stop a second. You believe Joaquin's dying words refer to the gold taken in that robbery."

"Yes."

"Okay. It appears Deacon believed Joaquin Murrieta—the Joaquin Murrieta mentioned in your bible there—buried the stolen gold in the mountains north of Robbers Roost and went looking for it."

"Your point?"

"Thanks to Al and your family bible, I do too."

"And?"

"I just want to make sure we're in agreement, here."

"I believe we are."

"Great." He craned his neck. From the position of her finger on the page, he could see additional lines written there. He was more than curious. "What else did Carmella write?"

Continuing to trace the faded writing with the tip of her index finger, Theresa Montero's voice took on a haunting tone as she read: "The morning sun shining through the window of my resting place points the way to the glory I've sought my whole life."

After a quiet moment, she brought her gaze up from the page. "That's the last of his words she wrote."

Jack settled back in his chair to give the passage some thought. "That final entry, what do you think it means?"

She closed the cover on the bible and pressed the pages flat. "It could mean a lot of things. My guess is the words 'Resting place' refer to his deathbed, or even his grave."

"He died in Mexico, right?"

"That's what it says here in the bible."

"So obviously he did. That's confusing. He says all that he has sought and dreamed of lies in California. We agree that's the gold. And then his final words are: 'The morning sun shining through the window of my resting place points the way to the glory I've sought my whole life.' Again, the glory he refers to has to be the gold. He can't be in two places at one time."

"Maybe the words written here were the dying words of a man obsessed with a place he always dreamt of living in."

"Or they're the deathbed confession of a ruthless bandit." He gripped his chin in thought. "We're missing something, that's all."

"I'm truly sorry." She crossed herself, carefully returned the bible to the box, and gently closed the lid. "I really hoped that what was written here would help. But that's all there is."

"Tell me," Jack said, his curiosity getting the best of him. "What was it you were hoping to get out of this?"

"I'm not sure what you mean. I shared Joaquin Murrieta's final words with you because I hoped they would help you find your brother."

He held her firmly in his gaze and for the first time, noticed a faint three-inch scar on her left cheek. There was a story that went with it, he was sure. One he'd love to hear given the opportunity and a more fitting occasion.

For now, the scar would have to remain a mystery. A tiny imperfection that only made her more beautiful.

He grinned. "I know. But what was it *you* hoped to get?"

She was quiet a moment. Then she said, "My great, great, great, grandfather was a thief and a killer. I'm not proud of that. But so were the white miners who murdered his brother and his wife, and so were many of the men who were hired to hunt him down. I'd love to prove Captain Love was a fraud and a liar. And I'd love to find that gold stolen in 1862."

"And I want to find my brother—find the gold, find him."

Twelve days missing.

He stood and said, "We need to work together on this."

80

CHAPTER 15

Jack dropped his father's worn canvas daypack on the floor next to a window table in Nel's Diner and took a seat where he could watch the street and sidewalk out front. The blue long-sleeved cotton shirt and jeans he wore were faded and worn to the point of being comfortable, his waffle-soled hiking boots were stiff from sitting too long in the closet.

The plan was for Theresa Montero to meet him at the diner at six for coffee and breakfast. Remaining true to habit, he arrived with a handful of minutes to spare. He was surprised to see her walk inside a few seconds after he sat down. She was dressed in jeans, a tan long-sleeve cotton shirt, and a pair of two-tone green and brown Gore-Tex hiking boots.

Ten minutes early and ready to go. He liked that. He was anxious to start looking for Deacon.

"I trust you slept well," he said when she stepped to the table. He rose from his seat and slid a chair out for her.

"Dreamed, that's for sure." She settled in chair. "You gave me a lot to think about."

He retook his seat. The waitress—platinum hair, penciled-on eyebrows, and enough glossy ruby-red lipstick, eyeliner, and caked-on face makeup to conceal her age—appeared at their table and wrote down their order.

Della wasn't working. Jack was relieved to not have the

distraction.

"Speaking of thinking," he said when the waitress scurried off to the kitchen, "when I left your house last night, I got to wondering if you or your relatives have looked for that gold? You've got the bible, the clues. And I'm sure you've heard the story Al Brink told me and probably a hundred other people."

"My husband and I looked more than once," she said. "My father and his father looked. Friends have looked. I believe the gold is hidden up there in the mountains, someplace. But under what rock? In what hole? Over the years, we've all just sort of stopped looking."

Jack was still trying to figure her out. He shrugged. "Maybe it'll be different tagging along with me?"

She smiled. "I'm helping you find your brother. Finding the gold in the process is a bonus."

He did like her way of thinking. "Then I suggest we eat and get started."

Their bacon and eggs came and they ate. In Jack's case, that meant taking a few bites. Mostly he poked at his food. His appetite just wasn't there knowing Deacon possibly lay hurt or even dead somewhere in the woods.

"You're really worried," Theresa said, pointing her fork at Jack's plate.

"You can tell?"

"You're picking at your food."

"Yeah, I am. Guess I should hurry and eat so we can go."

"We can leave now if you want."

"Nonsense, you're still eating." He forked up half a fried egg. "Another few minutes won't matter."

Fifteen minutes later, Jack paid the bill and they stepped outside. His rental Jeep was parked in front of the Gold Trail Inn on the opposite side of the street. He looked at Theresa and asked, "Is there anything you need to get from your car before we go?"

"Only my daypack." She pointed. "That's my Outback right up there. The green one."

He arched a brow. "I'd have expected a Range Rover or maybe a BMW SUV."

She frowned at him. "Because I have money?"

He felt his face heat with embarrassment. "Well, yes."

She chuckled. "The Outback serves my purposes just fine. Besides, I do own another car—two in fact: my husband's Mercedes Sedan and his wedding gift to me: a 1965 Ford Cobra. I drive the Mercedes when it suites me, and from time to time Carlos uses it. But I only drive the Cobra on very special occasions."

A Cobra, really?

He wondered. But as hard as it was to believe she owned an actual Cobra and not a reproduction, he had no reason to doubt her.

"You are indeed a special lady."

She gazed into his sea-blue eyes. "I'll take that as a compliment."

The attraction of those dark brown eyes peering into his made it difficult for him to look away. "Please do."

Her gaze seemed to hang there. Shaking off the spell, he motioned a hand toward her car. "Shall we?"

She glanced in that direction. "But of course."

Her Subaru was parked at the curb a couple of doors up the street from Nel's. He walked with her and waited while she gathered her lightweight nylon daypack from the rear storage area. The pack had seen some use.

She closed the rear hatch cover and looped one of the pack's straps over her shoulder. "Ready when you are."

They checked for cars. Seeing the roadway was clear, they trotted across the street to where he'd parked his Wrangler.

From the middle of the roadway, Jack could see something was wrong with the Jeep. The front passenger's side of the 4x4 slumped toward the curb in a way that suggested a flat tire. It only required a quick look on his part to satisfy his suspicion.

"We can take my car," she said, peering down at the ruined sidewall.

He squatted next to the tire, fingered the one-inch slice, and audibly exhaled an exasperated breath. Having to change the flat was an inconvenience, but that wasn't what irritated him. The tire had been fine when he walked past the Jeep on his way to the diner. The person who slashed the sidewall had stuck a knife into it in clear view of him sitting at the window.

He should have paid attention.

"The tire will need to be changed anyway," he said. "It'll only take me a few minutes."

He was removing the jack from under the rear seat when he noticed Marsh walk up to the Jeep and stop next to the front fender. Square jaw, thick lips, cruel eyes, broad chest, heavily muscled shoulders and arms, huge wrists, hands to match—the man was a monster.

Exactly how Jack remembered him.

He took a solid grip on the lug wrench with his right hand and waited to see what the big man was up to. It was Marsh's play.

Marsh kicked the flat with the pointed toe of his shiny brown cowboy boot. "Shame," he said, "A new tire with a hole in it."

"Accidents happen," Jack said.

Marsh didn't like him. That was obvious. And though Jack was not normally quick to judge people, he'd already decided he didn't like Marsh. So why was the man there?

"Funny," Jack said. "I didn't peg you for an early riser."

"Only when it suits me." Marsh turned his hard eyes on Theresa who stood watching. "If I were you," he said to her in a cautious tone. "I'd be careful about the company I keep."

She mocked him with a sardonic smile and said, "That's why I refuse your pathetic invitations to dinner. Once was more than enough."

He laughed. "If you ask real nice, I'll give you another chance."

Jack had enough of Marsh and his mouth. Before Theresa could respond, he asked in a none-too-friendly tone, "What is it you want, Marsh?"

"You're not from around here." Marsh hardened his gaze. "I suggest you go back to where you came from."

"A threat, Marsh?" Jack wasn't looking for trouble, but he was ready for it if the asshole wanted to bring it on. The man wasn't that big. He tightened his grip on the lug wrench. "Sure it was a threat. I wouldn't have expected less from a jerk off who beats up on women."

Marsh grinned and said, "You and me, out there in the street, I'd like that. But not today. My advice to you is to go the hell home—wherever that is—and stay there."

Jack kept his eyes carefully focused on Marsh and said, "Just as soon as I find my brother."

Mash peered back with icy coolness. "What if I told you he's shacked up with a nigger somewhere and doesn't want to be found?"

A filthy-mouthed bigot, too. Jack didn't think it was possible for him to like the man less. But he did.

"I'll find Deacon," he said. "And when I do, I'll leave your quaint little town. Until then, do yourself a favor and stay out of my way."

Marsh did not appear concerned about Jack's threat. He glanced at the toe of the boot he'd used to kick the tire and calmly polished it on the back of his pants leg.

Eyeballing his shine job, he said, "Forget about your brother. From what I saw, he wasn't much. The worthless little shit's probably wandered off and gotten himself lost, or dead, or something."

Marsh was cruel because he liked being cruel. Jack decided he didn't want to listen to any more of the man's shit.

"If something bad has happened to him," he said, "I'm coming back here for you."

Marsh laughed again. "Is that right? Now why would you do that?"

Jack narrowed his eyes. "Perhaps because I'll be mad as hell and will want to take it out on someone I don't like. But then I think you know why."

"I'll choose the time, tough guy. And when it comes, I'll break you in half." Marsh made a snapping motion with a pair of hands that looked big enough to break anything and walked away without another word.

Jack let the lug wrench drop to the floorboard and watched him go. Then he looked at Theresa and said, "That asshole asked you out on a date?"

Theresa shot a hard look in the direction of Marsh's back and said. "The man's a pig."

"That's an understatement," Jack said. He returned to the chore of changing the flat tire.

He was frustrated and angry with Marsh. More time wasted. He tried hard to keep control, but lost it when he reached to unbolt the spare.

He scanned the sidewalk on both sides of the street for Marsh and said, "That filthy, rotten, slimy sonofabitch. Spare's slashed, too."

"I was serious," she said. "We can take my car. We'll stop at the Texaco station and ask Henry to fix the tires. Then we'll find your brother."

CHAPTER 16

Jack kept his eyes focused on the uneven ground. The loose rock and the ever-present layer of decomposed granite that acted like tiny ball bearings under the soles of his hiking boots made walking tricky at times. Enough so that he had to concentrate on the trail at his feet. But even then, he couldn't resist glancing up every few seconds to admire the countryside.

"Let's take a break," he said and sagged against a granite boulder protruding from the ground next to where he stood. A blue jay squawked in a tree behind him and fluttered to an oak tree down the hill.

"Peaceful out here, isn't it?" Theresa said, slightly out of breath.

Jack wiped sweat from his forehead with the back of his hand. "Kind of like being on the ocean only with trees."

"Strange that you put it that way."

"Not really, I'm a marine biologist." He twisted a cap off a bottle of water he'd removed from his pack and offered it to her. "I spend a lot of time on my boat at sea, working."

"That explains the tan." She accepted the water and gazed wistfully at the San Joaquin Valley lying beyond the foothills below them. "My husband and I visited the beach on occasion—Santa Barbara, Monterey mostly. And we took a one-week Caribbean cruise, once. Other than that, I haven't spent much time around the ocean."

He twisted the cap from a bottle he'd removed for himself and smiled. "After we find Deacon—you and me, on my sixty-foot catamaran *Pono*—a couple of weeks sailing around the Hawaiian Islands might be just what the doctor ordered."

"*Pono*? That's an odd name."

"Hawaiian . . . it means *making things right*."

She gave him a long appraising look. "Is that what you do . . . make things right?"

He'd done that, on more than one occasion. And it had almost cost him his life. He wanted to change the subject.

"You know what's strange?" He scanned the trees, rocks, and brush thickets half expecting to see a set of eyes staring back at him. It was ridiculous, he knew. But he couldn't shake the feeling someone was there spying on them.

"What's that?"

He motioned his water bottle at the hillside around them. "A person can hike through these mountains knowing full well no one is close around and still feel like they're being watched."

"I know what you mean." She too scanned the hillside. "A hundred and fifty years ago, men swarmed over every rock, gulley, slope, and creek searching for gold. Maybe they never really left."

Jack gulped down a third of the water in his bottle and grinned at her. "You believe in ghosts, do you?"

Her expression sobered. "I believe in heaven. And I also believe it's possible some people's souls take their time getting there. There are moments when I'm hiking in the hills around town here that I feel the presence of my great, great, great grandfather. At times the feeling is so strong I've stopped suddenly and turned around thinking he was standing behind me."

Jack slid the water bottle into his pack and nervously glanced around. It still felt like someone was watching them. "I'll say this, if Joaquin Murrieta's spirit is doomed to wander these hills, I'm glad you're on my side."

"Me too." She flashed him a smile and motioned ahead with her hand. "Shall we?"

Before he could take a step, a loud rumble of thunder drew his gaze skyward. Through the gaps in the trees he could see dark, threatening clouds building fast overhead. The jumbled boulders creating the natural fortress suitably named Robbers Roost loomed on the hillside above them. They hadn't even really begun to look for Deacon, yet. Damn Marsh and his bullshit games.

"Looks like we're in for it," he said.

Theresa averted her gaze from the threatening sky and shot him a pinched look that clearly showed her concern. "These thunderstorms can build sudden like. Usually not this late in the season, though; and certainly not this early in the day. It must be a scorcher down there."

"It's not all that cool up here." Jack peeled the ball cap off his head, stroked back his sweaty hair with the fingers of his free hand, and slid the cap back on. "I don't particularly relish hiking around up here dripping wet, but it looks like we might not have a choice."

"Rain can fall pretty hard in these mountains." There was caution in her voice. "Lightening gets to flashing around, we don't want to be up here in the middle of it."

"I know, but I've got to find Deacon." He took off walking. Robbers Roost was right there ahead of them. He was determined to keep going.

From just beyond the granite outcropping, Jack studied the lay of the land to the north. He knew enough about hiking to know the quickest way to move about in the hills was to follow an established trail. Whether they are made by man or animal, the trails are there because that's the easiest way to travel.

There was one here, an old well-established trail by the look of it. And the trail led in a northerly direction from Robbers Roost.

He spent the next minute picturing himself in Joaquin Murrieta's boots. Not wanting to rush into a decision, he eased himself into Joaquin's thoughts, trying to reason out what the bandit might have done all those years ago.

Joaquin Murrieta—going by the entry in Theresa's family bible—was most likely wounded in the shootout with the posse; possibly so was Snake-Eye Carlos Sanchez. They were burdened with three hundred pounds of gold bars. It would've been slow noisy going for them to ride high into wild country busting brush along the way before turning north. The best choice would have been to muzzle the horses and sneak away from those rocks as fast and quiet as possible. That meant following a trail.

Was this the trail Al's great, great Uncle Donald spoke of?

He was sure it was.

Now he hoped Deacon read it the same way.

He hooked his thumbs under the straps of his pack and slid the straps farther onto his broad shoulders. Looking at Theresa he said, "According to Al, the posse followed your great, great, great, grandfather's trail north from here. My guess is this is the way they went."

"My husband and I followed this trail several miles. There's a lot of country back in there."

"I'm sure there is." He shot another worried glance skyward. "Let's just hope the weather cooperates."

They hadn't walked more than ten feet when the bulging dark clouds began to spatter rain. A half a minute later, electricity cracked in the air overhead. Hair stood up on the back of his neck and on his arms. Not more than a second passed when a rumble of thunder shook the ground they stood on.

Theresa grabbed Jack's arm. "It's not safe to be up here. We've got to get off this mountain before these clouds really open up on us."

Jack knew she was right. He hated leaving his brother out there another day, but hiking in the mountains in the middle of a lightning storm was no place to be. And if the clouds did cut loose, the grass and dead leaves blanketing the trail would be slippery as ice. They could easily fall and break a leg, or worse. What good would he be to Deacon then?

He stared at the trail ahead of him.

Dammit!

Theresa tugged his arm, clearly urging him to move. "I know you want to find your brother, but I'm serious, it's not safe to be out in this storm."

Jack shot her a strained look.

A second crack of lightening split a tree two hundred feet down the hillside from them.

They both ducked out of reflex.

He straightened and stared at the smoldering stump.

"Now, Jack!" She grabbed hold of his arm and pulled. "It's not safe."

"Deacon's out there," he said. "I feel it."

"We'll find him, but not in this storm."

"But—"

"You won't do him any good if you're dead. Think about it."

He glanced at the smoldering tree, then the trail, then her. He said, "Let's get out of here."

Taking the lead, he took off walking down the path the way they'd come. Marsh had better not get in his way again.

CHAPTER 17

"You don't suppose that hole yonder will fill up with water do you?" Kyle stepped into the downpour, turned his face to the heavy black clouds hanging low in the sky overhead, and opened his mouth wide.

From the relative dryness of the leaky roofed porch, Hector stood watching his brother getting soaked trying to catch the rain in that gaping maw of his. For a moment, he considered attempting it himself.

"Can't see how it would," he answered. "That pit's a good ten foot across and twelve foot deep."

Kyle's lips curled into one of his goofy grins. "Make a right good swimming pool, wouldn't it?"

Hector scratched the mop of red hair on his head. Slowly, a smile formed. "I like the way you think. We could get us some women with big tits, two or three cases of beer, and have us a right fine pool party. But it'd have to rain like a week straight to fill that hole up."

"Remember Mary Lou?"

Hector's smile broadened into a wide grin. "If we could drag her ass up here, we wouldn't need no other women but her."

"Think there's a chance?"

Hector's expression sobered. "She got locked up, remember?'

"I've still got those pictures we took of her." Kyle opened his mouth to the downpour, caught a few drops, closed it, and cast

Hector a look. He asked, "What you think about this rain?"

"I think it's coming down hard enough right now, but it'll be gone by morning the way it always is. Nowhere near enough to fill that pit."

"Maybe we should throw a tarp over it just the same. I'd sure hate for our friend to swim out of there or drown before we make up our minds if we's gonna kill him or not."

Again, Kyle turned his gaping mouth to the rain.

"Now you're using your head," Hector said. It was the smartest thing he had heard his brother say all day.

Kyle swallowed, wiped his dripping freckled face with his hands, and peered solidly at Hector. "A course I was using my brain. I ain't near as dumb as people make me out to be."

"You sure ain't," Hector said.

He darted into the cabin, grabbed a sturdy plastic tarp, carried it onto the porch, and tossed it onto the mud at Kyle's feet. "You're already wet; go ahead and do it."

"Aw come on," Kyle said. "We can toss some of those little rocks at him before we cover the pit. It'll be fun."

Hector chuckled and joined Kyle in the rain. He patted him on the back. "Come on, little brother. At least we don't have to take him any water."

Kyle picked up the dripping tarp, took a step, stopped, turned, and shoved it at Hector. "Hold this. I'll be right back."

"Come on, Kyle." Hector watched his brother step inside the cabin. "If ya gotta pee, pee on him. Won't matter none."

Kyle trotted outside a few seconds later and held up a ham bone with a few ounces of meat and gristle attached to the hock. "Don't have to pee. I grabbed this. I'm no dummy, remember? Now we don't have to feed him dinner."

Again, Hector patted Kyle on the back. "Let's go have us some fun."

* * * *

Deacon blinked against the falling rain and peered up at the two brothers. The moth-eaten blanket he had draped over him was sopping wet. He was soaked to the bone, cold, and absolutely miserable. Why the dumb-shits stood at the edge of the pit, looking down at his wretched carcass, with water dripping from their chins was beyond his imagination.

"One of you didn't by chance bring me a dry blanket, did you?" he asked.

"You'll be dry soon enough," Hector said.

"And whiles you're a waitin' you can chew on this." Kyle tossed in the gnarled bone, leaned closer, and barked like a dog.

Deacon caught the ham hock, tore off a mouthful of meat with his teeth, and extended his middle finger at two dumbshits while he chewed. He'd grown used to eating their scraps. He was determined to stay alive long enough to return the favor.

Both brothers laughed.

"Screw you, you goofy sonofabitch," Deacon yelled, looking directly at Kyle.

Kyle tossed a small rock at Deacon's head and laughed even harder.

Hector joined Kyle's game and they both started tossing marble-sized rocks at Deacon.

With the palms of his hands extended above him, Deacon blocked aside the first half-dozen pebbles. Then one of the larger ones hit him square on the top of the head.

It hurt.

"Dammit," he said. Ignoring the onslaught of stones, he leaned down, picked up a chunk of granite the size of a golf ball, and nailed Kyle squarely in the balls with it.

Kyle gripped his crotch, his faced pinched with pain.

Hector stuttered half a word and lost the rest of it in laughter.

"What'd you go and do that for?" Kyle finally managed to say to Deacon. "I was only funnin' with ya."

"So was I," Deacon said. He picked up his ham hock, brushed the mud and gravel off it, bit off a chunk, and chewed.

He was in no mood to be messed with.

Hector finally stopped laughing long enough to point at Kyle's crotch and say, "He nailed you in the pecker, Peckerwood." Again, he laughed.

"You're the peckerwood." Kyle pushed Hector and they started wrestling on the edge of the pit.

Granules of decomposed granite tickled down on Deacon from where it had been kicked over the lip by their tussling. He stepped back. "Knock it off you dumb shits. I don't want you falling in here on top of me."

"He started it," Kyle said, gasping for breath. "He had no right to say that to me."

"Liar," Hector gasped back.

"Am not," Kyle said.

Deacon watched with a smile. He couldn't believe these guys. They were without a doubt two of the dumbest people he'd ever met.

Or wanted to.

All at once, Hector's expression softened. He straightened. And in a gentle voice said, "I'm sorry, Kyle. Let's get this tarp over the hole and go back to the cabin where it's dry."

Deacon wasn't about to argue with that. For the next couple of minutes, he anxiously watched Hector and Kyle lay scrap 2x4's across the pit and cover them with a black plastic tarp. The roar of rain pelting the sheeting was annoying at best, and at times even maddening. But that he could deal with. Anything was better than sitting there shivering in that miserable downpour.

He bit off another mouthful of gristle and meat and slumped wearily against the granite wall. He barely had energy enough to chew and swallow. But he managed. Then he slid to the soggy floor of the pit, crossed his forearms against his raised knees, and leaned his forehead on them.

He was confined to darkness, but at least he wasn't being rained on. And he didn't have to look at the faces of those idiot brothers.

A sudden chill raised goose bumps on his arms. He raised his head, pulled the wet blanket tight around him for what little warmth it gave and closed his eyes. Jack was coming for him. He could feel it in his bones.

But how long?

He sighed. He was cold, hungry, and at the end of his rope. And he was at the mercy of two of the dumbest men alive. And he could only imagine what they would think up next.

CHAPTER 18

By the time Jack and Theresa made it to her Outback where she had parked it in the turnaround at the end of the dirt fire road, they were drenched and muddy to their knees. The ominous black clouds had settled on the mountain like a scene from a Stephen King movie and dumped on them with a vengeance.

It was still raining hard.

Theresa clicked open the car's automatic door looks on the run from fifty feet away. They splashed to a stop next to the driver's and passenger's side doors, jerked them open, slid soaking wet onto the seats, and slammed the doors closed as though the scene had been carefully choreographed. For a full minute, they sat slumped in their seats, chests heaving. The last couple of hundred yards had been an all-out dash for the car.

"I hate to think Deacon's out there in this downpour," Jack said when he caught his breath. "But you were right about getting off that mountain when we did."

Theresa removed her cap and shook out her wet raven-black hair. "What I need is a long hot shower and some dry clothes."

Jack checked his watch: 11:45. He peered through the rain-coated windshield at the gloom of the thunderstorm. It wasn't even midday and already it seemed late in the afternoon.

Another day lost.

"It's only just now going on noon," he said amid his concern for his brother. "We can get cleaned up and meet somewhere for a late lunch if you'd like, or get together this evening for dinner."

"Let's make it dinner, The Grubstake Inn." She started the car and slid the gearshift into drive. "I don't eat out often, but that place is at the top of the list when I do. Best food in town if you like steak."

Perfect. He'd have been happy to have lunch with her. But now he had the afternoon to sort out at least some of what nagged him.

"Thick and medium rare," he said.

She glanced at him, smiled. "We'll pass the restaurant on the way into town. It'll be on your left. We can meet back there at 6:30, if that's all right?"

"I'll look forward to it," he said. "But I'd much rather meet up at my room and go there together. Or somewhere else if you like. Just so we don't run into Marsh."

* * * *

Showered and dressed in a fresh long-sleeved shirt and Levis, Jack sat slumped in the wingback chair, head back, thinking. Mash's behavior confused him. He'd done nothing to cause the big man to dislike him yet it appeared Marsh was going out of his way to be a jerk. The Jeep's flat tires were proof enough of that. So was Della's black eye.

Was Marsh the town bully flexing his muscles to mark his territory?

Was there something else motivating his behavior?

And what would the man do next, challenge him to a pissing contest in the middle of the street?

Jack pinched the bridge of his nose and squeezed his eyes shut. The thunderstorm was a product of nature. Marsh was a self-made asshole. There was no changing either one.

He sighed and sunk deeper into the chair.

His hope had been to quietly go about his business of finding Deacon and avoid Marsh and his macho bullshit. So far, that proved difficult. He sure couldn't figure out why Marsh seemed so intent on keeping him from looking for Deacon.

But that's how it appeared.

That, or Marsh didn't want him hiking into those mountains.

Ten minutes later, Jack stepped out of the Gold Rush Hotel and onto the sidewalk in front. A steady rain soaked the town and anyone caught out in the open. The afternoon's dismal weather added to his already gloomy mood.

He walked in the direction of the Nugget Saloon. From a half-block away, he spied Al sitting on a bench out front. Al had on the same red and green plaid shirt and the same faded-blue denim bib overalls. He was talking to one of his cronies from the day before–a man not quite as old or grizzled, but with a face that bore the lines of time nonetheless.

Al turned his head and squinted in the direction of Jack as he strode toward him. With the tip of his index finger, Al slid his wire-rimmed spectacles higher on the bridge of his nose and said, "You look like a man with something heavy preying on his mind."

Jack stepped the last few feet to the bench and stopped. "Besides my brother being missing . . . yeah,"–his expression hardened– "Marsh."

"You make friends fast." Al heaved himself off the bench and stepped toward the door to the bar. "I'll let you buy me a beer and we'll talk about it."

"Me too." The man next to Al rose to his feet. "This is a conversation I want to hear."

Jack gave Al's friend a good long look: honest sky-blue eyes creased deep at the corners from age and wisdom, faded blue work shirt, worn Levis, and a thick mustache that forty years ago could have put him in a Marlboro commercial. He nodded at the man and said, "Why not."

With a wave of his hand, Jack motioned Al's sidekick inside and followed him and Al in.

Al and his friend headed directly for the bar.

"Let's grab a table in back where we can talk in private," Jack said before they had a chance to slide onto stools.

He stepped to the bar and ordered the three of them a round of beers. To his relief, Della's brother wasn't working. He slapped a ten-dollar bill on the counter and handed Al and his friend their glass of brew.

They carried their cold mugs of draft to the back of the room and took seats at a table out of earshot of the half-dozen other patrons. Jack settled into a chair where he could watch the room and the door to the street.

"Normally," Jack said. "When I buy a man a drink, he tells me his name."

"My fault," Al admitted. "This here's a friend of mind."

"Bob Burline," the man offered before Al introduced him. Bob reached across the table in an obvious gesture to shake hands with Jack.

Jack gave the guy's hand a firm shake and said, "You were awfully anxious to hear what I had to say about Marsh. Why's that?"

Bob's eyes narrowed in unmistakable contempt. "The look on your face was clear enough. I don't like the man either. If you ask me, he's an asshole."

The corners of Jack's mouth curled up slightly in a grin he couldn't hide. "I assume Al told you why I'm here in town?"

"Yesterday, after you two talked." His resonant voice softened. "Sorry to hear about your brother."

"Thanks," Jack said. "But I have a hunch that isn't why you were anxious to join Al and me."

Bob said, "I understand your brother went looking for a shipment of gold bars Joaquin Murrieta supposedly stole nine years after Captain Love shot and killed him and Three-fingered Jack."

Jack noticed Bob's eyes shift from him to Al and back to him. Skepticism, it seemed. "You don't agree with the story Al told me?"

"We argue about it all the time," Al grumbled. "I think he does it just to piss me off."

"I just tell what I know," Bob huffed. He settled his gaze on Jack. "I grew up in Coalinga. You know where that is?"

Jack nodded. "In the coastal mountains on the other side of the valley, south of Pacheco Pass, I believe."

"Well I grew up there. My dad worked on an oil lease. When I was about eight, my dog died. My dad told me to bury him across the street with all the other dogs. It wasn't dogs buried there, it was Joaquin Murrieta and his bandit friends that Captain Love and his rangers killed. If you're interested, there's a historical monument

99

marking the spot."

"I tell you"—Al swore—"my great, great Uncle Donald knew Murrieta by sight and recognized the killer right off. In case you don't know, as many people who said the head in that jar was Murrieta, said it wasn't. Love lied, plain and simple. He might have thought he killed Murrieta but I don't think so. If you ask me, he was just after the reward."

Bob shook his head at Al. "Crotchety old fool. You and that scorched journal. Believe what you want."

"See how he is?" Al looked at Jack and tossed a sideways nod at Bob. "The man loves to piss me off, I tell you."

It was an interesting story—both sides of the coin—and Al and Bob obviously enjoyed the banter. But Jack wanted to know about Marsh. "So what's up with this asshole Marsh?"

Al focused on Jack and gripped his mug of beer as if holding onto it made it easier for him to talk. "Can't say for sure. He's got a lot of money, I know that much. Owns a used car lot up the road: Gold Rush Motors. Doesn't spend much time there, though. Let's his no-account nephew run it."

"A lot of people have money," Jack pointed out. "Doctors, lawyers, plumbers, real-estate brokers . . . their wives—what's Marsh's claim to fame, besides being an asshole?"

"He showed up in town about a year ago. That's when he bought the car lot from old Fred." Al shot a questioning glance at Bob. "Sounds about right, doesn't it?"

Bob nodded.

"Since then, he's pushed his weight around pretty good," Al continued. "He's managed to make a few friends here in town—spending his money and all—but the impression I get is that most people just try to avoid him."

Jack tilted his mug and eyeballed the foam. "Causes you to wonder how he earns his money."

"Except for what he makes selling cars, no one knows," Bob said. "At least no one I've talked to."

"And you say his nephew runs the car lot?"

"Buy's the cars and sells them," Bob said. "I don't know that Mash has spent more than a few hours there."

"A big lot, is it?"

"A dozen cars, maybe—high-end stuff. But I don't know that many of them sell. Not with the price of gas as high as it is."

Jack gave some thought to what Bob was telling him. "So it doesn't look like the used car business brings him in the kind of money you're talking about?"

Bob shook his head. "Not to me."

Al huffed. "I don't think anyone really cares."

"The law should." Jack took a drink and swallowed it. "The man shows up in town, buys a nothing car lot for his no-good nephew to run, flashes a pocket full of cash, bullies people, beats up on women. Not the sort of guy you want in your community."

"Della?" Al asked.

Jack returned his mug to the table with a solid thunk of heavy glass hitting wood. "Marsh gave her a black eye."

"Not the first time," Bob pointed out.

Jack looked incredulously at both men. "She doesn't report him?"

"She kind of has a history with men," Al said. "A shit magnet of sorts. Deacon was the exception. I think she liked him."

Deacon was easy for women to like. Jack said, "Just because she has a habit of picking dirt bags for boyfriends, it doesn't make it right for them to beat on her."

Al sighed. "No it doesn't. Guess she hasn't figured that out yet."

Jack gazed at the door without seeing. He visualized Marsh for what he was: A mystery man loaded with cash, a thumper of women—a bad combination that meant trouble.

"I know what you're thinking," Bob said. "Forget it."

Jack turned his attention on Bob. But his mind refused to let go of his vision of Marsh. "What's that?"

The muscles in Bob's face and neck visibly tensed. "Two or three months ago, I got a little drunk and made the mistake of looking Marsh in the face and telling him exactly what I thought of his heavy-handed bullshit. He hammered me to the ground before I even saw his fist coming; practically knocked me out. Hell, if he'll hit an old man for speaking his mind, he won't hesitate slamming those big chunks of granite into your handsome young face."

Jack slipped into thought. He was not surprised at the cold expression of anger that hardened Bob's features. He was sure *his* face bore that same look. Hatred did not come easily to him.

Marsh made it easy.

"What Bob's saying is watch your back if Marsh is around," Al added.

Jack said, "You can count on it."

CHAPTER 19

Theresa showed up at the door to Jack's room wearing black slacks, a blue long sleeved satin blouse, and shiny black pointed-toe cowboy boots. Her raven hair was wound into a bun on the back of her head, mile-long gold earrings hung to complement her slender neck. She clutched a small black purse elegantly in her left hand. Jack was dressed in Khaki colored Dockers, a yellow and lime-green flowered Aloha shirt, his Seiko dive watch, and scuffed deck shoes. Certainly an unlikely looking pair.

He knew they were sure to draw some glances.

On the walkway outside his hotel, Jack inhaled a deep breath and let it out. The thundershowers that drenched them earlier had stopped, leaving the street and sidewalks glistening wet and the mountain air filled with the fragrance of sodden earth and damp blades of spring grass turned golden by the summer's sun. Dripping pines and oaks dotted the hillsides around town. He'd forgotten how wonderful the mountains could smell after a good rain.

"Let's walk," he said, his gaze searched her face and settled on her brown eyes. He so wanted to kiss her.

"It's a good three long blocks from here," she said, her eyes locked on his. "You sure you're up to it after that hike in the rain today?"

She wasn't making it easy on him. It took every ounce of willpower he could muster to resist the almost overwhelming desire to pull her close and press his lips to hers.

"We'll take it slow," he reassured her.

"We will?" She continued to hold him in her gaze.

"If that's what you want?" He was surprised he got the words out with her looking at him like that. But the words flowed smoothly and naturally, and he wondered for a moment if he was talking about the walk or them.

"I suppose we should go." She finally tore her gaze from his and peered up the street in the direction of the restaurant.

"I suppose." He started them walking. It was near impossible to resist hooking his arm in hers.

Glancing around, he noticed only a few people moved about the sidewalks. It appeared not many in town trusted the weather.

That was just fine with him.

They strolled past the Nugget Saloon. He peeked inside and saw Al sitting at the bar with Bob. The vision of him sitting there in the bar with those two old sots made sharing Theresa's company all that more special.

In the distance somewhere ahead of them, a siren broke out in a shrill wail. He continued to walk, but cocked an ear to listen. An ambulance probably, or a fire truck, not the police. Their sirens, he recalled, have a distinct wail all their own. The harsh unyielding sound seemed out of place in a town that swept a person back in time a hundred and fifty years.

They climbed the slope of roadway leading north out of Old Town. From the top of the rise they could see—through a gap in the trees and buildings—the brown haze of the central San Joaquin Valley below and miles to the west of them. The presence of smog meant the rain had been confined to the mountains. Above the rolling grey-blue hills on the western horizon, the sun shined bright orange where it dipped low beneath the veil of dark clouds stacked against the Sierras.

"Gorgeous, isn't it?" Theresa stopped and nodded in the direction of the setting sun.

Jack stopped at her side and joined her in taking in the view. He'd seen hundreds of sunsets, all of them beautiful. This one seemed special. He knew it was because of the woman standing next to him.

"It is indeed," he said. But his words came with a tinge of guilt.

Deacon was on that mountain. Something had gone terribly wrong. Now he'd been left to endure another night in the cold.

But what choice was there?

Jack wanted to believe he could have done more to help his brother. But to what end. Lightening had forced him and Theresa off the mountain. Whatever was done would have to wait until morning. The weather would hold and he'd find Deacon safe and unharmed.

He was sure of that.

And he knew he shouldn't let his concern spoil their dinner plans. It was a magnificent evening to spend getting to know Theresa Montero.

"I'm glad we're doing this," he said.

"Me too." Her voice came soft and alluring.

He could tell by the golden sparkle in her eyes, that she meant it.

"I guess we should eat," he said a wonderful moment later. "If you're still hungry?"

"Are you kidding?" Her tone reflected all the emotion of a starving Pilgrim. "I think I could eat one of Al's old mules."

"My suggestion is that you hold out for one of those thick steaks you spoke so highly of."

They chuckled and continued walking.

From a half-block away, he noticed that the parking lot and the curb on both sides of the street in front of The Grubstake Inn were filled with cars. He pointed and said, "I'm glad we left your car parked in front of the hotel and walked."

"I can't remember a time when I've eaten here that it wasn't crowded," she said. "That's why I didn't argue when you suggested we walk."

"Oh?" He arched a brow at her. She didn't look.

She said, "Maybe there were one or two other reasons."

He grinned. "It *is* a beautiful evening."

At that, Theresa glanced up at the lingering cloud cover. She smiled at Jack, her eyes wistful. "Perhaps it's just the company?"

Jack returned her smile and eyed the ominous dark mantle

overhead. "Could be you're right."

The two of them were almost to the restaurant now, and Jack was greeted by the mouth-watering aroma of grilled meat and hickory smoke rising from stacks above the kitchen in back. Having only had a beer and a handful of peanuts for lunch, his appetite knotted his stomach.

Pausing on the walkway in front, he inhaled deeply and said, "Reminds me of barbeques and campfires."

She took a whiff of her own and sighed. "Wait until you sink your teeth into one of those steaks."

He grinned. "Big and thick and juicy, that's how I want it."

When they walked inside, Jack saw right off that Theresa was correct about the restaurant. The place was full of people. They waited twenty minutes before they were seated at the one empty table.

Jack glanced around at the crowded room. His gaze settled on the two tables closest to them.

Both tables were occupied: one had two women and two men close to his age sitting at it; at the other, sat a distinguished-looking mature gentleman and a white-haired lady that reminded him of Betty White. None of them appeared the least bit interested in anything other than the conversation going on at their own table.

"What would you suggest?" he asked without picking up the menu.

"Steak of course," she said. "Thick and medium rare, right?"

He had to grin.

It didn't matter what he ate. He enjoyed the time with Theresa. He hoped Marsh didn't show up there and spoil the mood.

He said, "Did I tell you how nice you look tonight?"

CHAPTER 20

For the first time since her husband's death, Theresa Montero's voice caught in her throat. Men flirted with her, and she parried their advances with the skill of a master swordswoman. But there was something about Jack that made it difficult for her to remain detached from his charm.

She wished their waiter would hurry with the wine.

"Thank you," she said to his flattery. The dinner suddenly felt more like a date than an innocent get-together.

"You make it easy to complement you." He raised his glass of water in front of him. "To elegance and beauty."

She felt her face flush. He was tanned as brown as she was naturally. A wisp of his wavy black hair curled down his forehead. His strong angular features and mesmerizing deep-blue eyes held her firmly in their gaze. The drift into intimacy had been gradual and inevitable.

But not by design.

And not totally unwelcome. No one before or since Leandro had matched her raw sexuality, her wanton desires with the same natural ease and unassuming charm. If she were to get up from the table and walk away right now, she might be able to forget Jack Ferrell.

Not likely.

"To life," she said, lifting her goblet.

He clanked his glass against hers. "To life."

She moved her glass to her lips, then lowered it when she noticed an abrupt change in Jack's mood. His eyes were open, his gaze centered on her, but his vacant expression told her he was seeing the trail, trees, and brush north of Robbers roost. Obviously, having to leave his brother out in the forest another night still bothered him.

But what choice did he have?

She peered at him over the rim of her goblet and said, "You still feel like you ran out on your brother, don't you?"

"It's that obvious?"

His eyes seemed to clear and focus on hers. She'd seen that look many times before, in Leandro's eyes when he looked into the past wondering if he could have done something to save their two-year-old son's life. She mourned her son's loss too, but over time had accepted his death as God's will.

People die—even children—and sometimes there is nothing anyone can do to prevent it. It had taken her five empty years to learn that, and three more after Leandro's death. It did little to lessen the loss of a loved one, but it had allowed her to move on. She wasn't about to sit there and watch Jack beat himself up for something he had no control over.

She took a sip of water, returned the glass to the table, dabbed at the corners of her mouth with her napkin, and looked directly at him. "I don't want to sound insensitive, but your brother is alive or dead. If Deacon's dead, he's been dead for days and by no fault of yours. Eventually we will find him. If he's alive after almost two weeks—and we believe he is—I'm sure he can survive another night or two on his own."

Jack just sat there, quiet.

She watched and waited. It was obviously painful for him to imagine Deacon lying dead or seriously hurt in the brush on the side of a mountain. And it was no consolation to be told that none of what happened was his fault.

A long moment later he said, "Would you feel that way if it was your brother out there?"

She fell silent, her gaze dropping to her hands. His words tore her heart as though it had been pierced by a lion's claw. She couldn't really blame him, but his insinuation hurt just the same. Maybe he wouldn't have been so quick to judge her if she had told him about the tragic death of her son.

But then scars that run deep are slow to heal. She'd only recently found the will to accept the loss of her only child and free herself of the guilt that for years threatened to devour her soul.

She peered into his eyes and said, "Honestly, I can't say I would for sure. But I'd like to think so."

His eyes remained focused on hers, then he shrugged. "I suppose if I were in your shoes, I'd have said the same thing."

"I believe you would have," she agreed and settled into her seat.

There was more about Jack she wanted to know. Perhaps it *was* time she opened up to him about her personal life.

Perhaps, but not tonight.

But that didn't stop him from opening up to her.

Maybe if his mind was on something else . . .

"You mentioned you are a marine biologist," she said. "What is it you do, exactly?"

"Exactly isn't a word I would use when discussing my work. Mainly I study and document the effect of reef deterioration on apex predators."

"Apex predators?"

"Giant jacks, groupers, barracuda, sharks . . . hunters of the ocean's reefs, the big-boys."

"I see. And there's no woman in your life?"

He peered down at his water glass, took it in his hand, and swirled the ice cubes. "Spending months at sea working with fish doesn't exactly lend itself to a lasting relationship."

"Sailors go to sea for long periods of time because that's what they do," she said. "And they come home from the sea. The women you meet don't understand this?"

"None that stayed around long enough to know what my life's work is about."

"Then you haven't met the right woman."

Their waiter brought their wine. They sat quietly and watched him fill their glasses.

When he stepped away from their table Theresa said, "Perhaps we should talk about something else."

Jack lifted his wine glass and said, "Let's talk about you."

She reached for her glass. That wasn't what she meant. Leandro's memory flooded her thoughts and all of a sudden she was weeping. Smiling pensively at Jack and weeping. She didn't sob or sniffle; her tears merely welled in the corners of her eyes, broke over her thick black lashes, and rolled slowly down her cheeks.

Jack quietly lowered his glass to the table and waited.

Theresa turned away for a long moment, then brought her head back around and focused her teary eyes on him. "A year ago I wouldn't have been able to have this conversation with you. Time seems to have made it easier. Or maybe it's you?"

He leaned close, and in a soft easy tone he said, "I can tell that you were very much in love with your husband."

Again, she looked at him. There was no mistaking the genuine sincerity in his voice and the glint of compassion in his blue eyes. But there was something else. There was a fire burning behind those eyes that made her heart flutter and her pulse quicken.

Foolishness.

She found it practically impossible to tear herself away from Jack's gaze. It was so easy for her to be loyal to Leandro when he was alive. When he died, she could think of nothing else. Now she was finding it exceedingly difficult to not be disloyal to his memory, or the memory of their dead child.

She bit her lower lip.

Jack, indeed.

"Are you alright?" he asked in that same concerned tone.

She lifted her napkin and dabbed at the tears. "Isn't it strange," she said. "I would trust you with my life and we've only just met."

"Strange?" Jack said. He straightened in his chair. "You're a strong woman. If you ask me, you've done a good job of taking care of yourself."

She chuckled. "You are a kind man."

That brought a toothy grin to Jack's lips. "Maybe not as kind as you think."

Their steaks arrived, and both Jack and Theresa eyed the two-inch-thick boneless rib-eyes with the intensity of a circling tiger shark.

The young waiter set the sizzling plates in front of them and asked, "Is there anything else I can get for you?"

She glanced at Jack and gave her head an almost imperceptible shake.

"Thank you, no," he said to their waiter.

She saw him refocus his gaze on her, and then noticed him narrow his eyes. At once, his expression hardened. She turned and looked behind her. Marsh was on the other side of the restaurant weaving his way past the tables, walking directly toward them.

"Why don't you do both of us a favor," Jack said when Marsh neared their table. "Find another restaurant to eat in."

"Relax, Jackie Boy." Marsh's tone was unmistakably condescending. "I just walked over here to tell Ms. Montero how nice she looks tonight."

"You've told her, now you can leave." Jack showed no sign of backing down.

"You need to be careful, Jackie Boy." Marsh smiled. "Bad things can happen in the forest."

Theresa noticed the angry glow in Jack's eyes. It was as if a breeze fanned the coals of a fire, and she knew he wasn't going to remain seated long. She needed to end this cockfight before it went any further.

She stood up quickly and faced Marsh. "It's time for you to leave."

"Is something wrong?" Marsh shot her back a blank look that suggested he couldn't understand why she would want him to go away.

She planted her fists on the curve of her hips. "As you can see, Jack and I are having dinner and we'd like to eat it in peace."

Jack grinned from his seat. His hands gripped the edge of the table. There was no doubting his readiness to rise to his feet in an instant if Marsh didn't take the hint to back off.

"If I were you," Jack said. "I'd listen to the lady."

"You dare grin at me," Marsh hissed. "Go ahead and get up. I'll break you in half for smiling at me like that."

"No," Theresa snapped. "No you won't. You're leaving right now."

Marsh turned his gaze on her and held it there.

She didn't flinch.

To the side of her, Jack watched and waited, his muscles taught, his nerves visibly steady. She knew what he must be thinking. This was not about her fighting his fight. He'd already shown he was not the type of man to let her or any woman do that. She was putting Marsh in his place, for her. And he knew that.

A tense moment passed.

"Go," she ordered, and pointed.

Marsh tore his gaze from Theresa and glared directly at Jack. There was no mistaking his intent.

"Jackie Boy," he said. "This isn't over."

Jack slowly rose to his feet and returned Marsh's icy glare.

Thirteen days missing.

"No it's not," he said.

CHAPTER 21

Jack stepped onto the sidewalk in front of his hotel and raised the flat of his hand to shield his eyes from the first glaring rays of sun rising above the high mountain peaks to the east. The morning sky was clear and bright. And only a few puffy white clouds remained floating about. The downpour the day before had left the air and the countryside scrubbed clean.

Confident and eager, he was ready to get back on the trail.

Theresa arrived out front of his hotel as planned. He was glad to find she shared his eagerness. And he was equally glad to find Marsh nowhere around. There would be nothing standing in the way of their finding Deacon.

"You want to drive this morning, or do you want me to?" she asked with clear enthusiasm.

Jack looked her up and down for about the tenth time. On this trip, she wore a Giants baseball cap, khaki safari shirt, dust colored hiking shorts that left her long brown legs exposed from the top of the knee down, and the same two-tone green and brown Gore-Tex hiking boots. Her raven hair hung in a single braid that dangled to below her shoulders.

She looked fantastic.

He could only imagine how he appeared to her. He wore the same light-blue long-sleeved cotton shirt rolled to the elbows and the same faded and threadbare jeans—washed in the bathtub in his room and hung to dry on the towel rack—and the same stiff hiking boots.

"Nice outfit," he said, giving her another onceover.

"After yesterday, I decided shorts and a ball cap were more appropriate."

He laid his daypack on the rear floorboard of the Jeep, next to Theresa's, and smoothed the cover flap over the bulge clearly visible to anyone curious enough to take notice. He thought it best to not be too obvious.

"I'll drive this time. You navigate." He hadn't wanted to stop looking at her, but standing there gawking got them no place. They needed to find Deacon.

He climbed in his Jeep with one hand on the steering wheel and said, "Now how about you climbing into that passenger's seat before I change my mind and leave you behind." He joked of course. And she knew it.

Still, he worried for her safety. And a big part of him wished she'd let him go it alone.

But he knew that wasn't going to happen.

Theresa dropped onto the passenger's seat and shot him a determined look. "I told you, I'm not afraid of Marsh. The man won't dare raise a hand to hurt me."

"Don't be so sure. He likes hurting women; you can bet on that."

He heard her suck in a breath as if suddenly struck by a terrifying vision . . . or a horrible memory. He watched her expression soften.

She said, "You're referring to Della of course?"

He was. After their run-in with Marsh at dinner the night before, he thought it best to tell her that Marsh had used Della for a punching bag. Now it seemed poor Della was turning into the poster child for Marsh's abuse. But Theresa's response made him think.

He nodded. "And I'm sure she's not the first."

She stared up the street in obvious thought. After a moment she said, "For almost a year now, Marsh has been quite open about his interest in my affections. It's almost as if he has dared any man to challenge his claim on me." She turned her gaze on Jack. "It's you I'm worried about."

He smiled and said, "Then we'll just have to make sure we are where he isn't."

She continued to peer into his eyes as if the future was written there. Clearly, she was deeply concerned about him getting hurt.

Probably for good reason.

"Buckle up," he said, nodding at her seatbelt. "Let's find Deacon."

"And that gold," she added.

He grinned. "And the gold."

They rode in relative silence as Jack drove north from town on Hwy 49, both of them taking in the serenity of the early morning. The sun was up now, warm, and bright against a blue sky. Only one car—and old Chevy pickup with rusted out fenders—passed them heading in the opposite direction. No cars were behind them for as far as he could see in the rearview mirror. It looked to be a glorious day.

He turned right onto Murphy's Grade Road and continued up the hill just as Theresa had done the day before. He'd take the same dirt fire road off to the left and park in the same turnaround. He remembered the way.

From time to time, he glanced at Theresa sitting in the seat next to him but kept his thoughts about Deacon to himself. Several times he noticed her glance back at him, but like him she kept what was on her mind, private.

Each of them on a personal mission of its own importance.

And this time Marsh hadn't held them up.

The vehicle that appeared in his rearview mirror five minutes up the road was just a fly speck in the distance. He gave it no particular thought until the vehicle roared to within ten feet of his rear bumper.

His eyes darted from the roadway ahead to the mirror. A Large black SUV—a Tahoe or a Navigator—driving fast on a two lane mountain road.

A knot twisted Jack's gut.

But his anger eased when the SUV slowed, putting a half-dozen car-lengths between them. Only an annoyance. He saw no reason to let the driver get to him. He'd pull to the right and give the car plenty of room to go around him if the jerk driver pressed further.

115

He shot a glance at the roadway ahead and then continued his vigil in the rearview mirror. The distance between them had narrowed.

A second later, he watched the SUV accelerate to within three car lengths of their bumper.

"Asshole," he muttered.

"What's this guy doing?" Theresa asked, peering over her shoulder.

"In a hurry, I guess." Jack eased the Jeep to the right and hugged the edge of the asphalt. The dirt shoulder was a two-foot deep gully carved by storm runoff. He chanced a glance into the rearview mirror and squinted to get a look at the driver's face. It was impossible to see through the glare of the rising sun on the SUV's windshield.

The vehicle pressed closer.

"I can't believe this asshole," he cursed. His eyes darted back and forth from the roadway to the rearview mirrors. Another foot to the right and they'd be in the ditch.

"Pull onto the shoulder and let him pass."

Jack shot her a strained look. "What shoulder?"

She jabbed her index finger at the windshield. "There, just ahead on the right. Pull over."

Jack took a quick look in the rearview mirror and then swerved his 4X4 into the turnout. The SUV—a shiny black Lincoln Navigator with paper plates and gleaming fancy chrome wheels—roared by. He concentrated on the passenger's side window, but the glass was tented dark black making it impossible for him to see the person behind the wheel.

A ghost driver driving a ghost car.

Heading somewhere, fast.

CHAPTER 22

Jack waited a few seconds and watched for the Navigator's break lights to come on. That didn't happen. The SUV was not slowing down. He eased the Jeep back onto the roadway.

He asked, "Did that SUV look familiar to you?"

"Not that one," Theresa said. "Still had paper plates."

He nodded. "Fresh off of the lot."

She leaned forward and peered towards the mountain on his side of the road. "Get ready to turn. The fire road we want is coming up on your left."

He made the turn and steered the Jeep along the narrow dirt road. On both sides the brush, oak trees, and pines clogged the hillsides. Ahead lay the end of the road and the trail they'd followed to Robbers Roost.

Bouncing along at fifteen miles an hour, he couldn't stop thinking Deacon had already been missing too long. Now he wondered if there was a quicker way up; a shortcut that would put them onto Murrieta's trail north and save time. A precious commodity he was sure Deacon was short on.

In spite of the urgency pressing him forward, the risk of breaking an axle or rupturing a kidney kept him from driving fast. The downpour the day before added a few extra ruts and holes to the dirt road but nothing the Jeep couldn't handle.

Four miles in, they arrived at the turnaround where they parked

Theresa's Subaru Outback the previous morning. He braked the Jeep to a stop at almost the same spot and climbed out eager to get going. The Jeep's tire tracks were the only tire tracks in the damp earth. Those left by Theresa's car had been washed away.

He spent a minute looking the area over. There probably was another trail leading up to Robbers Roost. But how much time would he waste finding it? He'd stick to the trail he knew.

"Ready when you are," she said.

The sun's rays caught her eyes, and he saw them sparkle with flecks of gold. He couldn't stop himself from smiling. "Then let's get moving."

He hefted his pack high onto his back and started walking, eager to cover the ground they'd traveled the day before. They'd been over it once. He could think of no good reason to waste precious hours searching the same area twice.

With Theresa scrambling up the trail behind him, he attacked the slope with a vengeance bent on making up for lost time. The prior day's thundershower had taken a toll here too. From practically the first step, the waffle soles of his hiking boots dug in as they threatened to lose their grip on the mud, damp grass, and a fresh layer of slick dead leaves.

Jack continued to push himself to the point of near exhaustion. Every third or fourth step the soles of his boots lost their grip, but each time he managed to grab hold of a tree trunk or limb to keep moving forward.

Forward; no turning back—there was no other way.

That morning he woke up afraid that his run-ins with Marsh, and his concern for Theresa's safety, would distract him from his goal. That wasn't the case. His determination to find his missing brother so totally consumed him he remained on track and focused.

At the top of the ridge, the slope turned more gradual as it dipped and rose its way toward Robbers Roost. Huffing for breath, he slumped against a tree to wait for Theresa.

Even though the morning air rustling the leaves overhead was pleasantly cool, sweat dripped from his brow and soaked his shirt at the chest and armpits making the fabric stick to his skin. He mopped his forehead with the back of his arm, fished a couple of bottles of water from his pack, and stood there taking in the view.

To the east, the Sierra Nevada Mountains rose rugged and densely forested. To the west, the foothills shrank and blended with the vast San Joaquin Valley floor. Ahead of them lay Robbers Roost.

He narrowed his eyes in that direction. Lost or hurt, Deacon was somewhere north of there on the trail of the gold bars stolen by Theresa Montero's long dead relative Joaquin Murrieta.

Find the gold, find Deacon.

A moment later, Theresa trudged up next to him out of breath and sagged against the tree, hands planted on her bare, smooth, brown knees. Pretty and determined. He admired her grit.

"We're making good time," she gasped.

He handed her one of the water bottles. "Have a drink."

She removed the cap, straightened, and took a healthy swallow.

He peered up at the blue sky. "How accurate is your weather man?"

She furrowed her brow. "What do you mean?"

"He predicted cooler temperatures and clear skies."

"Cooler temperatures means there's less of a chance for thunderstorms in the mountains." She looked up. "My guess is he might be right for a change."

Jack chuckled at the inference. "Then I suggest we keep moving."

She tightened the cap on her bottle of water and slipped it into a nylon-mesh pocket on the side of her daypack. "You want to lead or do you want me to take it for awhile."

He grinned. "You just try and keep up."

He led her past rocks, around tangles of brush, and under more oak and pine trees. Sweat continued to slick his forehead and trickle into his eyes. And he continued to mop his brow with the back of his arm. They stuck to the trail where the path dipped below a thicket of six-foot-tall Manzanita and rose gradually on the other side skirting the ridge above. Finally, they reached the granite boulders where they'd taken a water break the day before. Fifty yards ahead of them and a hundred yards up the slope loomed Robbers Roost.

Jack stopped, leaned against the boulder to his right, and glanced at the blue sky. Peering behind him at Theresa he said, "Weather man's on the mark, no clouds. Are you good to keep going?"

She pounded to a stop and hooked her thumbs under the straps of her pack. "I'm good if you are."

Again, Jack grinned. And he realized he'd been doing a lot of grinning since meeting Theresa.

He heaved away from the mass of granite, turned, started to take a step, and stopped. All at once, it dawned on him how quiet the forest around them was. No blue jays squawked and fluttered from tree to tree the way they had the day before when he and Theresa stood there.

He searched the limbs and listened.

Nothing. Not even the chirp of a sparrow or the chatter of a squirrel—none of the forest noises he expected to hear. Only the gentle breeze rustling the leaves overhead. It was as if the prior day's thunder and lightning had scared nature's critters away.

Odd.

He took one more quick glance around and saw nothing to keep them from going forward. He shrugged his pack high onto his back and focused on the trail ahead, ready to find Deacon.

The puff of rock dust from the boulder next to him, the sting on his right ear, and the resounding crack of the rifle seemed to come all at once.

CHAPTER 23

"Here, puppy, puppy." The man's voice came from beyond the rim of the pit where the tarp had curled back in the wind during the night.

Deacon immediately recognized the moronic drawl. It was Kyle, the idiot brother. Hector was stupid. Kyle was dumber than shit.

The sun was out and he could feel its warmth seeping into the hole. But it had been a long, wet, miserable, lonely night—even under the tarp—still a chat with a half-wit like Kyle was better than nothing. He'd gotten use to bandying with the fool and sort of looked forward to his pinhead comments. First, he'd wait to see what nonsense the imbecile was up to.

"You didn't drown on us last night, did you?" Kyle asked from up top.

Deacon looked but couldn't see him. He didn't answer.

All at once, Kyle was on his hands and knees peering into the hole like a kid peeping under the lid of a shoebox at his newfound pet lizard. "There ya are." He flashed his toothy grin. "Nice night?"

Deacon was in no mood for their crap, not even a little. He worked his aching legs under him, stood, and said, "Toss down some wood and matches so I can build a fire and dry out."

Kyle's head pulled away from the opening. Deacon could no longer see him, only a patch of bright blue sky where his face had been. But he heard Kyle say, "What ya think, Hector. Should we let him build a fire down there?"

"I don't know." It was Hector talking, and Deacon heard him go on to say, "He just might catch his clothes on fire and burn himself up."

"Might be fun to watch him dance." Kyle's voice had taken on an excited tone. "Come on, Hector. Let's do it."

Yeah, Deacon thought. Do it.

He could hear the idiot brothers' shoes scuffing the decomposed granite just beyond the rim of the pit. Were they really going to let him build a fire?

Listening to them rummaging around, he could think of little else. The tarp the two brothers stretched over the pit the day before had kept out the rain, but the dumbshits put it there after the downpour hit. He was wet, shivering with cold, and in need of a dry blanket.

"Hey up there," Deacon called out. "What are you waiting for?"

Kyle chuckled. "You want wood; we're getting you wood."

Deacon could hear the scuff of their shoes and some jabber between them, but he still couldn't see the two brothers. It sounded like they'd split up.

Suddenly the tarp over the pit pealed back as if sucked away by a sudden gust of wind.

A burst of glaring light made him look down, and at the same time squeeze his eyes shut and cover them with his palms. For a moment, he wondered if he would see again.

After a few seconds, he cupped the blades of his hands to his brow to block the glare of the midmorning sun and squinted up at Kyle and Hector. They were grinning down at him, clearly pleased.

"Assholes." Deacon flipped them the finger. He was way beyond talking nice to them. Even when he had, being his cordial self got him nothing. Besides, they seemed to respond better to the insults. It had turned into a game.

"What's the matter," Kyle scoffed. "You don't like the sun."

It seemed Kyle was on a roll as was usually the case. Deacon hadn't wanted to be messed with and he sure wasn't in the mood for the man's stupidity. What he had hoped for was wood and a match for a roaring fire to warm his bones. And some dry clothes and a dry blanket.

"I like the sun," Deacon said with certainty. "It's your face I have a hard time looking at."

"My face, huh?" Kyle's grin morphed into a snarl. He turned away, leaned down, and said, "How about I rearrange yours with this."

It looked to Deacon like Kyle stooped to pick up something. He couldn't tell for sure that's what the goofy sucker was doing, but he had a good idea what was coming. He raised the flat of his hand above him just in time to brush aside a four-foot-length of 2X4.

"You like that do you?" The voice came from Hector who stepped into view next to Kyle. Like Kyle, he peered into the pit. And in a not too friendly tone he said, "Be careful what you say to my brother. He's sensitive about his looks. So am I."

Deacon glared back. He had to keep in mind the brothers were twins. Even if Kyle's half dozen missing teeth, extra spattering of freckles, and crooked smile did make him the goofier looking of the two.

"If I looked like him," he said, keeping in mind to choose his words carefully. But not all that carefully. "I'd be sensitive, too."

"Looked like what?" Kyle grabbed another short 2X4, peered into the hole, and shook the board threateningly. "You better not be talking about me."

Deacon Laughed. "Relax, dipstick. There's one or two people in this world worse looking than you."

"That's better." Kyle's toothy smile returned, and he casually tossed down the board.

Deacon dodged the second piece of wood with a little more grace than the first. The 2X4's appeared to be scraps from a pile of lumber he'd seen stacked nearby when he was led to the pit.

"How about a few more of these," he said. "And some matches?"

Kyle and Hector tossed in a dozen more short lengths of 2X4 and an armload of splintered and cracked scraps of lumber that were perfect kindling. Deacon had to keep dodging to avoid the falling wood, but he managed to ward off the onslaught at the expense of only a couple of scrapes and bruises.

"You still with us down there?" Hector stood at the edge of the pit and looked in. He chuckled and dropped a flattened matchbook.

"You be careful not to burn yourself up with these, now. Matches aren't for children to play with."

Deacon caught the matchbook and opened it: four matches. *Asshole.*

He peered up at Hector. "You could've given me a few more."

"I told you Kyle and me are sensitive about our looks." Hector's expression sobered. "Me most of all."

'Yeah," Kyle said with a definite tone of indignation. "You're lucky ya got the matches we gived ya."

Deacon frowned. Hector wasn't the idiot his brother was. But Kyle made up for the two of them. "I'll tell you what, Kyle. You go get the meat and beer, and I'll start the fire. We'll have us a down-home, backyard cookout."

Kyle grinned at Hector and slapped him on the back. "What do ya say? We get us those ribs we have and cook 'em. I'm hungry enough to eat that jackass you found."

Hector shot a hard look at Kyle. "I didn't find him; he found me and followed me here."

"Sure, whatever. Don't really matter none." Kyle smacked his lips and said, "Now what do you say to us a cookin' up those ribs?"

"Good idea." Hector brightened, and then all-of-a-sudden frowned at Kyle. "But *he* ain't doing the cooking."

"Hell no." Kyle pointed his finger at Deacon. "And he ain't gettin' none of our beer, neither."

"You got that right." Hector put his hand on Kyle's shoulder and turned him away from the pit. "Let's go light up the barbeque."

Deacon watched the dumbshit's step away. The warmth of the midday sun did a lot to calm his chills. But the shadows in the bottom of the pit were growing longer by the minute. He needed to get the wood lit while his hands were steady enough to strike a match.

He only had four.

He had to make each one count.

CHAPTER 24

Deacon took his time arranging the small tepee of wood splinters over the pile of smaller slivers so that tender would catch fire easily and hold the flame long enough for him to start larger pieces of kindling burning. He wanted to do it in one try.

He tore a match from the book, closed the flap, turned it over, and brushed the red tip across the abrasive strip.

The match flared.

He dropped the matchbook and carefully cupped the fragile flame with his palms. He let the fire build then slowly lowered it to the splinters.

All at once, his hand began to shake uncontrollably.

Shit!

He tried to will himself to stop, couldn't.

The match flickered and went out.

Reassuring himself he had three more, he picked up the matchbook, tore out a second match, and struck it.

The match-head fizzled and went out.

Dammit!

He couldn't believe his luck. But he still had two left. And he'd damn sure make them work.

He took a deep breath and held it. His shaking seemed to calm some. Saying a silent prayer to himself, he tore loose a third match and brushed it across the striker. The match-head flared to life.

At once, he cupped the flame with his palms and waited for it to catch hold.

The flame caught, and he lowered it to the tepee of splinters.

The wood began to darken. Again, his hand began to shake, and he concentrated hard to calm the trembling.

His fingers steadied, and the flame curled the end of the cardboard match into a black, ash strip.

He let himself breathe.

Already, he could feel the burn on his fingertips. A small price to pay for fire. He forced the pain from his mind and held the match to the shards of wood.

Still the tiny tepee refused to catch fire.

Come on, Baby.

Another second and he would have to let go.

He clinched his jaw against the pain. There was more darkening of the splinters, but still no fire.

Dammit!

Finally, he had to let go, and he dropped the match on the splinters. He jammed his seared thumb into his mouth and watched the remaining quarter inch of the match continue to burn.

He couldn't take his eyes off the dying flame.

Come on . . .

As if his unyielding will alone made the difference, the tepee flared.

Yes!

The flame grew into a tiny blaze, and he gently added a couple of pencil-sized shards of wood. The freshly added pieces caught fire, and he placed on two more shards of kindling about the same size. He waited for them to catch. It only took a few seconds for the dry wood to ignite. Satisfied with his effort, he stacked on a couple of chunks an inch or two square by about a foot long. He straightened and watched the larger pieces crackle.

With the scraps of lumber burning nicely, he angled one of the 2X4's against the granite wall of the pit and kicked the board dead center with the side of his foot. The wood cracked.

He drew in a breath and kicked the 2X4 again.

This time it broke.

Satisfied with the result, he tossed aside the pieces and repeated the process with the remaining 2X4's. Some snapped easier than others, but within a couple of minutes, he had a neat pile of firewood. And three, four-foot-long 2X4 studs left to hang his damp clothes from.

He lifted two chunks from his woodpile and added them to the flames. With the fire burning nicely, he didn't want to stand there idle and waste the heat or the wood it took to keep the blaze going. He still had one match, and if he was lucky, enough wood for one more fire.

Stripping naked, he draped his wet clothes on his makeshift drying rack and set his boots next to the fire. Then he spread his soggy wool blanket out flat on the granite floor close to the blaze so that the blanket could dry. With the help of the sun, it wouldn't take long.

There was nothing he could do now but wait and warm his aching bones. He sat on his bare butt close to the fire's heat, closed his eyes, and tried to ignore the growl in his stomach.

"Hey you down there, here's something you can cook"

Kyle's voice brought Deacon to his feet. The idiot was relentless.

He looked up just in time to see a four-foot long diamondback rattlesnake fly over the rim of the pit.

The enraged serpent landed at Deacon's feet, raised his head, and lashed out with it fangs at the same time that Deacon screeched and jumped backwards.

Dammit!

Deacon put another step between him and those venomous fangs.

The diamondback bit the air a second time, then coiled into a tight circle with his tail pointed at the sky, its rattles buzzing a warning.

"Kyle, you asshole," Deacon yelled with a quick glance up.

Kyle laughed from beyond the pit.

The rattler was anything but funny. Knowing the two of them could not live together in the confines of the hole, Deacon stared at the angry snake for close to a minute before he remembered the imposing viper was good to eat.

Chicken; tastes like chicken.

Keeping his eyes focused on the rattler's flickering forked tongue, he yelled, "Kyle, throw me down a stick I can use for a skewer."

He hoped Kyle was still there.

"Catch," Kyle said, several long seconds later.

Deacon looked up and saw a branch as big around as his little finger and half the length of broom handle arch into the hole. He caught the stick, turned, and grinned at the snake.

CHAPTER 25

Jack wasn't about to stand there and let himself or Theresa get shot. He grabbed her by the arm and pulled her to the ground with him. And at the same time, he shrugged off his daypack and let it drop.

It surprised him how quickly and naturally his fingers found their way under the flap and onto the walnut grips of the loaded revolver inside.

Without hesitation, he withdrew his father's prized .357 Colt Python ready to swap lead with whoever had done the shooting. Crouched behind the boulder for cover, he carefully scanned the trees and rocks on the hillside ahead, above, and behind them for the bushwhacker bent on putting a bullet in him.

Nothing.

Keeping low and exposing as little of his head as possible, he focused his gaze on Robbers Roost. On the high ground above, nature's stronghold loomed like a massive granite fortress. The shooter had to be up there.

"You've been shot," Theresa gasped. Then her eyes widened even more.

He knew at once she had seen his gun. Reaching up with his free hand, he gingerly probed his injured ear, winced, looked at his fingertips, and saw the blood. A lot of blood, but the wound seemed minor.

Just deep enough to make him bleed.

"I'll live," he said. He pointed a bloody finger at the boulder next to her. "Slide behind that rock and keep your head down."

The threat came from above. He turned his gaze on Robbers Roost and held it there. A hundred and fifty years ago Al's great, great Uncle Donald caught up with Joaquin Murrieta at this exact spot. Donald himself had possibly taken cover behind the same rock. Had Donald's men truly fired first, killing one of the bandits? Or had Murrieta and his cutthroats fired down on the posse, drawing first blood?

Just as the gunman had today.

For sure, more than one honest man died that afternoon. He wouldn't let history repeat itself.

* * * *

Jack and Theresa hadn't moved from the cover of the boulders. He checked his watch: forty-five minutes. No other shots had been fired.

Theresa peered at him from behind her rock. She seemed content to remain hidden there a while longer. Not him, he had enough of lying on his belly in the dirt like a lizard waiting to be stepped on. Besides, his gut told him the shooter had meant to fire just that one shot.

"We've been hunkered behind these rocks for the better part of an hour," he said. "I'm going to see if the person who shot at us is still up there."

"No, Jack." She reached out and placed her hand on his arm before he could move. "That's exactly what he could be waiting for."

He glanced back at her. "You going to stay huddled down here in the dirt all afternoon waiting for the sun to go down? I sure don't want to have to stumble out of here in the dark."

She tightened her grip. "And I sure don't want you walking into a bullet."

He held her in his gaze and sighed. He really did like this woman.

"Trust me," he said. "Neither do I. Besides, something tells me the shooter's long gone."

Her fingers slid hesitantly from his arm. He could tell by the way she looked into his eyes and the way she moved her hand, she truly did not want to let him go. He didn't much like the idea either, if his gut instinct was wrong. Still, he felt he had little choice.

Even so, he didn't have to rush into the open like a young buck in heat.

He set the revolver on the ground beside him, dug his binoculars from his pack, exposed just enough of his head to allow him a look, and focused the field glasses on the rocks where the shot had most likely come from. A half-minute later, he slid the binoculars back into his pack.

Theresa watched him from her rock hiding place. There was unmistakable concern etched in her expression. He knew the question she wanted answered.

"I couldn't see anyone," he said.

Her eyes didn't waver. She said, "It doesn't mean he's not out there."

She was right, and she knew it. So did he. But he had to do something.

"Wait here" he said. "I promise I'll be careful."

Before she could voice further objection, he took a tight grip on the butt of the .357 magnum and slipped from the safety of the boulder.

Although he remained largely convinced the shooter was long gone from the area, uncertainty made him cautious. Keeping low and moving from rock to rock and tree to tree, he carefully checked the woods in front of them.

Nothing.

Still cautious, he circled high on the slope thirty yards to the north and took cover behind the trunk of a large digger-pine. From there, he peered down on the jumble of boulders below.

Nothing.

Had the gunman been behind those rocks, he'd have seen him. That much he was sure of.

"It's safe," he called out.

Stepping from behind the tree, he stood for a moment staring down at where he'd been standing when the shot was fired. Theresa

Montero stood there now, gazing up at him, and in plain view. That meant he'd been an easy target. So what was that shot all about?

An accident?

Or a message: Stay away?

Again, his gut confirmed his suspicion. Only one bullet had been fired at them. And that shot was no mistake. Someone didn't want them following Murrieta's trail north.

Why?

The gold? Something else?

Had the shooter fled along the trail to the north; and was he hiding there now, planning another ambush?

One thing was for certain. If the asshole had intended for the bullet to hit its mark and missed, they couldn't count on being lucky a second time.

His heart said keep going, but common sense and caution told him the safe thing to do was to take Theresa home and come back in the morning, alone. He could almost guarantee the shooter wouldn't hide out in the woods all night waiting for them.

Now he could only wonder if his brother ran into the same unfriendly welcome.

If Deacon had, and was dead, his remains weren't there now.

They'd have smelled him.

And without a body what could be done.

He could go to the local Sheriff for help. But what proof did he have that the shot was anything but an accident? After all he and Theresa were on U.S. Forest service land.

People shoot guns there.

Besides, what reason could he give the authorities for why someone would want to shoot a man and woman hiking in the hills: to keep him from finding his brother? And so what if his brother was missing. Was it by his choice? There was nothing indicating foul play was involved. Even having heard Al's story, he couldn't say for certain his brother wasn't alive and well and simply wandering the mountains in search of *Murrieta gold*.

Everything about the shooting was absurd. But he couldn't chance Theresa getting hurt, or worse.

In the morning, he would return to the mountain alone, and

ready.

He skirted the granite fortress and started down the slope to where Theresa stood waiting for him. He hadn't walked ten feet when he noticed a fresh boot imprint. And a few feet away, another one, the outline of the pointed toe clearly visible in the damp earth.

The tracks led him to a gap in the boulders—a sort of pathway to the center of the granite fortress. It was there that he noticed the same boot tracks leading out. He followed the tracks to a large slab of granite on the backside of Robbers Roost out of view from where he and Theresa had taken cover.

He stepped onto the flattened boulder, squatted, and scanned the area. The ground fifty feet to each side and a hundred feet beyond was littered with small rocks and course gravel. The tracks disappeared from view and it was his guess as to which direction the shooter had taken from there.

He was past being afraid. But a chill of uncertainty brought goose bumps to the skin on his arms and raised the hairs on the back of his neck.

A sparrow fluttered and chirped.

His eyes narrowed with suspicion. Perhaps even now, the shooter watched from the concealment of the thick brush, contemplating, waiting.

He couldn't be certain, but he had a feeling their reaction to the gunshot dictated the shooter's next move.

What he did know for sure is he big man who fired the shot—from the size and depth of the boot impressions—knew the country; and knew exactly what he was shooting at.

And he'd drawn first blood.

Jack would not forget that. Nor would he forget he had to leave Deacon out there one more night.

If Marsh *was* the man behind the gun, next time he wouldn't find it so easy.

CHAPTER 26

Deacon drew his legs up tight in front of him and folded his forearms across his knees. He winced at the unrelenting granite floor, repositioned his butt, and lowered his forehead onto his arms. The barbequed rattlesnake had quieted his rumbling stomach. What he wanted to cap off the afternoon was one or two of Kyle's beers.

But the dickhead wouldn't give one up.

Kyle had refilled the water jug, though. And that was better than a cold beer, almost. Deacon chuckled to himself, thinking. From the music and the sound of Kyle's and Hector's hooting and hollering, the two were having themselves a real party. Perhaps he could sweet-talk Kyle out of a beer once the idiot and his stupid brother were good and drunk.

Possibly, but for now, he was content to sit there and let his mind work on something other than staying warm and dry. He'd thought of little else since the thundershowers the day before.

For two weeks, he'd spent endless hours staring at the walls of the pit. And each night in the darkness of his hole, he blindly probed the cracks and niches in the rock with his fingertips. The granite walls were for the most part relatively smooth. But there were chips and gouges, some of them almost deep and large enough for a hand or foot hold to climb out by. With some chisel work on his part, the fractures could easily be enlarged and reshaped to accommodate his fingers and the toes of his hiking boots.

If he had a chisel.

He peered over his forearms at the blackened rusty four-inch-long door hinge sitting on the granite floor next to the charred boards. The coals had cooled. But an hour before the wood had been ablaze. And the moment he noticed the hinge in the fire, he'd dug it from the hot embers with his cooking stick and set it aside to cool.

At the time, he didn't know what the hinge could be used for. Still, the hinge-plates were solid metal—so was the pin holding them together—and sturdy pieces of metal were always useful for something.

And now he knew just what that something was.

His mind was working clearly, again. The food and water had refueled the cells in his brain. And like the broad side of a broom, had brushed away the cobwebs clouding his thoughts.

He rocked forward onto his hands and knees, crawled to the hinge, and picked it up. Rolling onto his butt, he leaned his back against the wall of the pit and eyeballed the metal parts.

What he needed was a chisel.

He picked up a hand-sized rock that looked like it could take some pounding and beat the hinge-pin out of the hinge-plates. The stone cracked in half but not before it did the job. Setting the two plates aside, he picked up the pencil-sized metal pin. With a thick flat head on one end, it looked like a fat nail with a blunt point. It would do. Now what he needed was a hammer. A rock—he now knew for sure—would just crack and break apart.

He found what he needed in the charred remains of the fire: Nails. The old boards had been full of them.

All he had to do was nail one of the hinge-plates to the narrow side of a short length of 2X4. The thick metal would make a suitable hammer head. And it wouldn't crack into a hundred pieces in his hand.

He sorted through the nails and found the ones he needed. And then he checked the boards left in his pile and found one that had split lengthwise at an angle leaving it slightly tapered at one end and fat at the other. It would make the perfect handle. He could even use the rough surface of a rock to remove splinters and round off the edges on the smaller end to make a comfortable handgrip.

A renewed optimism fueled his effort. When he was done fastening the hinge-plate to the board by using one stone and then another to drive a dozen small nails into the wood through the four screw holes in the plate, he had a respectable looking mallet with a sturdy metal head capable of driving the chisel into the rock.

He picked up his makeshift hammer and eyeballed his handiwork. He had to grin.

Eager to give the crude sledge a try, he peered up at the rim of the pit. From the sound of the goings-on topside, the idiot brothers were still at it, barbequing or partying or whatever it was the two of them were doing. Their gangster rap was cranked loud enough on their ghetto-blaster to bust eardrums, even in the bottom of the pit.

And that was exactly the distraction he needed to begin his work.

Now if the idiot brothers' continued partying true to form, he'd see if his plan worked. He hefted his mallet and picked up the metal pin.

The many hours he'd spent studying the walls of the pit hadn't been wasted. He knew right where to begin work: On the rock face in front of him where there were a suitable number of gouges and fractures leading to the top. With some chisel work and luck, the notches would provide hand and foot holds sufficient for him to climb out by.

A particularly loud and obnoxious song about bitches and drugs and guns and killing started to play. Seizing the perfect opportunity to make some noise of his own, he placed the metal pin against a vein of quartz and swung the mallet once, twice.

A golf-ball-sized chunk fell away.

Perfect.

He raised the mallet for another strike.

Suddenly the music stopped.

CHAPTER 27

Hector jumped to his feet and switched off the boom box. But it was already too late. The wide-eyed look on his face said he knew he and Kyle were in deep shit with the big man.

Marsh frowned at them through the windshield of his shiny black Lincoln Navigator.

Idiots.

He shook his head in disbelief. Hector and Kyle had been sitting with their backs to him. That ghetto-crap music playing so loud they hadn't even heard him drive up. He was sure it was only by accident that Hector happened to notice the big SUV sitting there and *him* watching them through the windshield.

He opened his door, climbed out, and slammed the door hard enough for the idiot brothers to know he was pissed.

Both brothers stared.

Marsh glared back at them.

Almost immediately, his gaze focused in on Kyle.

Fucking moron.

Marsh shook his head in disbelief. The freckle-faced stooge was too stunned or too dense to realize he needed to move his ass. He just sat there in his chair with a half-eaten rib poised at his barbeque-sauce-smeared mouth.

The veins in Marsh's neck bulged.

"Put down that damn rib," he said. "And stand up, you

boneheaded idiot!"

Kyle shot to his feet and tossed the half-eaten rib over his shoulder and into the pit fifteen feet behind him.

"What in the hell is going on here?" Marsh directed his question at Hector. Kyle was a waste of time.

Hector offered a shaky grin and said, "Me and Kyle, we was just havin' us a little barbeque is all."

"Don't give me that Barbeque shit." Marsh threw the butt of his Cuban cigar onto the dirt, ground it into the course soil with the toe of his boot, and strode toward Hector and Kyle. "Listening to that stupid music and getting shit-faced is what you two were doing. Those plants are ready. I want you both in those fields working, not sitting here drinking beer and eating ribs."

Kyle brushed the back of his hand across a smear of barbeque sauce on his face and said, "Me and Hector has been working hard." He motioned his honey-glazed hand in the direction of eight haystack-sized piles of sundried marijuana plants down-slope from their shack. "Already pulled and stacked half those plants, maybe more. Another day or two in this hot sun and those buds will be dry enough to cut and package."

Marsh pointed a massive index finger at Kyle. "You keep your mouth shut. I'm not in the mood for any of your idiotic crap."

Again, he looked directly at Hector. "I drove in here without either of you hearing me. Someone else can do the same thing. I can't risk losing this crop because you two morons are too stupid to realize that."

Kyle sidled up next to Hector and said, "But no one else knows which road to take to get in here."

Marsh had no intention of responding to Kyle's idiotic comment. Hector at least, had had enough sense to keep his mouth shut for once. He brushed past the two brothers and stepped in the direction of the pit.

Hector and Kyle exchanged worried glances.

Marsh shook his head at the bottles and cans as he walked.

"Clean this mess up," he said. "And I hope you're not throwing trash in that hole."

"We ain't," Kyle said, bringing Marsh to a halt.

"*Ain't?*" Marsh shot Kyle a hard look. "You damned well better not be."

Kyle stood there with his mouth closed.

After a moment, the muscles in Marsh's neck relaxed. He took a step closer to the pit, pointed his index finger, and continued: "If that Barney Fife Sheriff of ours grows a spine and comes nosing around this place after we're gone, or some lousy do-good deputy, or especially those state DEA bastards, you can bet your ass they'll be sifting through everything looking for names, including any trash you've thrown in there. Now the two of you might not mind having your names and fingerprints dug out of this shit, but I damn sure don't want mine turning up here."

Hector shrugged. "We don't—"

Marsh thrust his hand up in front of him, cutting Hector off. "Don't even start."

He turned and took a step closer to the hole.

Hector and Kyle exchanged worried glances.

A *heehaw* from the donkey stopped Marsh in his tracks a few feet short of the rim of the pit.

Marsh turned and looked.

Dammit!

There seemed to be no end to Hector and Kyle's stupidity. He pointed his thick index finger at the donkey and shot a scathing glance over his shoulder at Hector that made the young man take a step backward. Marsh still did not want to talk to Kyle. "Where-in-the-hell did that jackass come from?"

Kyle grinned and said, "He followed Hector home."

Marsh focused his flinty stare on Kyle. He couldn't believe the freckled-faced redheaded idiot insisted on talking to him when he clearly didn't want to hear a word from the stupid ass. He was putting an end to their nonsense, now.

"Did it ever occur to either of you two dumbshits that the owner of this ugly jackass might come here looking for him?"

"How—"

Again, Marsh cut Hector off with a dismissive hand. Another excuse. He didn't want to hear it.

Without a word more, Marsh pulled a two inch-barreled .38

caliber revolver from a holster sewn into his boot, cocked the hammer back, and aimed the gun at Kyle's head.

Kyle cringed.

Marsh kept the revolver pointed directly at him a few tense seconds, then stepped close to the donkey, and shot the long-eared beast between the eyes at point-blank range. The animal dropped to the ground like a sack of rocks. He didn't even twitch.

"You want to barbeque?" He pointed at the dead donkey. "Cook that."

Hector and Kyle just stared at the dead burro. A tear formed in the corner of Kyle's eye and streaked his cheek. Hector sniffled.

Kyle ran the back of his hand across his cheek. "Me and Hector couldn't never . . ."

The veins in Marsh's neck swelled. He marched past the twins and continued on to his SUV. He had his fill of Hector and Kyle. At the driver's door, he turned and faced the brothers who stood staring at him with stunned looks plastered on their freckled faces.

Dammit!

Jack Ferrell's single-minded determination, Theresa Montero's insolence, the idiot brothers' stupidity—he was so pissed he considered shooting Hector and Kyle dead and be done with them.

And he would. But first, he needed them to harvest the marijuana.

He jabbed an angry finger at the brothers and said, "I don't want to find you two pulling any more shit like this. In fact, get your asses to work bagging what's dried. You've got three days. I'm sure you lazy asses can accomplish at least that much." He nodded at the carcass. "Now bury that jackass, and I mean bury the son of a bitch deep. I don't want to come back here and find you've just tossed a few shovelfuls of dirt on top of it. Got that? And keep a sharp eye out. Anyone you catch nosing around here, kill 'em."

"But me and Hector, we—"

He opened the driver's door of the Navigator, climbed inside, and slammed the door shut cutting Kyle off before he could get started.

Idiots!

Next time he *would* shoot them both.

CHAPTER 28

The unmistakable sound of a large caliber pistol shot silenced the countryside. An eerie stillness as resolute as death fell on the pit. Deacon flattened himself against the cold stone wall and waited.

An eternity.

He'd heard shouting, deep angry tones directed at Hector and Kyle—about trash and the pit; and about the donkey Kyle mentioned earlier. He was still trying to put a face to the voice. It sounded familiar. But from the bottom of the hole, it was hard to know for sure.

He cocked his head and peered nervously at the rim of the pit. More importantly, the man sounded big and mean tempered.

And he carried a gun he wasn't afraid to use.

The man's vicious berating of Hector and Kyle, suggested he was most likely the brains and money behind the dope. The gunshot, no doubt, had been fired by him.

But who was shot?

Deacon didn't want to think the asshole had blasted a hole in one of the idiot brothers. He wasn't exactly fond of Hector or Kyle, but he didn't exactly dislike them either. They'd kept him alive. He'd give them credit for that much.

Now one of them might be dead.

The goofy shits.

He felt an almost unbelievable flood of relief when he heard

Kyle speak up and mention Hector's name. They were both alive, but he knew now the burro had taken the brunt of the man's anger.

With his back pressed tight to the wall, he kept his gaze focused on the rim of the pit in the direction of the angry voice. His thudding heart threatened to beat its way through his chest, and he was sure every beat could be heard from above. He forced back his fear with the understanding there was not a thing he could do but keep absolutely quiet and wait and listen and hope he wasn't discovered.

More like pray he wasn't discovered.

Hector and Kyle had obviously kept his presence in the pit a secret. He didn't even want to venture a guess how the ill-tempered asshole would respond if he found him there. A shot in the head for sure. After all, the cold-hearted bastard had just shot that poor donkey.

He held his breath, waiting, watching. But all he heard was a mouthful of angry muttering from the big man, followed by the deep-throated roar of a V-8 engine, and the fading crunch of tires on gravel.

At last, he let himself take a deep breath. He was safe for now—at least from the brute in the car.

But for how long?

Too much had been said. Too much had been heard. This wasn't going to be an easy situation to talk his way out of.

The bastard in the high-powered car would surely return. And when he did, what or who would he shoot next?

CHAPTER 29

Jack struggled to put his thoughts about Deacon aside and focus on the two-mile hike back to the Jeep. No Sunday-afternoon stroll in the forest. Not with a trigger-happy gunman prowling the woods.

He hefted his pack onto his shoulders, took a firm grip on the butt of the Colt, withdrew the revolver from where he had it tucked under his belt, and said: "Let's get moving."

The look on Theresa's face suggested she wanted to say something. But she kept her silence and shrugged on her pack. She hooked the straps with her thumbs in an obvious gesture she was ready to head back and stood there, waiting.

Jack didn't feel like he needed to say more. She knew it was hard for him to leave Deacon out there. And she knew he was leaving because of his concern for her safety.

But what choice did he have? They had been shot at once. They may still be a target. He had to get her to safety before he did anything else.

Planting his feet solidly on the dirt and dead leaves of the pathway, he started down the uneven slope he and Theresa walked up that morning. An easy trek downhill, but he couldn't take anything for granted. He and Theresa were headed back, but that didn't mean they were out of danger.

With Theresa following close behind, he scanned the trees, rocks, and brush ahead of them. He didn't have to remind himself

143

that the man was armed with a high-powered rifle. Nor did he have to tell himself that if the guy was any kind of marksman at all, he could easily put a bullet in them from a couple of hundred yards away.

But only if the shooter had a clear shot.

That wasn't going to happen.

Every tree or large rock provided another spot for an ambush, every thicket of brush. But the same trees, brush, and boulders that offered the gunman cover and concealment, worked for them as well. Jack did not plan on slowing down or stopping in a clearing long enough to give the shooter time to line them up in his sights.

He pushed hard and when they were a half mile above the fire road, the trees thinned enough so that he could see the ribbon of brown snaking its way to Murphy's Grade Road. So far, they walked under cover of the trees without any sign of the shooter. But the turnout where they had parked the Jeep, remained. If the shooter waited to catch them out in the open, that was the perfect location for an ambush.

At the edge of the trees, Jack stopped and peered into the openness of the turnout. The Jeep beckoned to him like an exotic large-breasted woman on an otherwise deserted white sandy beach.

No matter how much he wanted to go to it, he had to be content to sit back and stare.

That or chance being shot.

He accepted the risk and stepped cautiously into the open. Having had the protection of the forest, the expanse of naked ground between him and the Jeep was unnerving.

In front of him, a set of fresh tire tracks caught his eye. They weren't there when he parked the Jeep.

He'd have seen them.

The skin on his arms prickled as a chill swept through his body. He swore under his breath that someone watched him from the shadows beneath the trees. Those mysterious unseen eyes again.

Ghosts from the past.

Murrieta?

He took one more glance around, stepped closer, and saw the now familiar pointed-toe boot impressions.

His earlier suspicion had been correct.

He couldn't say for sure the man who shot at them was Elliot Marsh. But the trigger-happy asshole with the gun had parked there after they were far enough up the trail not to hear him drive up. Then he'd hurried ahead to lay in wait for them at Robbers Roost.

And the shooter had been alone.

He tucked the revolver into his belt and stepped closer. The single set of boot impressions led from the driver's side of the mystery vehicle, around the Jeep, past it toward the mound of dirt and tree slash pushed into a berm at the end of the road, and back to where they started.

It was obvious boot-man exited and reentered the vehicle on the driver's side. The deep angled gouge left in the damp soil by the off-road tread of front tires when the driver cranked the wheel to steer back onto the roadway was clearly visible.

And since there were no pointed-toe boot impressions on the trail they took, the bushwhacking sonofabitch had taken a different trail up the mountain. And he knew he'd beat them to the top.

Jack turned and waved an all-clear to Theresa.

"So he did follow us here?" she said, nodding at the boot tracks at her feet.

He pointed at the berm. "And it looks like he hiked in through there."

She stepped beside Jack and peered in that direction. "A shortcut?"

"That's my guess. One thing's for certain, the guy knew exactly where he was going and that he'd beat us there."

"But why would he do that?"

"My thought is he doesn't want us poking around up there."

"Doesn't make sense."

"To me either." He placed the palm of his hand on her shoulder and nudged her in the direction of the Jeep. "There's nothing more we can do up here . . . not today, anyway. Let's head back to town."

She took a step and stopped. "You notice anything odd about the Jeep?"

Jack looked. "The tires have air in them, if that's what you mean."

"Look again." Her voice reflected her suspicion.

He did. The Jeep's hood was ajar.

"Sonofabitch!" He clinched his hands into fists.

Theresa was already walking that direction. He trotted past her to the Jeep and lifted the hood. He sighed at a tangle of wiring piled on top of the engine.

"That doesn't look good," she said.

"It's not," Jack said without a glance her direction.

"Can you fix it?"

He reached in and picked up a wad of wires. He'd made minor repairs to the engines on his boat a number of times. This was more than minor.

"Not this." He tossed the wires on the engine where he found them. "I'm afraid we'll have to call Henry."

She shook her head and said, "Between you and your brother, you're turning that service station of his into a profitable business."

"I just hope my cell phone works up here." He located the number he had stored in his cell phone and hit send. He got Henry on the fourth ring.

"Henry," he said. "This is Jack Ferrell. I—"

A chuckle from Henry cut him off in mid sentence. Jack could imagine what Henry was thinking.

"You're going to make me rich, boy. What's wrong now?"

"You know that fire road off of Murphy's Grade, the one hikers take when they want to hike into Robbers Roost?"

"Where your brother's truck was found abandoned." The humor was gone from Henry's voice.

Jack sucked in a breath. He said, "We're parked at the end of the road. Some asshole yanked the wiring loose from the Jeep's engine. I need you to come tow us the hell out of here."

"Who'd do an ornery thing like that?"

Jack huffed. "I have my suspicions. But we'll leave it at that. And don't go shooting your mouth off about what's happened."

"No one's going to hear about it from me."

"Good. Now get up here while I'm still young."

Hank laughed. "I'll be there in driving time."

Jack closed his phone and sagged against the fender. Now for the wait.

He turned to Theresa and said, "Henry's on his way."

Theresa stepped around the bumper to where Jack stood looking at her. "From the way you spoke to Henry a moment ago, I take it you're not going to report any of this to the Sheriff?"

Jack shook his head no. His gut told him police involvement would only add more complications to their quest. "I make it a rule to not involve the authorities in my affairs unless I have to."

"And you don't think someone shooting at you is reason enough?"

"I've been shot at before. I think our friend with the pointed-toe cowboy boots missed on purpose."

"I'm not so sure."

Jack heaved himself away from the fender and looked directly at Theresa. "Think about it, without proof we'd be wasting our time."

"But someone shot at us. Our word counts for something."

"The land up here"—he waved a hand at the forest and mountains around them—"it's U.S. Forest Service land . . . public land. People shoot guns up here. Who's to say that shot was anything but an accident?"

"What about ripping the wires loose on the Jeep? That certainly wasn't an accident."

"Cars parked in remote areas get vandalized. Kids with nothing better to do, nasty-assed drunks misdirecting their anger—we can't say for sure the person who shot at us did this." He nodded at the mass of wiring sitting on the Jeep's motor. "And I doubt the Sheriff will call in a forensics team to build a case. Not based on our assumption someone shot at us on purpose, and certainly not for a misdemeanor vandalism."

"There has to be fingerprints."

Jack lowered the hood into place and pointed at the fender. "See the cloth marks where the dust has been wiped away, and these." He pointed at the top of the hood. "Whoever did this was careful. I think we'd just be opening ourselves up to a bunch of questions we don't have answers to. And there's the treasure to consider."

He knew the risk he was taking. And what was on the line if he was wrong. It was a chance he was willing to take.

Theresa bit her bottom lip, and a few seconds later said, "So we don't call the Sheriff's Office?"

Jack nodded.

She held him firmly in her gaze.

The look in her eyes told him she wasn't altogether in agreement with his decision. He'd learned to trust his intuition, it hadn't failed him yet. But that didn't mean he was right. And it wasn't just him lined up in someone's rifle sights.

He sighed and added, "Unless you insist. And we can always call in the cavalry if things get too rough."

She glanced at the hood of the Jeep, and then slowly scanned the forest around them. "I'll play it your way . . . for now."

CHAPTER 30

Deacon slid his back down the rock wall and planted his butt on the granite floor. A hard, sharp object dug into his right buttock. Cringing, he reached down, dug the annoying protrusion from under him, and eyed the chunk of milky colored stone.

The piece of quartz he'd chipped loose from the wall. He frowned. Figured he'd bruised his butt on it.

Would make a good rock to throw at Kyle, he thought. Maybe bruise *his* butt with it if the fool goes back to playing his games.

Giving the jagged stone a last look, he turned it in his fingers ready to toss the piece of rubble aside, stopped, and narrowed his eyes at the chunk of quartz. His brow furrowed in disbelief.

Flecks of yellow.

He held it up to the sunlight and studied the color more closely. *Gold!*

Not a lot—he couldn't help thinking—but not a little either. The deposit he held pinched between fingers was way more than he'd panned out of the North Fork of American River in the last six months.

Gold was a hard to come across. He'd been quick to find that out.

And so had the hard-rock miner who dug the pit looking for the stuff. He'd missed the vein and given up. But the gold had been there all this time, an inch or two away.

Until now.

The belief there was more of the precious yellow stuff concealed in the lode bearing rock had his mind working. He tucked the piece of gold-laden quartz into his front pocket, grabbed up his makeshift mallet and chisel, and stood facing the fracture in the wall where he'd chipped the chunk from.

Even in the shadow of the slanting sun, the dull yellow metal of his dreams stood out bright and beautiful.

And it was there for the taking.

Right in front of him all this time, he couldn't believe it. He'd gone into the mountains looking for a cache of stolen gold bars, put there by one of California's most notorious bandits. What he found was a vein of lode gold deposited by Mother Nature thousands and thousands of years ago. How rich the strike was, he didn't know.

But given some luck and a lot of work, he'd soon have a good idea.

He knew that veins of lode gold often played out. The miner who dug the pit that now served as a cell, no doubt had that happen to him. All too frequently, a miner could miss the rich vein by only inches. And when the less productive vein he was chasing played out, the miner would simply walk away leaving behind a fortune far beyond his wildest dreams.

Deacon thought it ironic that like him, the riches here were held captive in a rock prison. He feared it would take a good deal more than his hinge-pin chisel and 2x4 hammer to probe the precious metal held deep in the quartz.

He rubbed the tip of his finger over the gold.

Jack was out there somewhere searching for him. And Jack would find him, soon. He truly believed that. He could feel it in his gut. All he needed to do was hold on and wait in the best possible way.

His lips curled into a smile. A little of the yellow stuff or a lot, it was just possible he could chip out enough to buy his way out of his predicament. Or at least make his confinement in the hole considerably more comfortable.

Buoyed by confidence, he stood and faced the rock wall. A nervous flutter made him pause. He took a calming breath, held the hinge-pin tight against the vein of milky colored rock, and hit the flattened end hard with the makeshift hammer.

A small segment of quartz the size of the lump in his pocket fractured but held.

He hit the rock again, and this time the chunk broke free.

Using his fingers, he plucked the golf-ball-sized stone from the vein and held the piece of rubble up in front of him for a close look.

More gold, lots of the stuff.

His smile broadened into a grin. Now he'd see if his plan worked.

"Hey, Kyle," he yelled. "You up there? I want to talk to you."

He figured he'd try and work a deal with him first. No normal-minded person would trade for gold they could dig up themselves, or even take at will. Kyle was miles from normal. And then so was Hector.

"Hey, Kyle," he called out again after a few seconds with no answer.

You stupid sonofabitch answer me.

That's what he wanted to say. He listened.

Mumbling. And shovels being booted into the rocky ground. Metal against gravel.

Then nothing.

He rolled the piece of quartz between his fingers and anxiously eyeballed the spattering of gold. It wasn't like that muttonhead Kyle to miss an opportunity to screw with him. So what had him preoccupied?

They were digging, that was obvious. But why?

"Kyle," he hollered even louder.

The scraping of metal against dirt, stopped. He waited, wondering if Kyle had heard him that time.

"You shut up down there," Kyle shouted from somewhere beyond the rim of the pit. "Hector and me has some thinkin' to do."

Well don't sprain your brains, Deacon muttered silently. He exhaled a long slow breath, thinking about what he heard the big man behind the harsh voice say to them. The callous asshole had given the idiot brothers a lot to think about. And that wasn't good—them thinking. He had to get their pea brains working on something else.

"Kyle, seriously man, come over here." Deacon spoke in an

even tone he hoped was loud enough to be heard. Kyle was surely tweaked plenty by what just happened between them and their jerk boss without him thinking he was being yelled at a second time.

"You'll be happy you did," he quickly added. "I promise. I have something to show you."

Deacon noticed a man's shadow slant across the far wall of the pit. In the distance, the sound of digging resumed. Kyle or Hector, he couldn't be sure who had walked over to the pit. A second later, he saw Kyle lean forward and peer in at him.

Before another word was said between them, Deacon held up the lump of quartz for Kyle to see. Perhaps letting him get a peek at the hint of gold before any discussion would make the bargaining easier.

Kyle bolted upright and took a quick half-step back. "You ain't thinkin' you're going to hit me in the balls with that rock, are you?"

"No, Kyle." Deacon extended his arm as far as he could reach. "Seriously, look."

Kyle stooped with the flat of his palm extended defensively in front of him and peered hesitantly over the edge. "You sure you ain't going to throw that rock at me? I just might have to shoot you in the ass if you do."

"You can trust me," Deacon said. "But can I trust you?"

Kyle relaxed his hand to his side and straightened to his full height. "Don't see where it matters none."

"Sure it does." Deacon held him firmly in his gaze. "Now, can I trust you or not?"

Kyle scrunched up his face in an even more confused look than his normal befuddled expression. A long moment later he asked, "You mean like a dog trusts his master?"

Deacon had to smile. Oddly enough, he actually understood the seemingly childlike reasoning behind Kyle's response. In the eyes of Kyle and his brother, he was their pet like a dog or cat or any other creature in his situation. But that was going to change.

He hoped.

"Yeah, like a dog trusts his master," he said. He pointed at the yellow metal embedded in the chunk of quartz he held. "You see this, Kyle? It's gold. You like gold don't you?"

Kyle's befuddled expression broadened into a grin.

The look on Kyle's face was answer enough for Deacon. "Thought so," he said with a grin of his own. "Well, I've got a little proposition for you. You know what a proposition is, right?"

"What's going on?" Hector stepped into view next to Kyle. He held a shovel in his hand and pointed the blade at Deacon. "Our friend down there giving you shit, again?"

Kyle slowly turned faced Hector as though it was hard to tear his gaze from the gold. "Claims there's gold in that rock he's holding. Says he wants to make a deal."

"A deal?" Hector laughed and said, "Let's just climb down there and take it from him."

Kyle gripped his brother's arm and leaned close with an impish grin. "Could be there's more than that one rock down there."

Deacon heard enough to know what was on their minds.

"Before you two do anything stupid," he said. "Think about this. You've got a marijuana crop to harvest. My guess is the man who was here a little while ago will shoot you dead in your tracks if you don't have his dope bagged and ready when he wants it. So let me dig the gold for you. All I ask is for a little something in return."

Hector furrowed his brow in obvious skepticism. "And just what would that little something you're talking about be?"

"A hot meal of something besides your leftover bones and gristle would do for starters . . . and a peach. I would really like some peaches. And I want some time out of this stinking hole. You guys might not mind sleeping where you shit and piss but I do. So chain my legs to a tree if you want. But let me out of here for a while."

Kyle leaned close to Hector a second time and said, "I'm thinkin' we could get him to bury that donkey. And dig the gold for us, too. That way we wouldn't have to do more work than we already gotta do."

Hector scratched his head in silence. A long moment later, he hollered down to Deacon, "Toss me up that rock and I'll think on it."

Deacon figured he had them.

He eyeballed the stone between his thumb and finger, his mind confident. Once Hector and Kyle saw the gold, they'd for sure want all they could get their greedy little hands on. And they'd want him to dig it for them.

He tossed the chunk of quartz to Hector and waited.

When he saw the man's eyes widen and his mouth curl into a grin, he said, "And there's more, boys. So, do we have a deal?"

CHAPTER 31

Jack sat with the passenger's door handle of Henry Baston's ancient Dodge tow truck digging into his ribs. He had his right elbow hanging out the open window in his door to keep his broad shoulders from being pinched together like a taco. Wedged between him and Henry, Theresa sat pressed tight against him. The smell of her hair, her woman scent, and the warmth of her body touching his, made him quite aware of her feminine presence.

With her sitting so close, it was hard for him to think of anything but taking her into his arms and holding her tight. Still, he had Deacon to be concerned about. The absurdity of the events of the last couple of days was maddening. And he was going to get to the bottom of what was going on.

"So what are ya going to do about it?" Henry asked when the cab of his truck fell silent.

Jack knew Henry directed the question at him. "It's not going to stop me from finding my brother, if that's what you mean."

"I meant are going to report this to the Sheriff?"

Jack exchanged glances with Theresa. He gave a slight shake of the head to confirm his intentions. Henry didn't know they'd been shot at in addition to the Jeep being vandalized. And he wasn't going to know.

With Theresa looking at him, Jack said, "Think it'd do any good?"

"Nope," Henry shot back without the slightest hesitation. "But you could, anyway. Besides, the rental agency will probably want a report filed once you inform them of the damage."

Jack faced the open window in his door to escape Theresa's gaze. He saw enough in those eyes of hers to know she still wasn't all that thrilled with her agreement to keep quiet about the shooting.

"I'll be paying the repair bill myself," he said into the wind rushing by the cab. "So that won't be an issue."

"It'll be pricy."

"Just do the work." He peered blindly at the countryside. All he could see was Deacon's smiling face. "The money is the least of my worries."

For the moment, the interior of the tow truck fell silent. Jack faced the road ahead of them and focused his thoughts on what he'd say to Marsh the moment their paths crossed. He was certain they would. And the meeting was sure to be anything but pleasant.

Which suited him fine.

He'd been in tough situations before. And he'd looked into the cold black eyes of men set on killing him. There were times when he'd talked his way out of trouble. And there were times when he'd confronted trouble head-on. This was one of *those* times.

"You'll want your brother's pickup, I suppose?" Henry continued.

Jack mentally shelved his thoughts about Marsh. He had hoped Henry would release Deacon's truck to him without having to argue that it was all right to do so even though the vehicle wasn't actually his property. It appeared he wouldn't have to make that argument.

"Just as soon as the Jeep is unhooked," he said. "If that's all right with you? And if you can have me a key made?"

"Key's no problem. I'll add that and the storage cost to your repair bill."

Jack thought for a moment. Then he looked past Theresa at Henry and asked, "Do you happen to know what kind of car Marsh drives?"

Henry glanced back at Jack. "Last I saw, he was driving a red Ford F 350 diesel dually. Why?"

Jack wondered if he might be saying too much. He had no proof Marsh had shot at them. But then Henry seemed to be on his side.

"How about a shiny black Lincoln Navigator with paper plates and limousine tint on the windows," he said. "Know anybody who drives one?"

Henry furrowed his brow at Jack. "Boy, I don't know what you've gone and gotten yourself in the middle of, but be careful who you start pointing your finger at. There's a few sorts around here you don't want to mess with. Elliot Marsh is one of them. The Sheriff is another."

"Marsh—I've got him pegged," Jack said. "The Sheriff's a real hard-ass, huh?"

"Marsh's hard-ass, or so I hear."

Jack was glad he and Theresa had already decided not to go to the Sheriff with their suspicions.

He said, "That's why you doubted it would do any good to file report?"

"Doug Bell's a fair lawman most of the time," Henry said. "His priorities just get a little clouded when it comes to Marsh."

Jack chuckled. "The man probably likes his new car."

Henry added a chuckle of his own. "Funny how people can be, huh?"

"Yeah," Jack said. He peered through the windshield reliving the shot that almost killed him—"real damned funny."

Theresa said, "I knew Marsh owned that car lot. But I didn't know the Sheriff was in his pocket."

"I doubt many people do," Henry grumbled. "So don't think it's because you spend most of your time hiding inside that big home of yours."

"Don't mince words with me, Henry." She shot him a scathing glance. "I'm well aware of your reputation for speaking your mind. So what are you really saying, that it's wrong for me to like my privacy?"

"I think you're a pretty woman with a lot of life to live, and that it wouldn't hurt you to show up at the Elks Club on a Saturday night once in a while."

She focused her gaze in the direction of her fidgeting fingers. "You know why I don't go to those dances."

"The whole town knows," Henry said. "Leandro was a wonderful man. But he's gone and it wouldn't hurt for you to get out once in a while."

"Well I am out." She peered into Jack's eyes with just the hint of a smile. "I'm helping Jack find his brother."

Henry scratched his beard and grinned at Theresa, his gaze settling on Jack who watched the exchange. "Yes you are."

Seeing her look at him like that, Jack could feel the heat inside the cab of the truck ratchet up a few notches.

Did she know what she was doing to him?

* * * *

On their way through town, Jack found himself scanning the streets and parking lots for the shiny black Navigator with the limousine tint and paper license plates.

"That's the car lot Marsh owns," Henry said when they drove past Gold Rush Motors.

Jack didn't expect to see the mystery Navigator sitting in the front row next to the Hummers and Range Rovers. It made total sense for the vehicle to not be there. He checked anyway.

Nothing remotely close.

"Pull over at the hotel," Jack said to Henry as they neared the Gold Trail Inn. "We'll drop Theresa off at her car."

Jack noticed Theresa's thick eyebrows pinch together in a deep furrow.

He added, "If that's all right with you?"

She smiled and said, "It seems to me we are right where we were yesterday about this time."

He fought a shiver of growing desire. "Except it isn't raining."

She held him in her gaze. "No it's not, is it?"

There was no way he could ignore the thoughts swirling inside his head. He wished she'd told him she wanted to stay awhile longer. But then he was the one who opened his mouth and told Henry to drop her off at her car. That wouldn't happen again.

Not if he had anything to say about it.

But then she does like her privacy. He tossed aside the notion of spending the evening with her and said, "Same time tomorrow?"

She didn't answer. She just continued to hold him firmly locked in her gaze with that wonderful hint-of-a smile beckoning him to kiss her full lips. He could only wonder what thoughts smoldered behind those dark eyes.

A year later, she replied with a simple nod.

Henry braked the truck to a stop next to her car, and Jack reluctantly pulled on the handle boring a hole in his side. Sliding off the seat, he held the door open for her as she swung her legs out and stood up. It seemed their eyes kept meeting until she finally stood close in front of him, her lips inches from his.

He wanted to kiss her, bad.

She edged past him as though she'd read his mind and gracefully excused herself from an awkward situation.

Watching her climb into her car and close the door, Jack couldn't help but to admire her class. She was a real lady.

And all woman.

He climbed back into the cab of the tow truck and settled onto the seat, trying hard not to stare at her. Even so, he repeatedly glanced in that direction. And each time, he noticed her watching him.

CHAPTER 32

Deacon caught a whiff of the sweat soaking his already rank shirt at the chest and armpits. He made a mental note to ask for soap and a tub of water. Another day and even the lizards sharing his rock prison would move out.

He squinted at the dark blue sky and used the flat of his hand to shade his eyes from the glare of the sizzling afternoon sun. Unlike the day before, only a scattering of large puffy thunderclouds clung to the upper most peaks of the Sierras.

The temperature where he was standing should have been a dozen degrees cooler than it was. It sort of figured the weather chose this particular day to set some sort of record high.

He peered into the hole he'd dug and sighed. Then raising the pick over his head, he swung it at the ground. The solid *clunk* of unyielding rock reverberated up the handle and into his fingers.

He swung the pick at a different place in the hole.

Another *clunk*. More solid rock.

He tossed aside the pick. The entire bottom of the hole was solid granite.

Shit!

He plopped his butt onto the mound of dirt and rock he'd scooped into a pile and drew his legs up in front of him. Resting his elbows on his knees, he sucked in deep breaths and scanned his work. An hour and a half of nonstop digging with a pick and shovel and all he had been able to accomplish was a trench six feet long, two feet wide, and two feet deep.

Not even close to being a respectable grave.

But he had to somehow convince Hector and Kyle the hole was deep enough; that all they had to do was help him roll the poor dead jackass into the dirt trough so he could cover the thing up before the carcass started to stink.

Picking up the concrete block chained to his ankle, he stepped across the hole and stood next to the animal's head. For a moment, he considered the effort it would take to move the lifeless jackass. No small task.

He looked at Hector and Kyle and said, "Hey you two boys, you want to give me a hand over here?"

The brothers lounged in the shade of a nearby oak tree, watching. A dozen yards down-slope from the cabin stood several piles of marijuana plants heaped like haystacks drying in the sun. Something—Deacon realized—that hadn't been there the day he was tossed in the pit. The boys *had* been busy, but not today. Neither of them appeared to have the energy to get off their asses.

He waited a long moment and finally saw the redheads exchange glances and shrug. An unspoken agreement between them to move their butts and help—it seemed like a hard thing for the brothers to do. He continued to watch the twins drag their feet under themselves and plod in his direction.

To ease the unavoidable monotony of swinging a pick and shovel, he'd spent the past hour pondering Hector and Kyle's parental lineage: brother and sister, first cousins? Both brothers were—in his mind—the perfect poster children for birth control.

Only they weren't children. And this was definitely no child's game.

Even so, it was hard for him to think of Hector and Kyle as criminals. In fact, he found he rather liked the goofy guys.

Big kids, both of them.

With a sad story to tell, he was sure.

Looking at the pair now, he was convinced the twins' unkempt, butt-ugly almost-comical appearance, and idiotic childish behavior were contradictions to their actual age. Thirty, he guessed—give or take a few years.

Men. Both of them

"What do you think?" he asked. Admiring his skill with a spade, he had to chuckle.

"Hole looks big enough to me," Kyle said. He shot an anxious look at his brother. "It'll do, right?"

Hector shrugged. "Let's roll her in and see."

The three of them managed to scoot and roll the donkey into the trench. And to Jack's amazement, the bloated carcass lay wedged between the walls of the narrow pit with its legs sticking straight up as stiff as the handle of the pick lying on the pile of dirt next to it.

"I don't know," Hector said.

Deacon didn't want to give Hector or Kyle an idle second to think. No telling what the dumbshits would come up with if he did. Besides, there was a chance the situation would work out.

Hoping to put the twins' simple minds at ease, he began shoveling dirt onto the burro's round belly. Several hurried scoopfuls later, he pointed the business end of the rusted shovel at the oak tree and said, "You two go back over there and stand in the shade and let me work. There's no good reason the three of us has to get hot and sweaty."

Kyle grabbed Hector by the arm and tugged. "He has a point."

"He does at that," Hector agreed.

Deacon leaned on the shovel handle until he was sure the brothers were walking away. Then he went back to work.

It'd take a while.

And he didn't want to push himself.

Finally, he peered down at the dirt piled atop the donkey and sighed. Good enough.

Mostly.

He heaved one last scoop of dirt onto the mound, tamped it into place, and tossed the tired spade aside. A trickle of sweat dripped from his brow into his right eye causing it to sting as though his body had sent a reminder his system had let go of its last grains of salt.

He knuckled the burn away and leaned forward resting his hands heavily on his knees. His body was right. It had endured about as much abuse as it could take. Only he still had some energy in reserve just in case. But he wouldn't let Hector and Kyle know that.

Picking up his concrete anchor, he hobbled into the shade of the oak tree, plopped onto his butt, and leaned his back against the coarse bark of the trunk to rest.

"There you go, boys."

"Looks good to me," Kyle offered.

Kyle was easy. Hector was the brother Deacon worried about.

For a long quiet moment, he watched with amusement as Hector stood with his arms crossed against his chest, his gaze fixed on the mound of dirt covering the donkey.

The hole was way too shallow, of course.

And now Hector and his brother eyeballed the four hooves sticking straight up out of a mound of decomposed granite and rock.

He held his breath. He'd have to bucket in a ton more dirt or pick and shovel a new hole somewhere solid granite wasn't sitting a foot or two under the top soil. Neither scenario gave him much comfort.

"I just don't know," Hector said.

Kyle threw up his hands in obvious frustration and said, "But he couldn't dig no deeper."

"Yeah"—Hector scratched his mop of red hair—"but those hooves sticking out of the dirt like that don't seem right."

"We've got that chainsaw in the cabin," Kyle pointed out. "If we can get her to start, we can have him dig the thing up and cut the legs off."

Deacon realized he needed to come up with a solution fast or he really would wind up having to dig a new hole. Or hack the poor dead animal's legs off with their chainsaw. And that was something he didn't want to have to do. Nor did he want to have to do more digging. He'd barely had energy enough to shovel on that last spade full of dirt as it was.

"I've got an idea, boys." He struggled to his feet, lifted the concrete block into his arms, and shuffled over to a pile of junk lumber.

"What ya tryin' to pull?" Kyle asked.

"This." With his free hand, Deacon lifted a two foot by four foot sheet of half-inch thick weathered plywood.

"What ya gonna to do with that?" Kyle took a step forward with no attempt to hide the confusion showing in his voice.

"Watch." Deacon carried the plywood remnant to the mound of dirt, dropped his concrete anchor on the ground next to him, and positioned the sheet of wood on the pairs of hooves.

Not bad, he told himself.

With a smug smile and a nod of satisfaction, he turned his gaze on Hector and said, "A perfectly good table to roll your dope on."

Hector shrugged. "I think that'll work."

Kyle was all smiles. "Then we can have us a beer."

Hector slapped Kyle on the back and nodded over his shoulder at Deacon. "Him too."

Deacon sighed in relief. "And a bucket of water to wash off some of this dirt and sweat."

The two brothers walked into the cabin, and Deacon reclaimed his spot in the shade of the oak tree. The agreement the three of them had come to was turning out better than he'd imagined. He'd had to do their grunt work, which he realized going into the deal. But he was out of the hellhole of a rock pit, he'd wolfed down a huge bologna and cheese sandwich, guzzled a gallon of water, and in a minute or two, he'd be enjoying a cold beer.

If the twins stuck to their word.

CHAPTER 33

Jack steered Deacon's four-wheel-drive pickup into the parking lot across the street from the Texaco station and stopped a few feet away from the historical monument he'd spied his first day in town. It struck him as odd that he picked this particular moment to be curious about what was written there.

But he was.

With the truck idling smoothly, he slide from the cab and stepped in front of the tarnished bronze plaque. The words written there read:

ANGELS CAMP
HOME OF THE JUMPING FROG.
ROMANCE — GOLD — HISTORY
FOUNDED IN 1849 BY GEORGE ANGEL. WHO ESTABLISHED A MINING CAMP AND TRADING STORE 200 FEET BELOW THIS MARKER. A RICH GRAVEL MINING AREA AND ONE OF THE RICHEST QUARTZ MINING SECTIONS OF THE MOTHER LODE. PRODUCTION RECORDS OF OVER 100 MILLION DOLLARS FOR ANGELS CAMP AND VICINITY. PROMINENT IN EARLY DAY CALIFORNIA HISTORY. TOWN SITE ESTABLISHED IN 1873. THE LOCALE OF MARK TWAIN'S FAMOUS STORY, THE JUMPING

FROG OF CALAVERAS. FREQUENTED BY JOAQUIN MURIETTA, BLACK BART AND OTHER EARLY DAY BANDITS.
ERECTED AND DEDICATED BY CALAVERAS COUNTY CHAMBER OF COMMERCE, MAY 16, 1931.

He noticed the spelling of Joaquin's last name: M-u-r-i-e-t-t-a. Everything he'd read on the bandit had it spelled with two R's and one T. Odd, or was there so little known about this bandit that historians didn't really know how he spelled his last name?

He was sure it didn't matter.

What was important was that the infamous Joaquin Murrieta—however he spelled his last name—*had* robbed and killed in these mountains. He peered up the street at the hundred-and-fifty-year-old buildings. None of them were historical treasures of any major significance, but they oozed with antiquity. And Joaquin Murrieta was part of it.

Al Brink's story could very well be more than mere legend.

No matter. Deacon believed Al's account of the robbery as passed down by his great, great uncle Donald. Theresa Montero did too. And he couldn't deny his own belief everything happened *just* as Al described it. He'd find Deacon and then he'd prove them all correct.

He'd find the stolen gold.

Seated in Deacon's pickup, Jack drove the couple of blocks to his hotel. He parked in a space at the curb near where he'd been parking the Jeep. Perhaps Marsh wouldn't make the connection, and there wouldn't be any more vandalism to have to contend with.

He could hope . . . he could hope for a lot of things.

Theresa was still on his mind. He'd watched her drive away, and now he truly wished she hadn't.

There was so much about her he wanted to know.

Maybe he'd get his chance, yet.

A week together on his boat sailing around the Hawaiian Islands and there isn't much they wouldn't know about each other.

But that would wait. He still had to find Deacon, and he still had Marsh to contend with. The events on the mountain had left him good and mad and even if Marsh didn't fire that shot or vandalize the Jeep, it wouldn't take much more of Marsh's bullshit to push him over the edge.

When he noticed Marsh standing next to a red Ford F 350 diesel pickup with dual tires on the rear, he couldn't contain the anger that had been building inside him all afternoon.

He climbed out of Deacon's pickup and walked across the street and down two doors to where Marsh stood talking to a younger man on the sidewalk outside of Chinless' General Store.

"Jackie Boy," Marsh said when Jack was still a half-dozen steps away. "I'd like you to meet my nephew, Roy. If you need a car, and a little birdie tells me you do, he's the one to see. I'll make sure he gives you a good deal."

"I'm not in the market for a car, Marsh." Jack huffed to a stop a couple of arm's lengths away from the big man. "Not from you or your nephew."

"That's right, you're driving that rental Jeep." He chuckled and glanced around. "The junker's running all right isn't it? I don't see the thing parked anywhere."

"Someone ripped the wires loose from the engine." Jack held Marsh's eyes firmly in his gaze. He'd already noticed the man's pointed-toe cowboy boots. "Of course you wouldn't know anything about that, would you?"

"Well no, I wouldn't." Marsh straightened, his smile turned narrow and mean. "I thought it was the Jeep's tires that gave you problems."

A man as big and muscled as Marsh was certainly a person to be reckoned with. Jack knew that all too well. But he wasn't going to let the guy's size scare him off. His chest was broad and thick with muscle from longs hours of hard work on the ocean. His hide was tanned tough as leather. He could take a punch; and he could deliver one.

And he was mad enough to see if Marsh was as tough as he acted.

He took a calming breath.

"You and I know better, don't we?" Jack wanted to hit Marsh, bad.

Marsh turned to his nephew. "Jackie Boy, here, has trouble keeping air in his tires. And now it seems he has engine problems as well."

Roy laughed, but he remained standing a full foot behind his uncle.

Jack half expected the weasel-faced shit to step up next to Marsh and puff out his pathetic chest to show what a tough guy he was. Apparently it wasn't going to happen; not in this lifetime.

No-account nephew, that's what Al called him.

And Al was right. There was little doubt in Jack's mind that the punk might sucker-punch someone from the side or kick them in the balls if they were down on the ground, but he'd never go toe to toe with anyone.

Jack dismissed Weaselface for the useless shit he was and kept his mind clear and his eyes focused and his muscles ready. If there was going to be a fight, it would be between him and Marsh.

He still hadn't replied to Marsh's wisecrack. Out of the corners of his eyes, he spied the heavy-bladed Rambo-style Special Forces survival knife displayed in the front window of Chinless' store. Words were doing no good. He stepped past Marsh in the direction of the door without as much as a sideways glance at the big man or his nephew.

He felt their eyes bore a hole in his back.

"Get yourself a real car, Jackie Boy," Marsh called to him and laughed. His nephew joined in with a chuckle of his own.

Jack ignored their laughter and marched into the store, letting the door clang shut behind him.

When Jack stepped outside a couple of minutes later carrying the knife, he was glad to see Marsh and his weasel-faced-shit-of-a-nephew Roy standing on the sidewalk. He noticed them watch him as he walked directly to Marsh's shiny red truck. They weren't smiling.

Without a word from him, Jack thrust the razor-edged survival knife in the sidewall of the rear tire closest to the curb. Air hissed from around the heavy blade. He jerked the knife out and drove it deep into the sidewall of the inner tire. More air hissed. And when he pulled it out Marsh's truck slumped into the gutter.

"That won't pay for the tires you flattened on my Jeep or the precious time you cost me," Jack said, calmly sliding the knife into its sheath. "But it sure does make me feel better."

"You don't know that I flattened those tires," Marsh groused, tight-jawed. He balled his big hands into fists, but made no move to step closer.

"You and I know you did," Jack said. He tossed a nod at Roy. "So does that no-account nephew of yours."

"Screw you." Roy jabbed his index finger at Jack. "We'll kick—"

Marsh raised a big hand in front of his nephew's face, shutting him up. His hard gaze remained focused on Jack. "Don't think this changes a thing."

Jack narrowed his eyes at Marsh.

Fourteen days missing.

"Stay away from me," he said. "And leave Ms. Montero alone."

CHAPTER 34

Hector and Kyle rushed out of the ramshackle cabin in tandem, each of them toting a six-pack of Budweiser in cans. In addition to the beer, Kyle lugged a white five-gallon plastic bucket with water sloshing over the rim.

Deacon smacked his lips and watched the brothers stride toward him. He could already taste that beer.

Along the way, Hector collected two folding aluminum lawn chairs with at least a couple of broken webs trailing from each one and carried them into the shade of the oak. He positioned their seats so that he and his brother would be facing the mound of dirt and makeshift table marking the poor donkey's grave. And so that Deacon was in sight to off their left.

"Here," Hector said to Deacon and handed him a can of Bud.

"And the water you wanted." Kyle plopped the bucket down next to Deacon's leg, sloshing a wave onto his jeans.

"Thanks." Deacon set the beer aside and worked his way to his feet. When he was standing he said, "Kyle, you're all right. You know that?"

Kyle parted his lips in a broad grin that showed a mouth full of widely gapped yellow teeth and took a seat in the chair next to his brother. He quickly popped the tab on a can of beer and took a healthy gulp. With a loud belch, he looked at Deacon and said, "Don't you go wastin' that water now or else you can pump your own."

"Don't worry about that." Deacon groaned. He'd have sworn Kyle's belch curled the leaves above their heads.

With Hector and Kyle looking on, he picked up the bucket and stepped as far from where he was sitting as the chain shackled to his ankle would allow. To be dragging the steel tether in the dirt behind him made him feel a bit like a mangy junkyard dog. Hector and Kyle trusted him, but not beyond the length of the chain. And that was fine with him. He could play their game. He was out of that pit and he was about to enjoy a bath and a cold beer.

Satisfied he wouldn't muddy up his resting spot next to the trunk of the tree, he set the bucket of water on the ground and stripped off his shirt. Wadding the shirt into a ball, he dunked it in the water and mopped the black mat of hair on his chest.

"First time I ever watched someone besides my brother take a bath," Kyle cackled.

Deacon was way beyond caring if Kyle, Hector, or anyone else watched him wash the sweat from his body. If Kyle would have brought him soap, he'd have used that, too. But a rinse was way better than nothing.

"How'd you boys get into the dope growing business, anyway?" he asked while he wet-mopped the sweat from his neck, shoulders, and armpits.

"Our pa raised us to grow things," Kyle explained.

Deacon sopped up another shirt-full from the bucket and let the cool water trickle onto his chest, and back. He felt a ton better, already. "Your father didn't grow dope, did he?"

"Tomatoes," Hector spoke up. "We was raised on a farm down in the valley near Chowchilla."

Deacon knew the one-horse town they grew up in. It'd been made famous when a nutcase kidnapped a school bus full of kids. There was even a movie made about it.

"And that's where you learned to grow marijuana?" He shook out his shirt, dunked it in the water a few times, let it drain, shook it out again, and hung it on a limb to dry. He figured it wouldn't take long in the days' heat.

"Pa said we had a gift for making things grow," Hector continued.

171

"Made us work the fields from the time we was old enough to lift a hoe."

"What about school?"

"Stayed home and worked most of the time. Pa said we didn't need no fancy schoolin' if we was gonna work the farm."

"And your mother, didn't she want you to get an education?"

"Ma took off when we was little," Kyle said with a tone of sadness. "Pa told us it was because we had red hair."

Deacon didn't like Hector and Kyle's mother for running out on them. He liked their father even less.

He asked, "Did your dad beat you?"

Hector stood up and pointed his empty beer can at him. "Mister, I think you need to shut up now."

The last thing Deacon wanted to do was piss off the twins. That would get him nothing. And besides, they were connecting.

In a soft easy tone he said, "Sorry, I didn't mean to pry. It's just that I like you guys, and I think you got a raw deal growing up."

"It weren't so bad." Hector popped the tab on another beer and retook his seat. "Me and Kyle, we'd just run far out into them fields and play when Pa was in one of his moods."

Kyle reached over and patted his brother on the back. "We had fun, didn't we Hector?"

Hector tapped his beer can against Kyle's in a toast. "And we still do."

Deacon stood looking at the twins. Dumber than shit, both of them. But they had found a way to survive a crap-hole childhood. He couldn't help admiring the brothers for that.

"You two are all right by me," he said.

Hector smiled in Deacon's direction. "You know what me and Kyle is gonna do with the money we make off this crop? We're gonna buy us a tomato farm and raise the best tomatoes anyone has ever eaten."

Deacon could see their reasoning. California was on the verge of legalizing marijuana and the big man's illegal dope growing operation or any other similar to it would likely soon be a thing of the past. But there was *this* crop.

So that was it: one last big score—for them, and maybe even

for the man who shot that poor donkey.

The asshole.

He felt himself being drawn in by the brother's simpleminded innocence. But he couldn't forget he was their prisoner. The heavy chain padlocked tight around his ankle remained a cruel reminder.

He looked directly at the two. Their mean-tempered boss' visit remained engrained in his mind. His threats were real.

He said, "You do know that plan of yours will never happen if you kill me."

Hector and Kyle exchanged glances.

Deacon felt a quiver of uneasiness that hadn't been there a minute before.

"Hell, mister." Hector did the talking. "We never intended to kill you. We is just going to keep you in that hole long enough to get this crop of dope harvested and get our money."

Deacon realized he was holding his breath. He let himself breathe. Now that he knew their intentions, he could play the game a little longer. But only because he had no choice in the matter. He couldn't say what would happen when Jack got there.

And Jack was coming for him, he was sure of that.

He shot a smile back at Hector and Kyle and said, "That my boys, takes a load off. I wish you all the luck in the world." And he actually meant it.

Again, Hector exchanged glances with Kyle. Grinning like a kid with a shiny new bike, he said, "And now we have us some gold, too."

Deacon had almost forgotten about that part of the deal. More hard work for him, and more gold for them that rightfully should be his. But he'd given them his word and wouldn't break it as long as they stuck to theirs.

He shook his head and shrugged. "You sure do."

Leaving Hector and Kyle cackling like a couple of excited farm hens, Deacon leaned forward intent on keeping his pants as dry as possible, lifted the bucket with both hands, and emptied the contents over his head.

Dirtier than a baby's bath water, but cleaner than a horse trough.

The water felt wonderful.

With the deluge streaming from his face and neck, he

straightened and tossed his head back, sending a spray of rain-like drops flying into the air. Then he wiped his face with the palms of his hands, and used his fingers to comb back his coarse black hair.

He believed that at that moment, he felt about as good as a man could under the circumstances. He retook his spot against the trunk of the tree and popped the tab on his can of Bud.

For a moment, he watched it foam. There was no good reason he could think of to rush himself.

When he could wait no longer, he lifted the can and took a swig. It was hard not to swallow every last drop in a single greedy gulp, but he managed. Leaning his head back, he closed his eyes and let the cold brew trickle down his throat.

Never had an ice-cold beer tasted so good.

Now he could only hope the man with the nasty mouth and bad temper didn't come back and find him there. It'd no doubt be the death of him.

CHAPTER 35

Jack walked directly to his room. He needed a shower and a drink. He'd been sure his use of the knife on Marsh's tires would goad the big man into taking a swing at him. But it hadn't. And that surprised him. Not so surprising was he now knew for sure his suspicion that Marsh was responsible for the damage to the Jeep was right on. And seeing those pointed-toe cowboy boots was enough to remove any doubt about the shooting.

But had the bullet been intended to kill?

Watching his back took on a whole new meaning.

He and Marsh had had three face-to-face confrontations now—two of them heated exchanges: next to the Jeep, in the restaurant, and on the sidewalk in front of Chinless' store. He was pretty sure Marsh would not come after him in town, but out there in the mountains all bets were off. The shot was certainly proof of that.

Out there among the trees, one of them would likely die.

But only if Marsh forced the issue.

Jack tossed the knife onto the lamp table next to the chair, poured himself a shot of Don Julio tequila, and slugged it down. He was in no hurry to kill. He'd killed before and it wasn't something he enjoyed. Still, he'd be ready if that's what the situation called for.

And he wouldn't back off if Marsh came at him.

The knock at his door made him jerk his head to the side and look. Then he relaxed. Marsh wasn't the type to knock. If the asshole had come to settle the score between them, he'd have kicked the door in with those fancy cowboy boots of his. That wasn't going to happen. Not with witnesses around.

And certainly not in broad daylight.

He stepped to the door wondering who he'd find standing there. He doubted Marsh would send his weasel-faced nephew to take care of business any more than he'd come himself. The punk didn't have it in him. And it wasn't likely to be Della. There was no reason for her to be there.

Before he could get the door open, there was another knock—solid and without uncertainty. But not rude and demanding either.

He cracked the door, wedged his foot against the bottom, and peeked out. He didn't honestly figure he had anything to worry about, but he half hoped Marsh had put aside caution and come there to do something careless and stupid. And if that was the case, he didn't want the door kicked in his face.

When he saw who it was, he totally forgot about Marsh and swung the door open wide.

"I certainly wasn't expecting to see you here," he said. "Come in, please."

Theresa stepped inside. "I wasn't expecting to be here, either."

Jack eased the door shut. He had a broad grin plastered on his face, and he was sure she could tell he was happy she was there. Then it dawned on him something might be wrong. He didn't want to believe something bad had happened, but he'd noticed she wore the same clothes she had on when he last saw her.

He let his smile slip just a little—he was still glad she was there—and asked, "What happened? I saw you drive off."

She pointed at the tequila bottle sitting next to the two glasses on the lamp table. "Are you sharing?"

He picked up the extra glass, poured her a shot, and handed it to her.

"I don't drink alone," she said, pointing at the other glass.

"But of course. I'll join you." He poured himself two fingers worth.

She drained the glass without the slightest shudder and lowered it in front of her.

He waited.

Settling her gaze on him, she said, "I got as far as the front gate outside my hacienda and sat there. Finally, I decided I wasn't ready to go home. Not yet, anyway. So I drove straight back here."

He poured her another shot and watched her sip it. He'd wished she hadn't left, and by God she'd come back. He'd find out why soon enough.

"You can tell I'm glad you did." The smile that had slipped from his face was back. Maybe she'd read his mind.

He could hope.

Holding on to that notion, he realized he had hoped to get to know everything about her. Perhaps this was a start.

And that called for a toast.

"To finding Deacon. And to finding that stash of Murrieta gold." He clanked his glass against hers and downed his tequila in a single gulp. First that knife business with Mash, now Theresa. The afternoon was turning out better than he expected.

Theresa raised her glass in salute and downed the remainder of her drink. Again, her eyes focused on his. "I was driving back into town and saw you talking to Marsh. It didn't look friendly."

"You watched." He poured them both another healthy shot. He'd sip this one.

"I pulled over."

"Then you saw everything?"

"I saw you flatten his tires if that's what you're referring to."

"It seemed like the thing to do." He couldn't resist a glance at the Rambo knife sitting on the table. "I didn't think about it when you knocked, but you could have been the Sheriff."

Her lips spread into a smug smile. "He looked plenty mad when he stepped inside Ben's store after you left. But I don't think he'll file a complaint. My guess is that even if Sheriff Bell is in Marsh's pocket, Marsh doesn't want any form of law good or bad anywhere close to him right now."

"Could be you're right." Jack stepped to the window overlooking the street, pulled the lace curtain aside, and peered down at Marsh's red pickup. The truck sat there slumped in the gutter like a lame drunk.

Flattening those tires had been the thing to do. If for no other reason than it made him feel better. The score was by no means even, but it was close.

He said, "I'll really have to watch my back from now on."

"You're worried?"

"Yeah, I'm worried. I'm worried about Deacon."

"And Marsh?"

He turned and faced her. "Sure I'm Goddamned worried about what Marsh might do. I'm convinced the asshole shot at us. But that's not going to scare me off."

"That's what I wanted to hear."

Jack furrowed his brow at her. "You wanted me to admit Marsh scares me?"

She reached out and laid her hand on his arm. "A man who isn't afraid of a dangerous *pendejo* like Marsh is a fool or an idiot. You don't strike me as being either. I wanted to make sure."

"You say that as if a decision you're about to make, rests on it."

She stepped next to him, pulled the curtain back on her side of the window, and looked out. "That *was* Marsh's nephew with him, wasn't it?"

Jack was confused. Why would she ask about that jerk?

He faced her and said, "That weasel-faced shit was his nephew all right. Why?"

"He carries a switchblade in his back pocket," she said without turning to meet his gaze. "If you look closely, you can see the outline of it through those tight jeans he wears."

"So you've seen the knife, then?"

"In his pocket . . . and I've seen him click the blade open and stick it into a wooden post from ten feet away."

A knife . . . and a switchblade to boot, he thought. A fitting weapon for a backstabber.

He couldn't help asking, "And just how did you happen to see him use the post for target practice?"

"On Main Street," she said. "In front of me and a dozen other people."

He pictured the slits in the sidewalls of the Jeep's flat tires. Out in the open, on Main Street. Marsh was responsible sure as shit.

But Weaselface probably did the sticking.

"So the man likes to play with knives, does he?" Jack stood rethinking his opinion of Marsh's nephew. Weaselface was still a punk, and he still doubted the pigeon-chested shit would go at it toe to toe with another man. But he would sneak up and stick someone from behind.

And he'd take pleasure in doing it.

Theresa peered into Jack's eyes. "Do not turn your back on him."

Jack felt the haunting allure of her gaze. He so wanted to take her in his arms, weave his fingers into her black hair, and press his lips tight to hers. It didn't matter that they were standing in front of the window. It wouldn't have mattered if they were standing on the sidewalk out front in view of God and everyone on the street.

But did she want that to happen? Is that why she looked into his eyes the way she did?

He stepped to the middle of the room to put space between them. He gulped half his drink, turned, and looked her up and down. Even in those sweaty clothes, she was beautiful. And she was all woman.

He should have kissed her.

But he hadn't.

Stupid . . . A fool . . .

There were hundred ways to describe just how ridiculous he felt.

He wanted her. Simple as that.

His mouth went dry when he tried to speak. He took another sip of his drink and said, "You can bet I won't turn my back on either of them."

She was looking at him again. Those big brown eyes doing the talking.

Enough, already.

He was about to walk over and take her in his arms and do what he should've done a minute after she arrived at his room. But she chose that moment to step past him and into the bathroom.

She pushed the door closed, and he stood there staring.

Odd, but he figured she had to go. Then he heard the shower come on with a hiss of spray.

The woman—it seemed—was full of surprises. He decided that

179

called for one more drink.

And then he'd try hard not to think about her in that shower.

Ten minutes later, he was sitting on the edge of his bed tossing glances at the bathroom door when she stepped out. Her hair was gathered in a towel she'd wound into a turban, and she was wearing a second towel wrapped around her and tucked in between her breasts. She was absolutely gorgeous.

"It's your turn," she said in a tone as calm and natural as if they'd been lovers forever.

He knew she was naked under that Terrycloth wrap and it was difficult not to peel it off her right then and there. But that would only spoil the moment for both of them. There was plenty of time, and he wanted to do it right.

He stepped toward the bathroom, unbuttoning his shirt while he walked. At the doorway, he turned to her and said, "You are beautiful, you know that?"

CHAPTER 36

Deacon stood in the bottom of the pit and stared at his granite prison. Having spent several hours free of the hole's confining walls, he knew the shaft would close in on him with the charm of a medieval dungeon. The stone maw was even more dreadful than he imagined.

But at least he'd cleaned his filth from floor. And he'd talked the drunken brothers into giving him another blanket and the strip of three-inch-thick foam they used for a pad on a wooden bench sitting on the porch of their shack.

He'd sleep better with a cushion between him and the unyielding rock. But the added comfort had cost him his last chunk of gold-bearing quartz.

Now he had to dig more.

A bright crescent of yellow-orange on the stone at the rim of the hole told him the sun was well on its way down. About an hour of light was all he had left. But at least he didn't have the heat of midday rendering him out like a hundred and eighty pound pork roast on a spit. And he didn't have to worry about making noise. Plus he had the two-pound hammer and the chisel Hector had given him to do the job with.

He stepped to the vein of quartz and went to work on it with the hammer and chisel. The first three chunks broke loose with ease. When he examined them, he saw gold in each, one more than the other two. Again, it wasn't enough to make anyone rich, but if luck stayed with him, it was enough to buy a few good meals and more time out of the hole.

Returning to work, he chipped away at the vein, following it up until he could reach no higher. A couple of the pieces of quartz that fell away bore traces of the precious metal, but the others didn't. The gold deposits appeared to concentrate in the lower section of the vein. That meant he had to chip deeper into the wall of granite.

And that wasn't going to be easy.

The deposit of quartz he'd worked on angled up at roughly forty-five degrees. The layer of milky colored stone started about three feet above the floor of the pit and ended a foot or so beyond his reach, and stood out from the darker granite like a one-inch wide line scribed in chalk. The quartz he'd chipped away left a narrow channel in the surrounding stone an inch wide and two inches deep. He ran his finger along the groove and eyeballed it.

He was right; getting to the lode wasn't going to be easy.

In order to get at the gold-bearing quartz wedged between the granite, he'd have to enlarge the groove. There was no way around it.

Hefting the hammer and chisel in his strong hands emboldened him in a way that made him even more resolute in the task facing him. He felt he was quickly turning into a regular hard-rock miner. Backbreaking work to say the least. And all it took to keep his back into the task was the possibility of finding more of that wonderful yellow metal.

The sunlight was fading fast by the time he got enough of the granite chipped away so he could go to work on the lower section of quartz where he'd found the greatest concentration of gold. He was dog-ass tired, but excited to see if the vein proved to be as rich as he believed.

When the first chunks fell away, he saw traces of the yellow stuff imbedded in them but nothing close to what he expected to find. But that didn't mean the gold wasn't there.

He chipped away more quartz, hoping.

And that's when he saw the nugget.

But how big was it?

The exposed portion was the size of a marble. Its edges smooth and round like a woman's behind.

And just as beguiling.

"So you *were* hiding here all this time," he said, speaking fondly to the gold. "Do you know how many men have searched for you?"

He glanced nervously up at the rim of the pit and waited for the pairs of eyes to materialize and stare down at him. Surely, he was being watched. If not by Hector and Kyle, then by the ghosts of the miners who dug the pit, following the vein down until their dream played out.

He'd heard their mournful wail at night when the wind blew.

When the phantom eyes failed to appear, he forgot about the ghosts and their nightly haunting and dug the nail of his index finger into the soft yellow metal. Even in the poor light, he could see the scratch.

Gold!

More than what colored the rocks at his feet, combined.

That might be all there is to the nugget, he quietly cautioned his pounding heart. *But there could be more.*

Working carefully, he continued to chip away at the quartz until he'd exposed a seam of solid gold an inch wide and a little more than a foot long. It looked as though it had been squeezed into the groove like toothpaste from a tube. And it gave every indication of running deep into the granite wall.

He imagined what that would mean.

The Mother Lode.

If the vein was as rich as the nugget suggested.

Now his mind kicked into high gear. It was no longer a matter of an ounce or two. He'd gladly give that much to the brothers in trade for food, time out of the hole, and any other creature comforts he could think of. But no way was he going to turn this much gold over to them.

This was the strike of a lifetime and he intended to keep as much of it as possible.

While there was still light, he sorted through the quartz he'd already chipped away and picked out the chunks that contained gold. Those he set aside in a pile and covered them with dirt he scraped from the floor of the pit.

He'd left each of the brothers with a chunk of quartz to work on. Removing the gold without the proper equipment was difficult. And their effort seemed to be keeping them busy for the time being. But he was sure they'd soon be itching for more.

And he'd be ready for them.

But they wouldn't get the chunks of ore all at once. He'd play it cool when he made his trade and dole the ore out to the brothers one or two pieces at a time as if that was all he had until he found more.

With luck, the bits and pieces would keep them satisfied and out of his hair. And hopefully out of the pit.

That would give him time to go to work on the nugget.

He raised his tools and leaned toward the rock.

"What you doing down there?"

The hammer-head slammed into the wall of granite. He'd missed the chisel entirely. *Kyle.* He glanced up. The goofball was standing at the edge of the pit looking in.

He glared at Kyle and said, "Don't sneak up on me like that."

The smile slipped from Kyle's face. "Hector and me done beat those rocks to pieces and got the gold. It weren't much. So you best be digging more if you want breakfast."

Deacon huffed. He'd hoped they'd stay occupied for the evening. They hadn't.

With an exasperated breath he said, "Chipping away this rock isn't easy. If you want to do it, get your butt down here and swing this heavy-assed hammer. Otherwise, bring me my dinner and then leave me alone. I'll have more rocks for you to work on in the morning."

"You ain't getting no dinner."

Deacon hardened his gaze. "What do you mean? I paid you for dinner. You're not going back on your word, are you?"

Kyle shook his head from side to side. "It weren't enough."

"But that's what we agreed on," Deacon shot back. He was just starting to like the idiot brothers. He hated to think he'd have to reconsider his opinion of them.

Kyle's smile slowly returned. He said, "Ah, I was just funnin' with you. You'll get your dinner."

Deacon breathed a sigh of relief. They were holding to their word. But they'd gotten a taste for gold and he feared the yellow stuff had already begun to work its devil curse on them.

He waved Kyle off. "Then go get my food and I'll find you more gold."

Kyle turned and stepped out of sight. Deacon waited a moment to make sure the goofball didn't reappear suddenly. When it looked to him like Kyle had gone for good—at least for the time it would take to fetch dinner—he went back to work with renewed vigor.

Nightfall came fast to the mountains.

And he'd already lost light playing with Kyle.

A deep shadow had descended on the pit by the time Kyle returned. He had a paper bag in his hand, and he dropped it into Deacon's waiting hands. "Here's your diner. You want steak, it'll cost you big-time."

Deacon peered into the bag: a bologna and cheese sandwich. He was sure the brothers were eating better than that, but then maybe they weren't. At least the sandwich was thick, and Kyle had included a can of peaches.

He couldn't help but smile. The man was all right in his book.

"Thanks for the peaches," he said to Kyle. "That was right thoughtful."

Kyle's lips spread into his goofy grin. He said, "You'll need some light to work by."

"A flashlight would be great," Deacon said.

"Something better." Kyle stepped into the evening gloom beyond the lip of the pit and promptly returned with a gas-powered camp lantern. He lowered it to Deacon on a nylon cord and dropped the line in after it. And then he tossed in a box of wooden kitchen matches.

"Good thinking," Deacon said.

Again, that goofy grin creased Kyle's face. "Just find me and Hector lots of that there gold."

"You can count on it," Deacon said as Kyle stepped away.

It was already too dark in the bottom of the pit for Deacon to see the quartz vein clearly. He wasted no time lighting the lantern. With the glow from the lantern to see by it would be easy to work late into the night. He meant to take full advantage of the time. And he'd find out just how big that nugget was.

CHAPTER 37

Jack lay on his back half under the tousled sheet with Theresa on her side next to him. Her head lay nestled into the hollow of his neck and shoulder with his arm cradling her. Her thick raven hair spilled out and across his chest like black tentacles weaving their way into his mat of dark curls. It was night outside and the room had faded into darkness. The only light came from the street lamps and car headlights that filtered though the lace curtains and reflected off the ceiling and walls.

"Regrets?" she murmured.

With each contented breath, he could feel the soft swell of her ample breasts pressed warm against his side and the scratchiness of her pubic hair on his hip. He pulled her tight against him, nuzzled her hair, and tenderly kissed the top of her head.

"Not a one," He said.

"Not even one little one?" She snuggled against his chest.

"What is it you're worried about?" His voice remained soft and caring. He drifted his fingertips across the small of her back and wound them into a tight circle on her right buttock.

"I don't know. It's been a while. I guess I thought I might have forgotten how."

"Are you kidding?" He shifted his body so that he faced her. And before she could answer, he kissed her long and tenderly on the lips.

The touch stirred the coals of passion still smoldering deep within him. Her mouth was soft and willing. *Damn the woman could kiss.* Her lips parted and he thrust his tongue inside to taste the sweet interior of her mouth. Her arms found their way around his neck, and he could feel her giving in to her own passion.

And his.

The kiss went on for a full half minute before they allowed their lips to slowly separate. The tingling of arousal begged him to take her into his arms and make love to her a third time.

It wasn't just kissing she was good at.

* * * *

When Jack stepped out of the bathroom with the towel draped over his shoulder, Theresa was dressed and sitting in the chair. He didn't care that she was clothed and he wasn't. They'd spent part of the afternoon and all evening together lying naked in bed. Modesty, it seemed, was not an issue.

"I'm hungry," she said, rising to her feet.

He saw Theresa step toward him, and he met her half way. He slid the towel from his shoulder, looped it around her waist, and pulled her into him.

She wrapped her arms around his neck and kissed him on the lips. Then she flattened the palms of her hands against his chest and leaned against the pull of his towel until she'd put a few inches of separation between them.

"Too much for you or what?" His grin told her he was joking.

"How do you feel about grabbing a burger?" she answered. "That or pizza. There's not much else open at ten o'clock at night."

"A burger's fine." He pulled the towel from around her and stepped away to dress.

"I'm sorry about Marsh," she said.

"Why are you apologizing for that sonofabitch?" Jack said as he slipped on his Dockers. "You're not responsible for him being a dickhead."

"No, but I live here. And I hide in that big house of mine and pretend the Marshes of the world don't exist. I used to be quite active in the community. I could've pressured the sheriff into putting a stop to his bullying."

"Maybe, maybe not," he said, buttoning his trousers. "Some men just have a knack for getting away with things. Their run of luck usually ends when someone puts a bullet in them."

"Is that why you brought the gun with you?" Her tone was pointed.

"I've learned to be prepared," he said. "I'd have brought an Uzi if I thought I could get away with it."

"And if Marsh gets in your way again?" she asked. "Are you going to shoot him?"

He'd yet to mention his plan to return to the mountain alone. His mind hadn't changed. He took a deep breath and said, "Perhaps it would be best if you stayed in town from now on."

"Guns don't scare me, Jack." Her eyes were focused on his. "I might even bring one of my own. So don't count me out of this. I just want to be clear on what your intensions are."

For a couple of seconds, he didn't quite know what to think. Had he even heard her right?

Damn.

He stepped to where she was standing, gripped her shoulders, kissed her forehead, and eased away to arms length. "You never cease to amaze me," he said. "Let's get that burger."

When they stepped onto the walkway in front of the hotel ten minutes later, Jack noticed the night air had a chilliness to it that warned of a changing season. Theresa hooked her arm around his and snuggled in close. He knew she felt the chill too.

"Cold?" he asked. He liked having her by his side.

She peered up at him. "Not now."

He took a deep breath and let it out slowly. He didn't want to stop looking at her. Gazing into her eyes was like staring into pools of oil, and he felt their allure. It would have been easy to stand there sink into the soft warmth of her touch.

But he needed to be cautious. He remained confident Marsh would not bring the fight to town; he wasn't so sure about the man's weasel-faced, backstabbing nephew.

"If I'm not careful I could get used to this," he said, casually leading her in the direction of Deacon's pickup.

She held on as they walked. "You're referring to me, I hope."

Jack stopped next to the wooden post supporting the porch overhang, leaned against it, pulled her close and said, "It's not the cool weather."

There were those eyes again, drawing him in like the dark water of a desert oasis at night. The allure was too much for him to resist, and he leaned into a passionate embrace.

The solid thud into the side of the post where his head had been a fraction of a second before was distinct and loud.

Tearing himself from the kiss, he pulled Theresa onto the walkway behind the protection of Deacon's Ford Ranger. No distinct *crack* of a gunshot. He knew exactly what it was.

Looking up, he saw the glistening blade of a pearl-handled switchblade stuck deep into the wood.

CHAPTER 38

Jack wrapped his arm around Theresa and held her down. No one was on the walkway to either side of them, so Marsh's shithead nephew had to have been lurking in the shadows of the buildings across the street. One hell of a knife throw . . . even for an expert.

But he just might be that good. And he might have another blade waiting.

"Roy," Theresa said.

"You were right about him." Jack had figured the weasel-faced punk for a back stabber, but he hadn't thought of him as a woman killer. Until now. When Roy threw that knife, there was no guarantee which one of them he'd stick.

And Roy *had* thrown the knife.

There was no doubt in Jack's mind.

What Jack didn't know was had Weaselface been waiting for one or both of them to step outside the hotel? Or had he merely seized the opportunity when it presented itself. And was he acting on his own or at Marsh's direction?

Did it really matter?

The skinny fucker was spying on them, that was for sure. And he was ready to kill.

Jack raised his head and peeked over the hood of the truck. Only an idiot would have stuck around after throwing that knife, but he wasn't going to take anything for granted.

"Is he gone?" Theresa raised her head next to his and peeked.

"Long gone, if he's smart."

"What do we do now?"

"Have that burger."

He fished an almost-clean rag from inside the cab of Deacon's pickup, draped it over the handle of the knife. Marsh's weasel-faced nephew had probably worn gloves, but there was always a chance he hadn't. And who knew what other trace evidence was contained there.

He pulled the four-inch blade from the wooden post and carefully folded the rag around the knife. Sheriff Doug Bell's credibility concerned him enough that he doubted the man could be trusted, even in a case as obvious as this. For now, he'd hold onto the switchblade.

"I'll keep this pig-sticker for the time being," he told her. "That worthless turd is probably hunkered down in a sewer someplace so I don't think we have anything more to worry about, for tonight anyway."

"None of this makes sense," she said. "I feel like I'm in the middle of a gang war."

"Marsh isn't after the gold," Jack said. "I'm convinced of that. But he's up to his neck in something bad. And I'm afraid Deacon has stepped right smack in the middle of it."

"Drugs?"

"Could be. That would explain his willingness to kill. But if that's what this is all about, what does keeping us off that mountain have to do with it?"

Theresa peered in the direction of the window to Jack's room and said, "I feel like I could use another shower."

He had the same crawly sensation. It was a natural response when a person felt violated.

The knife slamming into the post above their heads had done that.

He followed her gaze up. He imagined she wondered if the punk had been watching their naked shadows doing a sex-dance on the wall of his room.

Or worse yet.

He turned and eyeballed the roof of the vacant two-story building sitting idle directly across the street. The perfect vantage point for a person wanting to keep an eye on them.

It sickened him to think the pervert climbed up there with binoculars for a better look.

The quaint little tourist town had suddenly turned ugly.

"You ready to go?" Jack was done standing there. He could see no good coming from peering into the town's dirty little corners or its dirty little people and their dirty little games.

But in reality, only a few of its citizens were bad. He knew of at least four that were good. Five if he counted Della. She was at least part good. But she had her dirty little game and her dirty little corner just the same.

Al and Bob, too.

Even Theresa had her skeletons.

And him most of all.

That realization made him want to laugh.

He would be sure and remind himself of that whenever he started to feel cynical about the town and the people in it.

When he focused his gaze on Theresa, he noticed her eyeing him quizzically. He said, "My mind was a bit preoccupied, sorry."

"I thought I'd lost you," she said.

"Not even close." He bent and kissed her.

She stiffened—but only for a second—then she parted her lips and wrapped her arms around his neck, giving fully to their shared passion.

When he dragged his lips from hers twenty seconds later, she gasped, "Wow! Whatever it was that was on your mind, I forgive you."

Jack smiled. He couldn't help himself.

She sure could kiss.

"You know," he said. "I completely forgot what it was I was thinking."

He moved in for another kiss, and she took a step back.

"What?" he asked.

"I'll have to go home tonight, you know that."

Her eyes baited him in. And her lips, too. He couldn't resist.

"All right," he said. "If you say so."

"But there's time." She reached for his hand and said, "We can go for that burger or we can have pizza brought in."

He took her fingers in his, put his other arm around her back with his palm flat on her shoulder, and pointed her in the direction of the door to the Gold Trail Inn. "Pizza sounds wonderful."

They stepped toward the hotel arm in arm. Half way to the door, Jack peered over his shoulder and fought back a shudder of uneasiness when he scanned the shadows across the street.

Fourteen days missing.

CHAPTER 39

Deacon hammered the chisel into the granite, keeping to a slow even pace. The rock cracked and fell away and the hole grew larger. From time to time small shrapnel-like chips had struck him in the face leaving tiny gouges that brought blood.

Tiny scars of progress.

He casually wiped away the blood with the back of his hand and continued the task freeing the nugget.

Time was not on his side. He had to make every minute count.

He'd only stopped the few seconds it took to take a bite of his sandwich or slurp down a peach. And the minute he spent putting the chisel to work opening the can.

When he finally let the heavy hammer and chisel drop to the stone floor, the time felt late: midnight or even 1:00 in the morning by the position of the big dipper overhead. He lifted the lantern by its wire handle and examined the twenty-inch-diameter dimple he'd chipped in the granite around the seam of gold, careful not to hack into the soft yellow metal.

He wanted to keep the nugget intact if at all possible. One this size would have value far beyond the current bullion price.

Looking at his work, the circular depression reminded him of a large stone bowl imbedded in the wall. Cave art for stone-age admirers. For him, access to the nugget.

Fatigue helped contain his excitement, but he was still

exceedingly anxious to hold the enormous chunk of gold in his hands and caress its smooth edges. In his dreams he'd made finds like this, but that's all they were: dreams. This was real and right in front of him.

Five pounds of the precious yellow metal, if it was an ounce.

And his for the taking.

The answer to his problems is how he viewed the money the nugget would bring. Much-needed repairs to the salmon boat, gas and groceries for another couple of years or more, maybe even a big-screen TV for his dad, and that was only the beginning.

Once he dug deeper, he'd know just how big the strike was. Then he'd figure out how to make sure the discovery remained his.

The twins' boom box had been silent an hour by his reckoning. He guessed that meant Hector and Kyle had gone to bed. He'd work quietly now. The loud clank of hammer against chisel just might rouse the brothers from their slumber and bring them looking.

He couldn't risk they'd catch sight of the nugget.

That would be the end of his dream and maybe the end of him. People kill for gold and Kyle already showed signs of falling prey to its beguiling allure. Hector had to be right there with him.

He leaned in close to the vein and held the lantern there. The quartz holding the nugget in place was mostly exposed. A few more chisel strokes would clean the last of the stubborn granite away. Then with luck, he could chip the nugget loose without breaking it.

The lantern put out a bright light. But sitting on the bottom of the pit, it left shadows in the crevices. He had to go at it, carefully.

When he had the lantern positioned to provide the most light possible, he went back to work using careful, gentle strokes of hammer and chisel to carefully chip away the remaining shards of rock holding the nugget. And with each stroke of the hammer, he was careful to make the least amount of noise possible.

Minutes passed; his caution with the hammer made the job agonizingly slow. The granite didn't give way easily under the light touch of the chisel. But that was the way the work had to be done. Or he would risk waking the twins.

An hour later, the quartz that held the vein of gold in place was fully exposed. Weariness made it difficult for him to concentrate.

He took a drink of water and mentally prepared himself.

Holding onto the vein of gold with his left hand, he gripped the chisel with his right and tapped at the quartz with the beveled end.

Slow and careful—like using a small rock hammer.

"Come to papa," he whispered.

He kept at his work with the chisel. Each chip or fracture brought more whispered words of encouragement.

"That's right. Come to papa," he said aloud.

"Don't be stingy," he said another time. "You've held onto the gold long enough."

The talk seemed to help.

He continued to speak to the gold as though he was actually coaxing it from the rock with his words. Finally, with some effort, the quartz cracked apart and the nugget fell away. The weight of the gold surprised him when it came loose in his hand. It was far heavier than its size suggested—like picking up a lead sinker in a sporting goods store.

He let the chisel drop and cradled his prize in both hands.

Bits and pieces of the milky stone remained attached to the soft yellow metal, but for the most part, he was holding a single piece of pure gold.

His . . . he'd mined it from the rock.

Those pairs of eyes returned, he could feel them bore holes into his back. He tucked the gold tight against his chest and peered into the gloom above him. Like before, there was only darkness and the stars in the night sky.

Ghosts.

He couldn't get over how real the sensation was that he was being watched. The pairs of eyes weren't there peering down at him, but then maybe they were and he just couldn't see them. Maybe there really were spirits of miners long dead that had been doomed to roam the mountain.

And maybe those restless spirits watched him now.

If that was the case, he could only hope their souls could finally rest. The precious metal that eluded them in the pit had been found.

Or perhaps they would remain in their mountain purgatory a little longer, curious onlookers waiting to see just how rich their claim had been.

And if they chose to stay, would seeing their lost riches unearthed cause them more unrest? Or eternal peace?

Either way, those long dead miners abandoned their claim and the rickety old cabin the brothers squatted in. He was on U.S. Forest Service land—public land. A new claim could be filed, but first he had to hold onto the gold.

And his life.

He scanned the pit. The logical solution was to bury the nugget so the twins wouldn't see it. Against the far wall was the fresh bucket of dirt he'd lowered down earlier in the day to cover his waste. He could use that. The twins would never dig through the mound to see what was concealed below.

And if there were more chunks of gold, he would bury them there too.

Suddenly it occurred to him he hadn't taken a moment to see if there were more riches contained there.

He quickly buried the nugget and carried the lantern to the vein. He held it close, but he didn't have too. From five feet away he could see the spattering of yellow metal. The quartz was full of it.

Gold!

The Mother Lode!

CHAPTER 40

At six the next morning, Jack flipped open his cell phone and dialed Theresa's private number. She assured him Carlos would not answer her cell phone. The call went through, and he waited.

He needed to slow down and carefully think through his next moves. The shooting and especially the incident with the switchblade the night before had changed the rules of the game. This was not a matter of finding Deacon lying injured and dying in the woods or at the bottom of a ravine having suffered an accidental fall.

The urgency of the situation remained.

But there was something sinister going on.

And Jack knew he couldn't rush into the mountains with reckless abandon hollering Deacon's name from every tree and rock. Theresa put it to him straight. If Deacon was lying out there hurt, he was probably dead by now. Another day or two wouldn't matter. But if he had unintentionally wandered into the middle of something seriously illegal, caution could very well save his life.

Jack had to believe that.

"Good morning," Theresa said into her phone after the third ring.

Immediately his mind filled with visions of their lovemaking. He smiled and said, "Can I meet you for breakfast?"

"You gave some thought to what I said last night when I left, I hope."

He made himself concentrate. "It makes sense to not rush off half-cocked."

"Then I insist we have breakfast on my terrace."

He had to chuckle at the thought that crossed his mind. "Marsh won't be there, will he?"

"No. And he never will be." Theresa practically hissed the words.

Jack grinned at the resolve in her voice. Theresa Montero was no woman to mess with. She'd already shown she could hold her own.

"I have an e-mail to send," he told her. "Then I'm on my way."

He flipped his phone closed and hurried downstairs. The clerk manning the front desk unlocked the computer screen for him, and he brought up his e-mail account. A couple of dozen unread messages greeted him. He quickly glanced over the subject boxes hoping to see one from Deacon saying he'd gone to Tahoe and was winning big. Not seeing one—no surprise there—he clicked on the new-message tab and went to work writing.

A dozen minutes later, he stepped onto the sidewalk in front of his hotel and took in the early morning with a sweeping gaze. The sky was light blue above the rugged horizon to the east, but the sun was slow to reveal itself on this side of the high Sierras. There were a few people walking the sidewalks, none of whom showed the least bit of interest in him. And across the street, a half dozen cars lined the curb in front of Nel's Diner. Marsh's red Ford F-350 dually wasn't one of them, neither was the shiny black Navigator with limousine tint and paper license plates.

That suited Jack just fine.

What he hoped was that if he and Theresa did not go back into the mountains this morning as planned, Marsh would get the idea his threats worked. With any luck at all, that would put Marsh on a different tack—one that allowed them to get a jump ahead of the big man.

And that might be enough to turn the tide.

From the beginning, they'd been two steps behind every time he and Theresa made a move to find Deacon. That had to change. The next time Marsh and his paths crossed on the mountain, he wanted to be the man holding the gun; not the one walking into it.

He climbed into Deacon's pickup happy to find all the tires had air in them and that there were no wires dangling from under the hood. The engine roared to life on the first crank of the starter.

At least he still had wheels that worked.

He dropped the transmission into drive, cranked his head to the side, and glanced over his shoulder at the oncoming traffic. A delivery truck rumbled by and he waited for it to pass. A car-length behind the truck was a white BMW convertible with the top up. He wondered for a moment if it was the same Beamer that came close to running down Theresa. The next car was over a block away.

Accelerating onto the roadway, Jack drove south on Highway 49 amid light commuter traffic. He was glad he didn't have far to go. Theresa was waiting for him. And he was anxious to see her.

The access road came up on his right. He slowed and made the turn. The only other time he'd seen the grapevines growing around Theresa hacienda was at night in the headlights of the Jeep. In daylight, the vineyard was even more magnificent. In the distance, her walled hacienda stood like a fortress on the hill. He could clearly see the hundred-year-old oak that rose majestically from the middle of the courtyard.

He found the security gate open and drove on through without stopping to show his face to the camera. He figured the gate had been left that way for him. He followed the gravel drive into the walled courtyard, around the right side of the stately oak, and on to where he'd parked the Jeep the night of his first visit there.

When Max the German Sheppard did not make an appearance, Jack climbed out of the pickup and walked around it to the porch. He pressed the doorbell and allowed himself a couple of seconds to admire the beautifully carved front door. Then he turned to make sure no snarling mouth full of teeth was sneaking up to bite him on the ass.

The sound of the door opening came as a relief. He turned and was glad to see Theresa standing there with a smile on her face.

He matched her grin with one of his own and said, "Good morning."

"Don't worry about Max," she said. "I have her inside.

"She's eaten her breakfast, I hope." He peered past her at the tiled entryway half expecting to see the dog snarling at him.

She stepped to the side. "Max has already had her pound of flesh for the day."

"Only a pound?" He was serious.

She chuckled and said, "Come in and we'll go out onto the patio and have some coffee. Maria will have breakfast ready in a few minutes."

He followed her through the house and onto the covered terrace at the rear. It was truly a grand home. Beyond the richly tiled patio, a concrete deck the size of a small parking lot framed a large swimming pool and Jacuzzi. Beyond that, the ground sloped down just enough so that he could gaze over the wall at the vineyard.

"Nice," he said with a nod.

"Leandro and I had some grand parties here." She quietly gazed out across the vast expanse of land. "He loved to entertain."

"And you?" Jack noticed her stare into the past.

She smiled and motioned at the chair on the other side of the patio table next to them. "Please, do sit down. Maria will bring us coffee."

"A thought occurred to me this morning," he said as she settled into a cushioned chair next to the table.

"Only one?" She arched a manicured brow.

He grinned. "Okay, two."

Maria stepped onto the patio carrying a tray with a silver coffee service set and two finely crafted porcelain cups that looked to be a hundred years old. He took the seat across from Theresa and quietly watched Maria set the tray on the table.

Theresa smiled at her and said, "I'll pour; thank you. You can bring out breakfast whenever it's ready."

Maria bowed. "Yes Senora Montero."

"As I was saying," Jack said when Maria walked away. "On the drive over, it occurred to me that since we didn't go back into the mountains this morning, Marsh might get the idea his threats worked. With a little luck, that could put him on a different tack and give us a chance to get the jump on him.

"And if he doesn't?" Theresa glanced at him over the cup she'd just filled.

"Then we go back up there and find Deacon and the gold and

be ready for whatever Marsh throws at us."

"By ready, you mean going armed?"

Jack nodded. "Do you think you could shoot a man if you had to?"

Theresa pointed at the scar on her cheek and said, "You see this? I wasn't always a lady."

CHAPTER 41

Jack forked up the last bite of his *huevos rancheros* and took a sip of coffee to wash it down. He returned his cup to the table and said, "You've kept me in suspense long enough. Tell me about the scar."

Theresa fingered her left cheek as though remembering. "I told you I grew up in East Los Angeles, and that we moved up here to Sonora when I was fifteen?"

"Are you saying you belonged to a street gang?"

"No. But that doesn't mean I didn't have to fight. The stitches were still in my cheek when my father loaded us and what little we owned into our car and drove away from there."

"So you were one of the lucky ones. You got out of that hellhole life."

"Yeah . . . me and my two sisters."

"Your sisters," he asked. "Do they live in Sonora?"

"Mom still does, my sisters are married and live in the valley." She stared wistfully into the coffee in her cup. "My father was killed in a mining accident two years after we moved to Sonora."

Jack picked up on the feeling of loss reflected in her voice. Her father had obviously played a big part in shaping her into the woman she'd become.

But her father paid the ultimate price early in his life.

The cruel hand of fate.

He failed to understand why truly good people die while truly evil people like Marsh and his weasel-faced nephew, live.

"I lost my mother to cancer eighteen years ago." He said. "It's tough. Believe me, I know."

She peered into his eyes and held him in her gaze. Then as though she was reading his mind she said, "And now Deacon is missing."

Jack thought about Providence's habit of rearing its ugly head. Deacon was without a doubt one of the good guys. The cruel hand of fate was not going to have its way.

Not this time.

He steeled himself and winked. "Not for long."

At that, her lips curled into a smile. "Have you and Deacon always been close?"

"As brothers growing up," he said. A tinge of guilt made him look away.

"But not so much, now?" she asked.

He said, "The last few years—I'm sorry to say—we lost some of that closeness. I'm only now discovering there's a side to my little brother I didn't know. Like his fascination with finding a cache of Murrieta's gold."

"Do you think there's a chance?"

"What chance is that?" he asked

"That we'll find those gold bars my great, great, great grandfather took in that robbery."

"You bet there's a chance."

"You say that as if you've done this sort of thing before."

He had to chuckle. "Funny you should put it that way."

"So I take it you have."

He took a sip of coffee and said, "You have no idea."

"Please," she said. "Tell me."

He focused his gaze on her big brown eyes and asked, "What do you know about Captain Cook?"

"Only that he got into a fight with natives over a boat and was killed."

"Kealakekua Bay on the Big Island of Hawaii," he added. "It was King Kalaniopuu's warriors who attacked and killed Cook in 1779 and cut his body into pieces."

"You know your history."

"I know my treasure," he said.

She said, "I'm listening."

"During WWII," he began, "a soldier stationed on the Big Island stumbled onto King Kalaniopuu's burial cave, which—in addition to a treasure trove of artifacts—held the king's bones and the last remains of Captain Cook. The soldier, it turned out, was an amateur antiquities dealer profiting from other discoveries he'd made while stationed in Hawaii."

"Not a good man," she added.

"Not at all," he said. "Till then his black-market antiquities operation had run smoothly, but the war caught up to him. In his haste to fly the antiquities to Oahu, he lost them when his plane crashed in the channel off Maui's west coast. My friend Robert and I recovered King Kalaniopuu's stolen remains, and those of Captain Cook. Since the bones rightfully belonged to the Hawaiian people, the artifacts were turned over to one of their priests, a *Kahuna*, for repatriation. In gratitude for what I'd done, I was given a box of pearls we'd found with the bones. My share bought me my boat."

She smiled and said, "You surprise me, Jack."

Her smile was contagious. He grinned and asked, "How's that?"

"What you've done, I'd never have guessed."

Only the half of it.

He said, "You know what they say about looks?"

"That they're deceiving," they said in unison.

They laughed.

Theresa had proven to be as good a listener as she was a kisser, and that made it easy for Jack to talk about himself. He changed the subject and talked a bit about having to leave college to run the family salmon boat when his father injured his back. And that he moved to Maui when Deacon was old enough to take over the operation. And he told her about going back to school and his love for the sea and the creatures in it.

To his relief, she didn't press for answers he wasn't prepared to give. The parts he glossed over were the times he'd killed men.

Truly evil men bent on killing him.

Perhaps the fickle hand of fate did at times deal a deadly blow to those who deserve it most. And now that he thought about it, no other explanation fit. He could have died a hundred times during his exploits of the last few years and yet he'd come through them alive.

"Sounds like neither of us had it all that easy," she said when he stopped talking.

He lifted his hand and made a sweeping gesture at their surroundings. "But life turned out not so bad."

She nodded, "For both of us, it seems."

He glanced at his watch and realized he'd been talking nonstop for nearly an hour.

"Sorry," he said. "I kind of got carried away there."

"You weren't boring, if that's what you're worried about."

He couldn't resist smiling for about the hundredth time. "What's nice is you make it easy for me to rattle on about myself."

She fell silent, and once again, her gaze dropped to her cup. After a moment, she peered into his eyes and said, "Joaquin Murrieta is my father's great, great, grandfather. That's how I'm related to him. I want to believe the good that was so much my father, makes up for at least some of the bad that was a big part of Joaquin."

Jack knew all about guilt. "You can't carry the blame for something a relative did a century and a half ago."

"No? Tell that to John Wilkes Booth's relatives."

"That subject has been hashed and rehashed," he said. "I think the relatives that are out there are too far removed to be blamed."

"Well, my father was a direct descendant of Joaquin. So am I."

He shook his head in confusion. "You're saying there are people around who blame you for Joaquin's thieving, murdering ways?"

"I'm saying I want history to be reflected truthfully."

"You've already told me why it's important to you to find that gold."

"I don't just want to find it, Jack." She leaned close, her eyes locked squarely on his. "I want to give it back."

Jack felt as though a light breeze could blow him over. "Something new?" he asked. "Or was that your intent all along?"

"I thought about it a lot last night on the way home, and again this morning," she said. "You could have been killed by that knife. Or I could have. Life's short. I know that only too well. I want to do something truly good before I die."

The knife had come close to sticking him in the head. That was for sure. But his thoughts had been how good Theresa felt in his arms. If he had died, he'd have died happy.

She was a damned good kisser.

He said, "That's certainly a noble thought. The question is, are there even any records around to say who the gold bars actually belonged to at the time? I hate making assumptions, but I'm assuming you're talking about returning the loot to a surviving relative . . . if one can even be found."

She leaned back in her chair. "We won't know that until we try."

He nodded. His mind was already working on the problem. "First, we have to find the gold."

CHAPTER 42

Kyle's voice drug Deacon scratching and clawing from a dream so wonderful and real he didn't want to let go of it. He opened one eye and let it close. The foam pad and extra blanket allowed him the first halfway decent sleep since being dropped in the pit. A full belly helped too. So did the satisfaction of knowing he would have enough money stashed to make his and his dad's life easier, at least for a while.

But first, he had to survive the hell he'd stumbled into. And that meant playing along with the twins.

"Asshole," Deacon grumbled, squinting up at Kyle. "The suns not even all the way up yet. What is it you want?"

Kyle pointed in the direction of the pile of rubble on the floor of the pit. "The gold you dug last night. And then you've got work to do."

Deacon hauled himself to a sitting position. He'd expected Hector and Kyle to wake up with gold on their minds. That precious yellow metal brought on a fever more contagious than any he knew of.

He was glad he had a plan.

"Figures," he said. "Toss me down a bucket and get me some coffee. While you're fetching me that eye-opener, I'll get you your rocks."

"They better have gold in them," Kyle said. Then he turned and

209

stepped from view.

Deacon took the opportunity to remove two golf-ball-sized chunks of gold bearing quartz from his stash and stuff them into his right front pants pocket. The others he reburied.

That done, he went to work gathering the rubble. A few of the stones Kyle had pointed to showed at least some color, but most didn't. That would, he reasoned, go a long way to supporting his claim there wasn't much gold to be found there. And it might keep them out of the pit. He'd thrown mud on the vein to hide the glint of yellow that would certainly catch their attention, but the ruse would only fool the twins if they were looking down from above.

"Here's your bucket and your coffee," Kyle said when he reappeared at the edge of the pit. Reaching out to arm's length, he lowered a white plastic pail down to Deacon by way of a rope.

Deacon took hold of the bottom of the bucket and called out, "Hey, what about breakfast?"

Kyle dropped the remaining coils of rope on the ground next to his feet and pointed. "In the bucket with your coffee. I'll be back in ten minutes. Then it's work time. And you'd better have some gold for us."

Deacon took care in lowering the bucket to where he could peek inside. He smelled his morning feast before he saw it: a greasy over-fried egg sandwiched between a respectable looking homemade biscuit and a large steaming mug of black coffee.

"Hey," he called out again. "Wait a minute."

Kyle returned to the edge of the pit and peered down at him without even a hint of the goofy grin that normally creased his face.

"What do you want?" he grumbled.

Deacon could tell from Kyle's strained expression and the harshness in his voice that the man was stressed. "Here's a piece of quartz I saved special for you." He dug one of the chunks from his pants pocket and tossed it up to Kyle. "You and Hector will have to sort through the rest. But I'm afraid there's not much gold in it. Now tell me what's wrong."

Kyle held the quartz in front of his face and narrowed his eyes.

His expression visibly brightened. Then just as quickly his smile faded and he said, "Yesterday, the man what shot that poor donkey, he gave me and Hector three days to bag up the buds we have dried. Plus we gotta get the rest of the crop stacked, dried, and bagged."

"Your boss?'

"Yeah . . . right." He peered down at Deacon. "Well, me and Hector decided there's no way we can do it alone. Not by tomorrow afternoon. That's why you're going to help us."

Deacon stood there thinking he didn't know a damned thing about harvesting marijuana. Not that he wanted to help Hector and Kyle flood the streets with a shit-pot full of weed. Then it dawned on him that if they were brining in the crop of dope, and if they kept to their word—which he believed they would—he'd be free to go in a few days.

That he *did* want.

Now he just had to hope the twins remained true to their word.

He gobbled down his egg and biscuit and washed it down with a few sips of coffee. The rest of his coffee he gulped down while he scooped the rubble into the bucket with his free hand. When Hector and Kyle weren't harvesting dope, they'd be busy sorting through the rock debris looking for gold.

And while they chipped and scratched and hammered for an ounce or two of the precious yellow metal, he'd continue to chip as much ore as he could from the Mother Lode.

He was getting out of there soon. The gold was going with him.

* * * *

Deacon cradled the concrete block in the crook of his arms and watched the twins walk away muttering to each other. His talk of long-dead miners peering down at him in the night had no doubt left them feeling uneasy. They kept glancing back at the pit, and he wondered if the wide-eyed look on their faces was one of uncertainty, or if they actually believed what he said.

He figured it was the latter.

And he wanted it that way.

To keep from tripping over the chain padlocked around his ankle, he gripped a handful of metal links, lifted his shackle to remove the slack, and shuffled down the slope a dozen steps behind

Hector and Kyle. The piles of dried plants were still there, much as they'd been the day before when he'd noticed them. Several of the plants now sat on the ground next to a makeshift table erected on a patch of flat ground in front of the cabin. A scattering of stocks and twigs littered the area.

The twins had been busy.

Kyle stopped and faced Deacon. A look of irritation in Kyle's expression told Deacon that Kyle was in a hurry to get started. He and Kyle watched Hector step to the table and begin snipping buds from the plants. The buds, he tossed into a plastic five-gallon bucket. Not exactly a sophisticated operation.

Deacon wasn't sure what he expected, but thought it somehow should have been more.

A minute later, he stood on the pockmarked earth in a clearing, staring at what was left of the six-foot-tall marijuana plants growing there. He recalled seeing three such dope crops rising among the trees on his way to the pit the day Hector and Kyle took him captive.

That made for one hell-of-a-lot of dope.

And a lot of work.

Some of which—from what he could see—had already been done.

But that was only a good start.

According to Kyle, each of the remaining plants had to be pulled from the ground, lugged uphill to the cabin, and piled to dry. Deacon didn't need to be told that was his job. He exhaled an exasperated breath. Not an easy task lugging his concrete anchor along with him.

He turned to Kyle and asked, "How many plants are out here?"

Kyle smiled with the pride of an expectant father. "All together—counting the ones we have drying—I'd say we ended up with two thousand, maybe twenty-five hundred. We planted almost twice that, but we had to cull the males."

Deacon chuckled. "How do you tell which is which, peek under their leaves?" He didn't really give a shit how it was done. He was just trying to get Kyle to lighten up. The boy was behaving way too serious.

Kyle cracked the hint of a smile. "Hector and me knows the

difference. The females are full-figured like a good woman."

Deacon wanted to laugh. "You like ladies big, huh?"

Kyle's smile broadened into a grin. "Sure do."

Deacon was glad he'd finally gotten Kyle to smile. "Show me how you water all these plants. I know you don't irrigate by hand."

"Nope," Kyle said. "We made us a drip system.

Kyle led Deacon over to the stream splitting the narrow canyon and pointed to a small dam. "See that thirty gallon trash can with that PVC pipe coming out of it?"

Deacon noticed it right off and had already visually followed the piping into the field. "Gravity fed. That's pretty smart."

Again, Kyle grinned. "I thought of it."

Deacon slapped Kyle on the back and said, "I knew you were smart."

He didn't mind paying Kyle the complement. It seemed to lighten the mood even more, and that was just what he wanted. Kyle was a whole lot easier to get along with when he was smiling.

"So how do you want to do this?" Deacon nodded at the dope plants swaying in the breeze.

"You ain't going to try and run off on me, are you?"

Deacon hefted the chunk of concrete. "Can't run anywhere with this ball and chain."

"Nope, but you could try."

"You still going to let me go when you get this dope harvested?"

"Me and Hector was serious when we told you that. We don't want to kill no one."

"Then you can trust me."

"You still gotta wear that chain."

Deacon shrugged and said, "Show me what to do. I want to get this done and get out of here."

Kyle led Deacon back to the dope plants. Taking hold of a fat stalk, he heaved the plant from the soil. "Since you is chained to that block of cement, I'll do the carrying. You pull."

Deacon had to laugh. Chuckling, he pulled a plant and tossed it aside. "You'd better hurry or you're going to fall behind."

Kyle was already on the move with the first plant. "We'll see," he hollered back.

Deacon waved the twin off.

The morning turned into an exhausting sprint to keep from falling behind. The hard work took its toll on his ravaged body. But he stayed with it and by midday, he was cruising. Plants littered the ground where he'd tossed them. Kyle couldn't keep up.

Gasping for breath, Kyle walked up to him and asked, "Do you know how to work a Seal-a-Meal?"

Deacon did.

"Why?" he asked.

"Hector needs help."

Deacon thought about how many times he and his father used Seal-a-Meal to package and freeze select fillets of salmon for themselves and friends. Packaging marijuana—he was sure—was one use for the machine that wouldn't make it into commercials.

Not this Christmas season, anyway.

"You don't know how?" Deacon asked, looking squarely at Kyle.

Kyle pointed at the anchor chained to Deacon's ankle and said, "You can lug these plants and that chunk of concrete up this slope if that's what you want. Or you can stand up there at that table and seal bags. Your choice."

Deacon grinned and said, "Back home, they call me the Pro from Dover."

Kyle cocked his head, obviously confused by Deacon's response.

"It's a saying," Deacon said. He waited for a hint of understanding from Kyle. It didn't come. He added, "It means I'm an expert with one."

At that, Kyle smiled and nodded as if suddenly getting the point. "Oh yeah. Good. You gonna help Hector."

Deacon turned to follow Kyle, then stood his ground when the redhead raised his hand in a gesture for him to stop.

"What is it?" Deacon found himself trusting Kyle. Something was wrong. Then he heard the high-rpm groan of an engine dragging a vehicle up a grade in low gear.

Kyle turned and pointed. "Into the field, hurry."

Deacon didn't argue. He took a step in the direction of the bushy six-foot-tall plants.

"Hurry!" Kyle shoved him from behind.

It wasn't necessary. Deacon shot him a hard look over his shoulder and kept going. He was already moving as fast as he could with his ball and chain. He had enough adrenalin pumping to keep going all the way down the canyon and out of the mountains. If that was the way he wanted to play it.

Four rows in, he stopped and crouched down for a look.

Peering between the leaves and bulging buds of the marijuana, he saw a big red Ford pickup with duel tires in back appear over the rise in front of him. The truck had a box trailer hooked to its rear bumper. It pulled to a stop next to the cabin.

CHAPTER 43

Jack followed Theresa into a cavernous parking garage. When she'd offered to show him her wedding present, he jumped at the opportunity. But his heart was only half in it. Deacon was still out there, most likely caught up in something seriously illegal. He might even be dead. There was only one way to know for sure.

Go back up on the mountain and find him.

But not yet.

Jack itched to make something happen. His hope right now was that his ploy worked and they ended up a step ahead of the man, which was where they needed to be.

But first, he wanted to hear back from Robert regarding the e-mail he'd sent him that morning.

The frustrating part was he had no idea when that would be.

He wasn't sure he could wait.

And then he saw her car. Ten feet away sat Theresa's vintage Ford AC Cobra Mark III. Equipped with a 427 cubic inch high-performance engine rated at 485 horsepower with a top speed of 180 miles per hour, the Cobra was the fastest production race car produced in its time. Her 1966 was cherry.

Unable to resist the urge, he quickly stepped to the driver's door and peered into the cockpit, careful not to touch. Then he took his time making a circuit of the Cobra. Painted midnight blue with two parallel white competition stripes down the middle, the car all but

216

begged him to run his hands over her classic lines.

He resisted, of course.

"I've never seen one up close," he said. He didn't even try to contain the excitement showing through in his voice.

"There were only three hundred Mark Threes produced by Carroll Shelby in 1965 and 66," she explained. "Each one has a serial number that's recorded."

He leaned down and examined the paint on the hood.

"Are you looking for cracks?"

He grinned. "You're surprised I'm familiar with the problem?"

"Not many people outside the Cobra circle are."

He refocused on the hood. "The torque from all that horsepower stresses the aluminum body cracking the paint, right?"

Her smile told him he was right.

"Thirty one unsold Mark Threes were detuned and made street worthy," she continued. "They were called S/C for semi-competition. Today, they are the rarest and most valuable. This happens to be an S/C."

Jack was a bit embarrassed to inquire how much the car was worth, but he couldn't resist. He looked at her and asked, "What do you mean when you say valuable?"

She looked him solidly in the eyes. "In excess of one and a half million."

All he could do was stare at the car and smile.

The tone of his cell phone jarred him back to reality. He saw the name and flipped it open. He said, "You'll never guess what I'm looking at?"

"A pretty woman," Robert answered into Jack's ear.

"That too. I'm also staring at her honest-to-goodness Mark Three Cobra."

"Women, vintage race cars, people trying to kill you, I can't leave you alone for a minute. I knew I should have gone there with you."

Jack sighed. He and Robert had beaten the issue to death, at least twice. But then that was Robert.

He said, "I needed to do this alone."

"You told me."

"I still feel that's what I need to do."

"And you are," Robert said. "Reel your tongue in and listen."

"You got the information?"

"Enough to know you need to be careful."

Jack said, "You've got my undivided attention."

"Good," Robert said. "I called a friend of mine who works for the Bureau of Narcotic Enforcement there in California. I asked to have Elliot Marsh's name and age run through their computer to see what popped out."

"And?" Jack said.

"Marsh has never been arrested," Robert said. "So he doesn't have a rap sheet. But his name has come up in a few BNE cases: primarily marijuana production and distribution. But BNE also believes he was connected with at least two meth labs their agents took down three years ago in eastern Kern County."

"Suspected, but no arrests?" Jack asked.

"He's slippery," Robert said.

"And no small chicken."

"Not at all. And as you see, just as hard to catch."

"I'm not surprised." Jack sighed into his phone. "He's made friends in the right places, here."

"The local cops?"

"The sheriff." Jack practically hissed the words.

"A good man to have on your side if you're a crook." Robert shot back.

"And some local business people," Jack added.

"Probably members of the County Council."

"He's not dumb," Jack said. "He just chose to screw with the wrong person."

"Don't get cocky" Robert said. "I'm sure this guy has dealt with bigger and badder people than you are, my friend."

"I'm sure he has. And that just might give me the edge."

"I'm not following."

"If he thinks I'm little more than a minor annoyance, he might not see me coming when I hit him head on."

"You've got a point."

"So what's his MO?"

"The man floats in and out of towns—on the average not more

than a couple of years in any one place—and operates under the front of legitimate business ventures."

"Like a used car lot?"

"And a tow company. And an automotive repair shop. He's owned a couple of each. He buys and sells his businesses as quickly as he moves from town to town."

"The man works fast. And he knows how to make the right contacts."

"You said he owns a used car lot, there. Kind of tells you what the man's up to."

Jack chuckled. "He should have stuck to selling junkers."

"Doesn't pay enough," Robert said. "Are you aware that illegal marijuana production in California supplies fifty percent of the marijuana consumed in the United States?"

"I thought the stuff came north across the border," Jack said. He could count on Robert to have the facts.

Robert said, "The practice now is for dope growers to bring illegals across the border from Mexico to tend the crops here. In fact, that big fire in the mountains above Santa Cruz last summer was started by one of their campfires that got out of control. BNE investigators believe other Northern California fires started the same way."

"Bastards cost the state a lot of money." Jack said.

"And damage to the state's forests," Robert added.

"That too," Jack said. He added, "But if California legalizes marijuana—and it looks like they will at some point—that should all but end illegal cultivation operations here in the U.S.—especially if the other states follow suit."

"And you can bet they will," Robert assured him. "Every state wants a shot at those tax dollars. But right now they're sitting back waiting to see what California does."

"Probably should have been done a long time ago," Jack said. "So what did you find out about Roy Briscoe?"

"My contact is still checking. I'll get back to you when I know more."

"Make it quick." Jack flipped his cell phone closed and stood there.

"You look worried," Theresa said.

"We were right about Deacon walking into the middle of something seriously illegal."

"Marsh?"

"At the head of it all, by the looks of it."

"So how do we deal with him?"

Jack wanted to play by the rules and did whenever possible.

Fifteen days missing.

He straightened his back with resolve and said, "We do whatever it takes to get Deacon out alive."

CHAPTER 44

Deacon remained crouched low in the marijuana field. From his vantage point peering through gaps in the leaves, he had a good view of the red truck and could slip deeper into the forest of dope if he needed to.

He was sure the man behind the wheel was the big mean-talking bastard who shot the donkey dead.

The asshole!

He hawked a wad of saliva into the dirt in disgust. The poor dumb donkey didn't know any better than to stand there and look stupid while he was drilled between the eyes with a bullet.

That, he swore, would not happen to him. Not as long as he had a good pair of legs under him.

Making himself comfortable on the ground among the stench of cannabis, he settled in to wait. He had no idea what to expect. But he did know one thing for sure.

The big man already proved he could kill.

* * * *

Marsh stood beside his pickup, waiting for Hector and Kyle to join him. They had to have heard him coming, and should have been there waiting for him when he pulled up. Damn their halfwit asses. Next time he was using illegals. He might anyway if the idiots didn't get their sorry butts over to the truck and unhook the trailer like they were supposed to.

Dammit!

He'd just shoot them dead now rather than later.

But he couldn't do that. Getting illegals up there to do the work would take days he didn't have. He needed that dope packaged and ready to go. The deal had been made and the buyer wasn't the type to wait. And there was that legalization bullshit looming on the horizon. Time was against him. He had to move now or risk losing a million dollars.

He forced himself to take a deep breath and let it out slowly.

At least Hector and Kyle were working. And they did grow great dope.

He decided he'd let them live a little longer. They'd be dead soon enough. And he'd bury the bodies deep.

"Get your dumb asses up here and unhook this trailer," he yelled, waving the redheads over to the truck with a sweep of his hand.

Glancing in Kyle's direction he said, "Let's go, little brother."

Kyle dropped the plant he held and hurried to join Hector. "What'd we do now?" he asked, clearly confused. "We's getting the dope bagged as fast as we can."

"Says he wants us to get over there and unhook that trailer." Hector peeled off his rubber gloves, stuffed them into his pocket, and slide on his leather work gloves. "Reckon we was supposed to read his mind."

"Then we better go." Kyle shot a worried glance in the direction of the dead donkey, steadied his gaze, and nodded. "I don't want to end up like that poor dumb jackass."

Hector looked that direction and said, "Let's hurry and get that trailer unhooked. I have a bad feeling about this deal."

They exchanged glances.

"Me too," Kyle muttered. "But we need the money."

"Don't do us no good if we aren't alive to spend it."

* * * *

Hector walked directly to the trailer: a five foot wide by eight foot long enclosed U-Haul. Stolen, of course, and the license plate had been changed. He was sure of that. When the trailer was finally found abandoned on a street somewhere, no one would be able to trace it back to Marsh.

And the dope would be long gone.

He let Kyle unhook the tongue and said to Marsh, "We filled thirteen boxes already. And we're not planning on stopping for lunch."

Marsh eyed the filled containers. "How many bags are in each box?"

"Eight. A pound each," Hector said.

"And you're getting close to a bag off of each plant?"

"Like I promised."

"And how many plants did you say you ended up with?"

"Females, at least two thousand, maybe as many as twenty-five hundred."

Marsh stood with his brow furrowed.

Hector watched the big man work his brain. Something he'd already done. Thirteen plastic containers with eight bags in each one amounted to one hundred and four bags. The bags, he knew, sold for a thousand each. Their cut was ten percent. Ten thousand four hundred dollars. When they were done, they'd have twenty times that.

Marsh said, "Yesterday, you told me you had half the crop dried. I gave you three days to get it bagged and ready to go. At this rate, it'll take you two morons a week to finish. Tell me now, are you and that idiot brother of yours going to have that dope ready to go by tomorrow afternoon or do I have to get people up here who can?"

"Me and Kyle will get it done," Hector said.

Kyle stood next to his brother and nodded. "That's right. Me and Hector will get it done."

Marsh narrowed his eyes in a hard look, and there was no mistaking what the look meant. "See that you do. Or else . . ."

Hector winced. He was confident he and Kyle could get the buds bagged in time. It would mean working straight through the night without sleep. But they would do whatever they needed to do to get paid.

And stay alive.

One more big score and they would have enough money to buy their tomato farm.

He glanced at Kyle and then peered nervously at the crop of marijuana plants two hundred feet away. Hopefully their captive hadn't run off on them. They had little choice but to trust he'd stay put.

For his sake. And theirs.

He clapped his brother solidly on the shoulder and said, "Let's get this trailer unhooked and go back to work."

Kyle grinned and said, "I'm with you, brother."

They wedged rocks against the tires to keep the trailer from rolling down the hill and lifted the tongue off the towing ball. Hector then braced himself against the weight of the trailer and said to Kyle, "Roll that big rock over here so we can prop the hitch up on it."

Kyle didn't move.

Hector lowered the tongue to the ground and straightened. Kyle stood with his mouth agape and his arm outstretched, fingers pointing down the canyon.

Hector turned and saw Marsh striding off in the direction of the field of marijuana plants.

CHAPTER 45

Deacon inched deeper into the forest of dope, silently cursing the heavy block of concrete chained to his ankle. The hulk with the mean temper and short fuse walked directly toward him. Another twenty feet and the asshole would see him for sure, if he hadn't been spotted already.

Now he remembered the voice, and the thug behind it. Marsh: the asshole who got in his face for taking to Della.

He was surprised he hadn't made the connection.

The big man had certainly left an impression.

He wormed his way through a gap in the fat stalks of marijuana and back another two rows before his feet nudged into a barrier of plants. To part the foliage like King Kong crashing through a jungle—he was sure—would betray his presence there and bring certain death.

This was not the way he was going out of this world: on his belly in the dirt like a reptile.

He chanced a glance behind him

More dope and no space between the plants to slip through.

Again, he silently cursed.

He brought his gaze forward. The big man kept his pace.

Another ten feet.

Deacon knew it was useless to try and slip free of the steel links padlocked tight around his ankle. He'd tried more than once.

Damned ball and chain.

He bunched his muscles ready to make a run for it.

His odds of making it out of the canyon alive—he knew—were slightly less than him winning the state lottery. But it beat being shot down like that poor jackass.

Zigzag, that's what he'd do. And sprint like an escaped slave running for his life, which he was. If he didn't run, all that would it get him was a bullet in the brain, a dusty unmarked grave in the middle of nowhere, and a shovel full of dirt in the face.

There was little choice.

He brought his feet under him like a cougar ready to spring and took a firm grip on his concrete anchor.

Now or never.

All of a sudden the big man stopped.

Deacon flattened.

No more than fifty feet ahead of him, the hulk turned and faced Hector and Kyle who trotted down the slope toward him.

Deacon watched and listened, not entirely confident in the twins' ability to keep Marsh's attention diverted elsewhere.

He stayed ready to jump up and run.

* * * *

Hector skidded unsteadily to a stop, the pea-sized grains of decomposed granite acting like tiny ball bearings under the soles of his high-top tennis shoes. He caught his balance and straightened. Whatever he did, he had to keep Marsh from taking a step closer to those plants. The big man bore the same menace in his eyes he did the day before when he shot the donkey dead. It wouldn't take much for him to kill again.

And this time he'd kill them all.

He stuck his arm out to keep his brother back. Marsh clearly did not respect or appreciate Kyle's contribution to the quality of the crop. If Kyle got too close, his presence there might set the man off.

The thought shot a chill through Hector that turned the skin on his neck and arms to gooseflesh.

"You wanna see quality." He jabbed a shaky index finger in the direction of the folding camp table with the Seal-a-Meal sitting atop it. "I'll show you some of what we're packaging."

"Humph." Marsh narrowed his eyes at the leafy stalks of marijuana swaying in the afternoon breeze. He stood staring for a moment; then he brushed past Hector, shoved Kyle aside with a massive paw, and strode off in the direction of the table.

Hector shot a nervous glance into the field of dope. When he saw no telltale shadow or silhouette betraying their captive's presence, he swallowed a sigh of relief and hurried after Marsh.

"Like I told you," he said when he was still a couple of steps behind the big man. "We got some really nice bud."

Marsh stopped and spun on Hector. "You'd better." His tone had the venom of a rattlesnake's bite.

Hector cringed at the rebuke. The man was definitely on the edge.

He stepped past Marsh in an arch that put several feet between them, dipped his hand into the plastic bucket sitting on the ground by the table, lifted a wad of fat green buds, and held it up. He hoped the sight of all that premium pot would calm his boss' temper.

"The whole crop is like this," he said. "Our best yet."

Marsh's hard set jaw and steel-eyed gaze hammered home the dread preying on Hector's mind. He and Kyle needed to get the dope packaged, grab their cut of the money, and get the hell away from there, fast.

"Those are ready to go?" Marsh asked, pointing at the plastic storage bins stacked a few feet away.

Hector dropped the buds into the bucket and lifted the lid on one of the bins. "Thirteen of them packed just like this. Eight one-pound bags weighed and sealed. One hundred and four bags total."

Kyle inched a step closer. "Hector and me did good, huh?"

Marsh furrowed his brow in a hard stare at Kyle.

The expectant grin slipped from Kyle's face.

To Hector, Marsh said, "There're a hundred of these empty containers inside the trailer. I suggest you and that moron brother of yours get back to work. You have until two o'clock tomorrow afternoon."

CHAPTER 46

Jack steered Deacon's pickup onto Highway 49 and accelerated in the direction of his hotel room. He intended to give Marsh the day to believe his threats worked. The plan still seemed sound, and he thought it best to stick to it. Even so, there was no way he could close his eyes to the fact that Deacon was in serious trouble and needed his help, now.

Marsh had killed more than once. Or so it seemed. Jack couldn't ignore that. But Deacon was alive.

He could feel it.

Since that first day on the mountain with Theresa, he had allowed himself to become distracted by concerns for her safety and even his own. Sure, being caught out in the open during a lightning storm is no place to be; and sure they had been shot at, even had a knife thrown at them. He'd been shot at before, and had come close to being stabbed a couple of times or more. But he'd never been struck by lightning.

The next time he set out to find Deacon, nothing would drive him off that mountain.

Theresa, too, had made her choice. She knew the risk. And she'd been quite clear when she insisted he was not leaving her behind. He'd do everything possible within his ability to insure her safety. But he couldn't allow his concern for her to jeopardize him rescuing Deacon.

Now he had to find a way to remain true to his plan for another eighteen hours.

Even though he wasn't sure what he would to do when he got back to town, he was at least moving and that was better than sitting on his butt at Theresa's hacienda sipping iced tea and attempting to talk pleasantries while his thoughts dwelled on Deacon's fate. She was a gracious host and he certainly enjoyed being with her. She was a lovely lady in every respect—strong, focused, and resilient. Plus she was a great kisser. But he could only sit with her at her place for so long. He had to do something productive to ease the guilt of leaving Deacon hanging out there in the woods another night.

Theresa understood completely when he finally excused himself from her company. She too struggled with the wait. The day that began with a wonderful breakfast and a step into his dream world of cars, had turned into an exercise of patience . . . for them both.

At first light, he and Theresa would be on the mountain. They would find and rescue Deacon . . . *alive*. And when the opportunity presented itself, the three of them together would put to rest Al's legend of lost Murrieta gold.

Glancing into his rearview mirror, he noticed a flashing bar of red and blue lights speeding toward him. No patrol cars had been in sight in either direction when he pulled onto the highway. He had no idea where this one came from.

Out of reflex, he checked his speed: *fifty*.

He let off on the gas a little, eased to the right, and waited to see if the patrol car passed.

The police cruiser maintained its speed then slowed and pulled up close behind him.

He knew his mind had been preoccupied with thoughts other than how fast he was driving. But he could not imagine that he had been going much more than five miles an hour over the speed limit, if that. He certainly wasn't racing down the road the way that Beamer convertible had been the other day.

Jack braked to a stop on the shoulder of the road.

Again, he peered in the rearview mirror and watched the police cruiser pull to the edge of the asphalt and park a car-length behind him. He'd expected to see a Highway Patrol unit, not a Sheriff's car.

It only took a second for him to understand what was happening. He was more surprised it had taken this long.

The crisp white Stetson worn in place of the standard issue Smokey-the-bear hat and the gleam of brass on the officer's shirt collars was all Jack needed to see to know he had been pulled over by Sheriff Doug Bell.

He studied the man in the rearview mirror: average height, graying at the temples, soft around the middle. A thick moustache trimmed to the corners of his mouth. Stereotypical mirrored sunglasses. A large-framed semi-automatic handgun holstered high on his right hip. Nothing about the man stood out as being particularly striking in any special way.

Local law bought and paid for.

The thought turned his stomach.

"License, registration, and proof of insurance, please," Sheriff Bell said. He held his right thumb hooked over the top of his shiny black duty belt just forward of his gun. He reached out with his left hand.

An engraved single action .45 cal Colt, fully cocked, ivory grips—Jack took notice. The smug upward curl of Doug Bell's lips told him the Sheriff knew exactly who he was talking to. A quick glance at the officer's nametag confirmed the man's identity.

"Of course Sheriff," answered Jack.

Careful not to make any sudden moves, he calmly dug his Oregon driver's license from his wallet and fished Deacon's registration and insurance card from inside the glove-box. He could see no need in asking why he had been stopped. He knew the reason. And it wouldn't take much on his part for the situation to turn very ugly, very quickly. For now, he'd play it cool and wait for the Sheriff to make his play.

"People don't usually speed through my town," Sheriff Bell said, eyeballing the paperwork in his hand.

Jack knew that was a crock of shit. He kept his opinion to himself and said, "Sorry, sir."

"This your car?" the sheriff asked, his tone pointed.

"My brother's."

"And he knows you have it?"

Jack could not see the sheriff's eyes behind the mirrored lenses. But he could feel them bore into him like the harsh bright-white light of an interrogation lamp. "I assure you, officer, there is no problem with me driving his pickup."

"So you took his truck without him knowing it." The smug hint-of-a-smile returned to Doug Bell's lips.

Jack stared directly into the mirrored lenses of the sunglasses. He was being hassled. And the sheriff knew he knew it.

"I rescued the truck from impound at Henry's Texaco station," he said. "But then I 'm sure you know that."

The slight upward curl at the corners of Doug Bell's lips disappeared. "I don't suppose there is much point in introducing myself."

"Not to me," Jack said before the Sheriff was able to say more. His expression remained firm. "Can we hurry this up? I'd like be on my way."

Bell stiffened. "When I'm done."

Jack felt his face heat. The Sheriff's point had been made. Not that Doug Bell's subtle warning changed a thing. There was no need for the man to push further. Yet he obviously felt the need to.

"Yes, sir!" Jack said with a tone of respect that soured his stomach. But he'd already pushed Doug Bell's buttons more than he intended.

"People around here don't like outsiders coming to town and poking their noses where they don't belong." Sheriff Bell inched his hooked thumb closer to his gun. "It would be advisable for you to remember that."

Jack caught the movement. And the implied threat.

He had his fill.

"By people," he said. "You mean Elliot Marsh?"

He noticed a nervous tic form at the corner of Bell's right eye. He'd struck a nerve.

"And by outsiders," he continued. "You're referring to me and my brother Deacon of course. You haven't seen him have you?"

Jack did his best to keep his cool. He was having trouble.

"I represent all of Calaveras County, Mr. Ferrell." Bell's evil smirk returned. "When I speak, I speak for every one of my constituents."

231

"Then you don't have a thing to worry about. Several of your constituents have welcomed me with open arms."

"You're referring to Ms. Montero, of course?"

"And others." Jack couldn't resist a broad grin. He figured Theresa Montero carried more clout in town than she let on. The sour look of frustration in Sheriff Bell's expression told him he was right. Having her on his side was probably all that stood between him and a cold hard bed in a jail cell.

"Where are you headed?" Doug Bell unhooked his thumb and handed Jack his driver's license, truck registration, and proof of insurance.

"To my room at the hotel," Jack answered.

The smirk on Doug Bell's face, returned. "See that you do."

"And stay out of trouble," Jack said. "You forgot that part."

"You've been through this before," Bell said. "Then I don't have to waste time spelling it out for you." He returned his thumb to his duty belt. "Have a good day."

Jack nodded and said, "I'll be seeing you."

To that, the Sheriff leaned close to the open driver's door window and said, "You'd better hope not." Then he marched back to his patrol car.

CHAPTER 47

Jack watched Doug Bell drive away. The Sheriff's presence on that stretch of road at that particular time of the morning confused him. Nothing he'd done that morning would give Marsh reason to believe the gunshot and the close call with the knife the night before hadn't been enough to keep him from going back into the mountains.

So why had he been pulled over?

The only answer he could come up with was that the Sheriff must have been insurance. Or on second thought, Bell could have acted on his own volition. But for him to do so would surely be out of character for a man whose strings were manipulated by Marsh.

And there was no doubt the Sheriff danced to Marsh's music. The nervous tic that formed in the corner of Bell's right eye at the mere mention of Marsh's name was proof of that. On his own, or at the direction of Marsh, Bell's veiled threats were real.

Anything to look good in Marsh's eyes.

Or believe he was something he wasn't.

Jack sank into his seat and fought back the indignation surging in his gut. He felt his anger rise to a boil and then reduce to a simmer. If he could hold it there, he'd be all right.

Nearly a full minute passed before he accelerated onto the roadway. This time he'd pay close attention to the speedometer. There was no need to press his luck with Deacon's fate riding on the line. But he sure wouldn't allow himself to be intimidated by a bucket load of Sheriff-for-hire's bullshit harassment.

Marsh and Bell would pay in the end. He'd see to it. Until then, it was as much their play as it was his.

But one question remained unanswered.

Was Deacon still alive?

More than ever Jack remained focused on the unpleasant business that lay ahead. There was no backing off, not because of Elliot Marsh or his no-account nephew, and certainly not because a small-town sheriff let greed get the better of him.

He drove along feeling cornered like an old bear with his back to a rock wall. He had no real proof, but Marsh, his nephew, the sheriff; they all seemed to play a part in what happened to Deacon. The big man most of all.

One way or another, Marsh had taken Deacon from him.

No one would get away with that.

A slideshow of childhood memories flashed inside Jack's head: Big brother watching out for little brother; Deacon's audacious behavior—not unlike his own venturesome spirit. Two peas in a pod, their mother had said. And he thought about the wedge of resentment that time and circumstances drove between them. He wanted those lost years back . . . and the chance to make things right between them.

He imagined Deacon caught in the middle of something he had no part in. No big brother to watch his back. Defenseless to prevent what was happening to him.

Jack could only hope the bastards had let him live.

The sonofabitches.

Even if they had Deacon tied up, gagged, and wedged into a crack in the rocks to rot, what further unimaginable brutality had been done to him—was *still* being done to him?

Vipers like Marsh took pleasure in exacting the most inexplicable cruelty imaginable.

And the Sheriff let him get away with it.

For money.

Savagery, unlike any Jack felt before, rose to a boil inside him. He wanted to hammer his fist into a face, gouge eyes, kick teeth out, break bone with his bare hands.

He wanted to avenge his brother.

He had to bring Deacon home.

Alive!

In his heart he knew Deacon hung onto life, even now. Waiting. But that didn't mean another day wouldn't be too late.

Now he wished he'd just gone back into the mountains alone, without telling Theresa he was going. But that was not going to happen, not now. Not enough of the day remained. And, and he certainly couldn't traipse around the forest in the dark. With a flashlight to brighten the way, he'd stand out like a lighthouse beacon on a jetty.

Dead, he'd do his brother no good.

Deacon would have to hold on one more night.

Jack pounded his fist against the steering wheel.

Marsh had brought the fight to him and he hadn't run. In the morning, he'd return the favor.

CHAPTER 48

Jack drove the now familiar route back to the fire road. Theresa sat in the seat next to him. He'd spent the long hours of the prior afternoon staking out Gold Rush Motors. There had been no sign of Elliot Marsh or his low-life backstabbing nephew Roy Briscoe. Or the shiny black Lincoln Navigator.

The afternoon had felt like a waste of time.

Especially the run-in with the Sheriff.

No reason for that.

Hate was a powerful word. And he used it sparingly. Marsh and his nephew were on the list. So was Doug Bell.

Bell was greedy-bad. Law bought and paid for, the worst kind. Marsh was downright mean-bad. A bully—he liked that people feared him. His nephew was sneaky-bad, and a backstabber.

All three fit the bill.

The more thought he gave Roy Briscoe and that deadly stunt with the knife, the more he wanted to shove the switchblade up the skinny dickhead's ass. And before the day was over, maybe he would. Right after he inserted the barrel of Marsh's gun where it belonged and pulled the trigger.

Both assholes deserved it.

But most importantly, Deacon would be out of there.

Alive!

He held that thought and mashed the gas pedal to the floorboard.

With a low-engine-growl of determination that Jack likened to a timber wolf homed in on the scent of prey, his brother's four-wheel-drive Ranger roared up Murphy's grade.

Deacon had driven to the mountains in his pickup; he'd be coming home in it.

In the early dawn light, he could see the fire road come into view on their left. A quick check of the mirror on the windshield showed empty roadway behind them. So far, no shiny black Lincoln Navigators or big red Ford F-350 pickups with duel rear tires had appeared in the rearview mirror.

And no sheriff's cars.

But that didn't mean someone wasn't waiting for them at road's end.

Jack slowed the pickup and made the turn. The truck bounced through a rut and settled on its springs when the tires gained smoother ground.

He and Theresa Montero had driven into the mountains twice during the past four days. And each time, the country on both sides of the roadway slid by him in a blur in their haste to find Deacon.

Not this time.

The dust billowing up behind the pickup, the blades of dry grass, the tangles of brush, the oaks and pines covering the hillsides, and every rock and shadow stood out in stark clarity. Even the first rays of the morning sun peeking through the treetops hurt his eyes as though the sunlight shown brighter than it had the previous mornings.

Jack flipped down the sun visor, and squinted when strobes of sunlight found the gap between the visor and the rearview mirror. The harsh glare tap-dancing on his eyeballs made it impossible for him to focus on the road. Or was it the thoughts racing through his head.

He slid on his sunglasses in spite of the early hour and glanced at Theresa who sat with her gaze fixed on the windshield. Beautiful, rock solid, determined, she remained true to her quest.

For the second time, he smiled inwardly at her choice of clothing. A detail he'd taken notice of when he picked her up at her hacienda earlier that morning. She wore faded green bush pants, a khaki long-sleeved button-down-the-front cotton shirt with the sleeves rolled to the elbows, the same two-tone green and brown Gore-Tex hiking boots, her Giants baseball cap, and like before her raven hair hung in a single braid down her back.

No real fashion statement, just take-care-of-business clothes. She was ready for the trail ahead.

He turned his attention back to the road a moment then faced her and said, "So far so good."

Theresa jumped at the sound of his voice. Not what he planned on.

She offered a thin smile and said, "So far."

He felt bad for startling her. They had ridden in silence for the last twenty minutes. None of the nervous chatter he might have expected from her under the circumstances. He should have seen she was caught up in thought just as he had been. They both had their ghosts . . . and their demons.

He shifted his gaze to the road and back to her. She reached into the side pocket of her backpack on the floorboard in front of her, fished out her sunglasses, slid them on, glanced in his direction, and then silently faced the windshield.

Nothing needed to be said.

He nodded to himself. The excitement that fueled their two prior trips into the mountains had been replaced with grim resolve and wariness. Both of them understood the risk they were taking.

If Deacon was in fact being held by drug dealers, getting him out of there would be no easy matter.

Jack fingered the bandage on his ear. Marsh had demonstrated a willingness to shoot someone. He doubted the big man would miss the next time their paths crossed. And that backstabbing nephew certainly didn't have any qualms about using that switchblade.

He couldn't help wondering about the men holding Deacon. Surely, they would be armed as well.

They might even share the same willingness to kill.

The .357 magnum inside his backpack provided him a reasonable measure of reassurance, but he regretted Theresa being with him. Killing was ugly business. He knew; he'd done his share. And he didn't want her anywhere around if people started shooting. Still,

she insisted on being there to do her part.
Even if there was a chance she would be shot.
Sixteen days missing.

CHAPTER 49

The pickup truck bounced through a rut, jarring Theresa from her thoughts. She settled back in her seat as the 4X4 leveled out, and tried to focus her attention on the fire road. The whirlpool of events from the last few days swirling inside her head wasn't making that easy; nor did sitting this close to Jack.

She hadn't expected to be drawn to him so easily. Even more surprising, she had easily reasoned away the guilt of having gone to bed with him. The attraction had been there from that day in town when he saved her life from that speeding car. And it wasn't just her. She'd seen the flicker of desire in Jack's blue eyes that day as well. And later; the times they were together. . . .

What she hadn't been prepared for was the guilt of betrayal to her husband. He had been dead three years. Enough time had passed. Plus Leandro would want her to move on. He was that kind of man. Still, she felt remorse as if she had defiled his name and his memory.

They'd had a good marriage. Solid.

Leandro had been everything she desired in a man. After his death, she'd entertained thoughts of male companionship but hadn't desired anyone until Jack came along.

Jack?

What was it about him that attracted her?

She couldn't help but wonder. Lots of men sought her affections and failed. Marsh had been an exception and he turned out to be a pig. She shuttered at the memory of his hands on her. Groping, hurting, tearing her clothes. And his filthy nephew's threats to keep quiet about what happened.

But no had meant *no*!

She'd dug her nails into Marsh's cheek and escaped with her dignity in tack. But the assault left her with a sense of vulnerability she wouldn't accept. And she dismissed men from her life without a second thought.

But not Jack.

So what was it, then? He was tall, ruggedly handsome, mysterious—a man much the same as the others.

Or was he?

Strip away some of the rough edges, she decided, and maybe he wasn't all that different from Leandro.

But would he stick around long enough for her to find out?

Was he serious about the cruise around the Hawaiian Islands?

She wanted to believe in him.

The sensible thing to do would be to keep him at arm's length. She could walk away now and not be hurt. The pain of Leandro's death and Marsh's insolence was all too fresh in her memory to reopen a wound that had only recently begun to heal.

Then again, perhaps Jack was exactly what she needed. The logical next step. After all, they had spent a fantastic evening together. Their lovemaking had come so natural—each exploring the other's pleasures without inhibition. It was as if they had been lovers for years. She'd almost forgotten how wonderful it felt to hold a man, and to be held.

But she had never imagined being a one-night stand.

If she had gone to him last night, would that have made a difference?

She had wanted too. Now she wished she had.

She refocused her thoughts on the danger ahead. Jack had warned her there could be shooting, that he may have to kill someone. She remembered the gang member she had seen gunned down on the sidewalk in front of their house in Los Angeles. The ugliness of that horrific moment was not a scene she liked to relive.

But she would not let that memory keep her from going into the mountains with Jack. If someone shot at them, they would shoot back.

She rested her hand reassuringly on the bulge in her pocket. She would not hesitate pulling the trigger if that's what it took to save their lives. And she could shoot straight. Leandro had taught her.

Even so, was it stupid of her to insist on coming along?

Was this truly about setting history straight? Or deep down did she have a death wish?

For a moment, she wondered why that thought popped into her head now. She had no desire to join Leandro before her time no matter how much she missed him. And she planned to live to be a hundred. She had no inner desire to cut life short.

Especially now.

So, was setting an obscure piece of history straight really all that important?

She realized there was no reason for her to even ask herself that question. It was, even with the risks involved.

Jack said it. They'd find his brother and find the gold.

She believed they would find his brother. And held onto the hope they'd find the cache of gold bars stolen all those years ago. Something no one else had been able to do.

Satisfaction curled her lips into a hint of a smile. For years, she'd done little more than talk about setting the record straight. Now she was actually getting out and doing something to prove history wrong.

And she was doing it with Jack.

CHAPTER 50

Jack straightened in his seat. A hundred yards ahead of them lay the end of the fire road. He could see the turnaround was clear of vehicles. Relief flooded over him, but he knew it was only a temporary reprieve.

Somewhere up the mountain lay trouble, lots of it.

And they'd find it soon enough.

He liked having Theresa next to him but still wished she'd stayed home. "You can change your mind, you know."

She cast him a sideways look. "And let you have all the fun?"

Jack chuckled. "Fun is it?"

She shrugged. "I'm not changing my mind."

"Well then, let's take a look around."

He parked Deacon's pickup at the end of the road. The sun rising above the treetops remained unusually bright. But the forest was bathed in deep shadows. He opened the door, climbed out, and hiked up over the mound of dirt, rocks, and tree debris that had been pushed there by the bulldozer cutting the road. Theresa followed him over.

Taking a quick look around, Jack found a trail leading up the mountain. The trek was steep, rugged, and in his opinion, not well traveled. But the path looked like it would take them where they needed to go.

When he looked closer, he noticed an impression in the soil.

He squatted, removed his sunglasses, and used his finger to trace a line around where the pointed toe of a cowboy boot had sunk into wet ground. And there were other boot tracks in the area, smudged and shapeless indentations left by someone moving fast.

"Our friend?" Theresa asked.

"My guess is they're from the other day." He stuffed his shades into his shirt pocket and nodded at the faint line of bare earth snaking up the mountain. "This is how he got ahead of us without being seen."

She squinted at the trail and nibbled her lower lip. "You don't think Marsh is up there waiting, do you?"

This was the first time Jack had seen her bite her lip. She was worried. And for good reason.

"I don't think so," he said. "But we won't take anything for granted."

She turned and scanned behind them. "At least we weren't followed."

"Not yet, anyway," he said. "And since the racks have dried out, my guess is no one has gone up ahead of us."

She faced the trail and said, "So why are we standing here?"

"I like your style." Jack said, and took off at a fast walk in the direction of the Jeep to retrieve their packs.

Two minutes later, he led the way up the mountain. It was no easy climb. The trail was narrow, twisty, overgrown, and rough. He considered himself to be in excellent shape. Diving and spending long hours at work on a boat toughens a man. Still, he soon breathed hard with each step.

He stopped and checked on Theresa. She had fallen behind.

Taking in a deep breath, he couldn't help thinking how quickly Marsh had gotten ahead of them the day they were shot at. The big man had to have the lungs and legs of a mountain goat.

Theresa pounded up next to him and gasped, "This had better be a shortcut or there is no way Marsh could have gotten ahead of us the other day."

Jack said, "I was thinking the same thing."

Theresa was breathing hard. He let her catch her breath and fished a couple of bottles of water from his pack. He handed her one.

"Good to go?" he asked.

"As soon as I have a drink of this water."

He twisted the cap from his bottle, took a drink, and peered at the trail ahead. He'd always believed that if you avoid truly bad men, they would avoid you. At least he liked to think so. But that hadn't turned out to be the case. Marsh, too, was proving his theory wrong. He'd have to rethink it.

He stowed his bottle and continued the climb.

At the top of the hill, he stopped and crouched behind the fat trunk of a pine tree. Even peering through gaps in the forest, he could see the jumble of granite boulders clear enough to recognize the formation.

Theresa dropped to her hands and knees next to him. He pointed to Robbers Roost no more than a hundred yards ahead of them.

She nodded.

He checked his watch. The trail they followed cut close to forty-five minutes off their previous hiking time. Marsh had plenty of time to make the climb and be there to ambush them.

He raised his finger to his mouth in a sign to be quiet. Then he motioned for her to stay put.

Another nod.

Jack didn't believe even for a second that someone had spent the night in the rocks waiting in ambush. But he wasn't taking any chances. He knew where the shooter would be lying in wait if he was there.

He drew his gun from his pack.

Keeping low and quiet, he scurried to the gap in the rocks where he'd seen the boot impressions leading into the fortress of boulders.

He stopped, looked, and listened.

The legendary quote regarding the gun maker Samuel Colt came to mind.

God created man. Sam Colt made them equal.

The .357 Colt Python he held in his hand, pointed and ready, put him and the shooter on equal ground here. Just as it had the men of the old west.

He moved cautiously among the boulders, taking his time.

Again he stopped. And again, he listened. He even sniffed the air for anything that would suggest someone was there ahead of him.

Nothing.

Finally, he reached the open area in the center of the stone fortress. It was empty.

The day they'd been shot at, he had been concerned about the boot tracks and where they led. Now he spent time examining the area. It didn't take long to find a packed spot in the dirt the size of a man's butt, a pile of cigarette butts next to it, and a couple of feet farther to the right, a spent .308 cartridge case.

He plucked a twig from the ground, inserted the tip into the open end of the casing, lifted it, and eyed the shiny brass.

Bad shot or intentional miss; the shooting had been no accident.

This time he was ready to shoot back.

He stepped from the rocks, slid the Colt under his belt, and waved Theresa up. He knew she watched from her hiding place behind the tree.

"Found a shell casing from the other day," he said. "And I saw where the guy sat and waited."

She pounded to a stop with their packs in hand. "Now we know how Marsh got up here ahead of us. That shortcut had to have shaved at least thirty minutes off the other climbs we made here."

"Close to forty five by my figuring."

"So now we keep going?"

He turned his gaze on the trail north. "You said you hiked up that trail before. How is it?"

"Not bad. Certainly a lot easier than the one we just climbed."

"So we can make good time, then."

"If it doesn't rain."

He thought about the lightening, and the smoldering tree. There could be another thunderstorm, and more lightning. It didn't matter.

Not this time.

Sixteen days missing.

He eyed the trail north remembering Al's story about his great, great uncle Donald, trying to visualize the scene and what followed that morning after the shootout.

CHAPTER 51

October 11, 1862

At first light, Donald stood twenty feet away from the outcropping of boulders, his eyes focused on the ground at his feet. Three bandits lay dead in the rocks behind him. Joaquin Murrieta and Snake-Eye Carlos Sanchez weren't among them. Neither was the gold. He couldn't believe the bandits had ridden away from there without being seen.

He stooped and eyed two sets of hoof tracks heading off to the north along a game trail. Clearly, they had. And they were traveling heavy.

"Adam, Duncan, Rollie." He stood and looked at each man in turn. "You men come with me. Quentin, Charlie, do what you can to get the bodies loaded onto horses and headed back to town."

He looked at Charlie who stood clutching a bloody handkerchief to his right bicep and asked, "You alright to do that?"

Charlie said, "Just a crease. I'll make out."

Donald nodded.

"Turn the bodies over to the Chinaman?" Quentin asked.

"First hold onto any personal effects," Donald said. "They'll disappear if you don't. And if Bob is still in town with that fancy photography equipment, have him capture a likeness of them. Be important for the law 'case they know who these bushwackin'

247

scoundrels are. That way we won't have to dig 'em later."

"And Morgan?" Quentin asked. "Gonna be hard on his wife."

Donald dug a five-dollar gold piece from his right front pants pocket and tossed it to Quentin. "Give this to her when you tell her what happened. It's not much for a man's life, but it's something."

"No it ain't," Quentin said, eyeballing the coin. He stuffed gold piece into his pocket. "But I recon it'll help."

Rollie settled onto his haunches near an opening in the rocks and dabbed at the ground with his fingertip. "There's blood here."

"Good," Donald said with a nod of satisfaction. "At least one of them's been hit. Should make the hunting easier."

"We're not catching the murdering bastards standing here jawing," Adam said. "I'll bring up the horses so we can get after 'em."

Ten minutes later Donald led Adam, Duncan, and Rollie along the trail north. None of them talked. Their gazes darted from the tracks on the trail to the trees and rocks around them. All of them watched carefully.

And each of them held their guns at the ready as they rode, taking it slow and easy.

The trail took them over a ridge and down into a shallow saddle. From there they began a steady climb into high country. The trail was narrow, twisty, and rough, but passable. Several times, they heard the warning cry of a mountain jay; the nervous chatter of a squirrel.

Donald watched a particularly noisy jay flutter across a clearing to the bottom limb of an oak tree fifty yards ahead. From the hoof tracks, he knew Murrieta and Sanchez had ridden through there. The presence of the bird told him they weren't there now.

The trail left by Murrieta and Sanchez was not hard to follow. The bandits were riding hard with a lot of weight. Given the pace and the heavy load, Donald figured their horses would give out soon.

And then he and his men would have them.

But that also made Donald more cautious. Murrieta and Sanchez could be up there now, hiding, waiting. He didn't want to ride into a bullet.

He gingerly fingered the wound in his scalp. The murdering

sonofabitches got away with it once. They wouldn't get a second chance.

At the edge of a meadow, he reined to a stop and turned his horse to face the others. "Best give them a rest, boys."

Rollie climbed down from his saddle with a creak of leather, held onto his reins with one hand, and relieved himself on a bush next to the trail.

"Think we're gaining on them?" he asked over his shoulder.

"They couldn't have gotten more than a couple of hours jump on us." Donald said. He pulled the cork from his canteen, paused with it raised in front of him, and scanned the trail ahead. "Riding with a heavy load the way they are. Rough country. At least one of them shot. My guess is we could come up on them any time."

The drum roll of distant thunder drew his gaze skyward.

Rollie climbed back into his saddle and said, "Don't like the idea of riding around up here in the open if lightening gets to flashing around."

Donald took a swig of water, shoved in the cork into the neck of his canteen, and said, "We might not have a choice."

CHAPTER 52

Jack withdrew the Colt from his belt, slid the six-shooter into its holster, buckled the rig high on his hip, and cinched it tight so that the holster wouldn't move around. With renewed confidence, he faced the trail leading to the north. That's the direction Deacon took. That's the direction they were headed.

"Ready?" he asked.

"After you," Theresa said with a wave of her hand to point the way.

He picked up his pack, shrugged it onto his shoulders, and started walking. The trail was wide here and Theresa moved up next to him. He slowed his pace slightly so she could keep up.

She did a good job of it.

He said, "You mentioned you followed this trail for several miles?"

"At least two or three. It's slower going, farther in."

He glanced around and said, "Mighty pretty country up here."

"If you're not worried about someone shooting at you."

"Good point," he said. "But it's still mighty pretty."

He kept a steady pace and studied the expanse in front of them as he walked. He couldn't imagine the trek being all that different from what Al described in his story. And like Al's distant uncle, they were heading up the path armed . . . and for much the same reason.

Only they weren't going back empty handed.

MURRIETA GOLD

He promised himself that.

Sunlight fell through the trees casting stick-figure shadows onto the ground in front of them; a gentle breeze rattled the dry oak leaves overhead and at their feet. Here and there squirrels chattered and scurried into trees and out onto limbs to watch.

"See those critters," he said. "Makes a person feel like they're a hundred miles from anything bad going on."

She looked. "There not worried. That's for sure."

He nodded. "Means we have a ways to go."

She continued to watch the forest creatures scamper and flutter about. After a ways, she dropped back a couple of steps and stayed there.

Jack noticed the trail had narrowed some. Not having her plod along next to him, made walking easier.

But he missed having her by his side.

He tried to not think about that.

The first mile was a steady climb up a ridge. At the crest, they dropped down into a saddle where the trail leveled out for a ways. The forest thinned out here: scattered pines and occasional thickets of Manzanita. It was hot walking and he called for a water break.

They plopped onto the ground with their backs to a tree and sipped from plastic bottles. In the distance, quail called to each other.

"There's another story," he said after a couple of minutes.

"What story is that?" she asked.

"Robert and me."

"I'm sure I'd love to hear it."

Her dark eyes focused on his. Alluring, attentive, he thought. She really did make it easy for him to talk about his adventures.

"Several Japanese mini subs took part in the surprise attack on Pearl Harbor in 1941," he began. "They were all sunk or captured, except one: I-16. A year ago, I stumbled onto the missing mini sub in the ocean off Kauai's Na Pali Coast."

"Interesting," she said.

He grinned. "The sub was only the beginning. I also discovered a skull the size of a grapefruit in the reef not far from the wreck. Not a child's skull, the skull of a three-foot-tall species of human

251

that lived 12,000 years ago. But the skull was no 12,000-year-old fossil. And that's where the story gets good. A lava tube led from the reef to a grotto in cliffs. Inside the grotto I discovered a village of tiny huts."

Her eyes noticeably brightened. "And?"

He sensed her excitement.

"Ireland has its leprechauns," he said. "Scandinavia has its trolls. Hawaiians have the mischievous *Menehune*. In hopes of solving the enigma once and for all, Robert and I assembled a team of scientists to explore the subterranean village and the adjoining caves. A lot happened. Much of it not good. What we found was a room carved from solid rock and lined with rows of wooden shelves stacked with irreplaceable antiques, gold coins, and just about every piece of junk you can imagine. We even found a first edition printing of *Robinson Crusoe*."

"And the *Menehune*?" she asked.

He took a breath and stared at the water bottle in his hand. He wanted to tell her everything, the truth, but he'd promised to never divulge his discovery of the last living *Menehune*. Or where he'd taken the survivors when their subterranean world was destroyed and they could no longer live out their lives in secrecy in the caves on Kauai.

He said, "The mountain caved in on us before we found them. Those of us who made it out were lucky to be alive."

"The antiques, the gold, the book," she asked. "All lost?"

"Not everything," he said.

A blue jay squawked Jack back to the present. They'd rested long enough. He stood and looked around.

"Al described an area like this in the story he told about his great, great Uncle Donald," he said. "They followed the trail through here and on up the hill ahead of us."

"The top of that mountain is as far as I've been," Theresa said. "It's not too bad a climb if you take it slow."

They'd needed the few minutes rest. But he also knew they were in a race against time. His gut told him Marsh was building up to something bad. If they were going to find Deacon alive, it'd be today.

"You opposed to taking it fast?" he asked.

She smiled. "Wait and see."

"Let's go then," he said. "We had our break."

She grabbed her pack by the straps, stood, and scanned the countryside.

He saw her look and did the same. The land around them was beautiful and there was a lot of it. He realized at once, what she must be thinking. The forest doesn't seem all that big until you start looking for something in it.

He drew in a deep breath through his nose and let it out.

His heart told him what he needed to know.

Deacon was up ahead somewhere, maybe over the next hill. He'd walked in on this same trail looking for Murrieta gold. The rain had washed away all trace he had passed this way. But he was out there, and alive.

And they'd find him.

He peered at the sun, then his watch. It was a quarter till ten. They needed to get moving.

When he glanced up, he noticed Theresa had seen him check the time.

"You're in a hurry to find Deacon," she said. Her gaze shifted from him to the trail ahead. "And you should be."

She knew what he was thinking. "I am," he said.

He lifted his pack and looped the straps over his shoulders ready to go. He paused. His gut said they were close to finding Deacon. He could think of little else. But with it came an undeniable concern for her safety. He had to say something.

He said, "I still feel you should have stayed at your villa and waited for me there."

She cast him a long look and said, "Your brother wouldn't be out here if my great, great, great, grandfather hadn't stolen that gold. My place is here, with you."

"My brother"—he chuckled—"is out here because he's my brother."

"Still."

It was his turn to give her a long look of his own. He liked her tenacity. And he liked that she insisted on being there with him. He couldn't help wanting to believe there was more to her desire to share his company than an obligation based on a long-dead relative's dastardly deeds.

"Promise me," he said. "If shooting starts, run. Run down the mountain and get help, but not from that sheriff. And don't worry about me. I'll be taking care of myself."

She matched his gaze. "I'll promise you this. I won't take any unnecessary chances."

There was no way he was going to get her to turn back. That was obvious. And he knew it was a waste of time to stand there bandying back and forth with each other.

"Let's find Deacon."

Nothing more was said. He turned and started walking, Theresa matching his stride a step behind him. Fifteen minutes later, the forest closed in on them again as they began to climb.

The trees were mostly pines, but also scattered oaks, and more thickets of Manzanita. The trail was rough: rocky exposed-root switchbacks snaking up the mountain. Several times, they reached a fork in the trail where he could see faint traces of a long-ago-traveled path that disappeared beneath an impenetrable barrier of Manzanita that had overgrown it. And each time they skirted the brush confident that was the direction Deacon had taken.

Near the crest, they came up on a massive pine bough lying across the trail. Jack noticed that the jagged end showed recent charring. Looking up at where the limb had split from the tree, he thought about the lightening. And he thought about their first day on the mountain when the lightning struck the tree near them.

Now he was glad they had left the mountain when they did.

"Lightening strike," he huffed, pointing to the burned end.

She glanced at the limb and then up into the tree. "Thank God it didn't start a fire."

He sucked a breath through clenched teeth and said, "Don't even want to think what that would have meant."

"Me either. I'm glad we weren't up here."

They stepped onto and over the limb. Jack was winded and glad they were almost to the top. From the sound of Theresa's labored breathing, he knew she was just as tired.

But what lay beyond the summit? That was as far as she had

hiked.

At the crest, Jack rested his hands on his knees and took a moment to just breathe. The mile-long trek uphill was not one for the weak hearted. He glanced at Theresa and noticed she had her hands planted on her knees as well. He saw her peer in his direction.

"I told you the climb's not so bad if you take it slow," she gasped. "You were pushing."

"I was in a hurry to get up here and see what lay ahead. You said this is as far as you've been."

She pointed. "We picnicked in that meadow."

Peering through the gaps in the trees ahead, he could see the forest opened into a grassy meadow four or five acres in size. He glimpsed green grass there, which meant water—a stream. Perhaps the one Al spoke of.

CHAPTER 53

Jack and Theresa stood side by side next to a fair-sized shallow stream that cut maybe a foot deep into the floor of the meadow. They faced a narrow canyon leading to the east: high sloping sides, maybe a hundred yards wide at the mouth, the stream flowing steadily out of the middle of it.

Jack could visualize this as being the creek Al described. Joaquin Murrieta and Snake-Eye Carlos Sanchez rode up this canyon packing three hundred pounds of gold bars. It was here in the water that Donald and his men lost the bandits' trail. Deacon had walked the same ground.

The canyon is where Deacon went. That's where he ran into trouble.

Jack would put odds on it.

For a moment, he pictured the two bandits: desperate, bleeding, hungry, and bone tired; their nerves frayed to the breaking point. Was it in this canyon that Murrieta and Snake-Eye Carlos Sanchez hid the gold?

Deacon would have wondered the same thing.

The question in his mind now was whether or not he would find his brother lying up there dead.

"According to Al, his great, great uncle lost Murrieta's trail in a stream," he said to Theresa without looking at her. He dropped to his haunches, scooped up a handful of water, and let it trickle through his fingers. "I'm betting this is the one."

"And you think Deacon's up there?" she said.

"That's where I'd have gone if I was him."

"Looking for the gold?"

"Yep."

"So he's there?"

"We hope. But who's with him."

"The men holding him prisoner," she said without hesitation.

"If they're still there."

"So now we find out?"

Jack stood and adjusted the heavy holster and pistol strapped to his hip. On the trail up, he'd cursed its weight. Now he drew comfort from it. If he'd lived here during the hey-day of the Mother Lode, he'd have been with that posse.

"Definitely," he said.

He checked his watch: 11:05. They'd take it nice and slow.

But first, he wanted to get a feel for the place before heading into the canyon. Now that they were here, there was no need to rush. And there was always the possibility he had missed something.

On the opposite side of the stream, the trail they followed up from Robbers Roost continued northward not much more than a narrow swath in the meadow grass with a few patches of dirt showing here and there. Even on their side of the water, the path was little more than a well-traveled game trail. The way he saw it, few hikers ventured this far in. And of the ones who did, not many hiked beyond the grassy meadow and its babbling brook.

He knew Deacon was up that little valley. But he took a moment and scanned the mud on both sides of the creek for shoe tracks that would suggest his brother had crossed and continued on. There weren't any that he could see. Possibly the rain washed them away.

Or they weren't there to begin with.

Deacon ventured into that oversized gorge just as Murrieta had done. And he hadn't walked out.

Yet.

Jack turned his head to look upstream and noticed Theresa stride off into the canyon. Hurrying, he caught up with her about twenty yards in where a fallen pine tree lay rotting in the grass.

257

The tree had lain in the dirt for some time. It'd be there long after they were gone.

He wasn't happy she'd wandered off.

"When we go," he said. "We take it slow. And stay close to me. No more wandering off. Trouble starts, drop to the ground and get behind something if you can. And if you get the chance, hightail it the hell out of here and on down the mountain."

She locked eyes with him. "Joaquin was here, Jack. I feel his spirit."

He hoped she'd paid attention to what he told her. He didn't press and said, "Let's just pray he's on our side."

"He is," she said. Her eyes softened. "Leandro and I had a son. I want you to know that before we go any farther. He drowned in our swimming pool when he was two. He'd slipped out of the house without me knowing it. If I'd been there, I could have saved him. I wasn't. "

Jack didn't have to ask why she had shared the death of her son with him. He knew why. He also knew they were going to find Deacon alive.

"Thank you," he said.

Without any further talk, they followed the stream bank in. Jack glanced at the canyon him thinking the area must have changed a lot in the last hundred and fifty years. A bandit looking to hide a lot of gold bars fast would have sought out a large rock or tree for a marker he could find later. Murrieta would have done the same thing. Only the inscription in Theresa's family bible suggested that was not the case.

The morning sun shining through the window of my resting place points the way to the glory I've sought my whole life.

Murrieta was not talking about a rock or a tree.

About a hundred yards into the canyon, the basin widened by maybe half again as much. He continued walking, Theresa a step behind. Then it dawned on him the birds had stopped singing. The jays that had been welcome company were silent. Here, the brush and trees kept him from seeing much more than twenty-five yards in any direction except where the stream cut its path.

He stopped. Theresa did too.

A sudden chill brought goose bumps to his skin and set the hair on his neck and arms standing on end.

Was it the presence of bandit ghosts from a violent past?

Or was it human flesh and bone ready to kill?

A scene from a movie flashed inside his head, a favorite of his: Gary Cooper walking down the street in HIGH NOON. One man walking alone ready to face the danger awaiting him.

Alone.

"What is it?" she whispered.

He raised a finger to his lips. "*Shush.*"

His eyes remained focused on the brush and trees. He'd been shot at before and had no problem shooting back, and would this time. He'd even kill if need be.

Nothing moved.

In a quiet voice he said, "I think you should hunker down behind something and wait here. I'll check ahead and come back for you if it's safe."

"Forget it," she huffed. "I'm not about to hide in the rocks like a frightened child. I'm in this with you all the way. I thought I made that clear."

He stiffened. "You did, more than once. But I'm getting a really bad feeling."

"So you keep trying?"

"I told you before; I don't want to have to worry about you getting hurt."

"Then don't."

"Aren't you afraid you might get shot?"

"You're asking if I'm afraid of dying?"

"Yeah, okay, if you want to put it that way."

"Not since Leandro died in that plane crash."

"No way you're talking death wish?" At times, he'd wondered.

"Not at all. It's just that I've come to understand that you can't change fate. No matter how healthy or careful you are, if it's your time to go nothing you do will change it."

"Still. . . ."

"I told you not to worry about me. I'll take care of myself. You take care of you."

They'd already talked to long. And she'd made her point. He said, "Let's go."

CHAPTER 54

Deacon struggled to keep moving. Kyle had let him sleep when he collapsed in the dirt too exhausted to continue. But not for long enough. He'd been shaken awake and put back to work sealing bags of fat buds by lantern light hours before the sun showed itself. He didn't know how the twins kept going.

Crystal meth, he guessed. Or cocaine.

He'd pass. But he sure could use a gallon of coffee. And some food.

Hector and Kyle weren't eating either.

Another sign they were flying high.

And that gave him something else to think about. What if one of them keeled over before the work was done?

He straightened and arched the kinks from his back. Two o'clock tomorrow afternoon, he'd heard Marsh say.

Not a request, a threat.

And here they were. Time was running out.

A trickle of sweat streaked his forehead and settled in the corner of his eye. Not even enough salt left in his system for it to burn. He wiped the perspiration away with the back of his hand and glanced at his work. He was back to pulling plants. Hector was bagging the last few buckets of the buds. Kyle was helping him. They just might make the two o'clock deadline.

But that was not the part he looked forward to.

In a few days, he'd be allowed to walk out of there. Hector and Kyle promised. But first, he had to help them get the rest of the dope harvested. He was doing his part. Now he hoped they did theirs.

He glanced up at the inferno beating down on him and estimated that the time approached noon. Another two hours, perhaps a bit more before Marsh showed up.

He hoped, anyway.

No way did he want to be caught standing in the middle of the man's dope field. He'd be lying next to that poor dead jackass for sure.

They weren't making a table out of him.

Steeling himself, he went back to work tugging the fat stalks from the soil. The six-foot-tall plants did not want to come out easily. But even with the added labor, he managed to keep a steady pace.

For how long, though? His arms felt like they were coming off. And probably would if he didn't stop soon.

Two minutes later, he saw Kyle running down the slope towards him.

Energy fueled by pharmaceuticals. He shook his head.

He watched Kyle skid to a stop a few feet away. The boy was still wired. He could see the wild look in his eyes.

"Hector is finishing the last bags now," Kyle chattered. "But we're going to keep working."

"I'm spent," Deacon huffed. "I need to eat and get some rest."

"You just—" Kyle stopped talking and listened. A jay fluttered up from the trees down the canyon.

Deacon cocked his ear, but didn't hear anything.

"Hurry," Kyle said. He pointed his grimy finger toward the cabin.

Deacon lifted his concrete ball and chain and started up the hill. He glanced at Kyle asked, "What's going on? You hear something?"

"Maybe. Maybe not. But you're going back in your hole."

"What the hell, Kyle? We agreed."

"Me and Hector need to check what's going on. Can't do that if you're not in your hole."

Deacon peered over his shoulder at the canyon beyond the field of dope. Kyle had heard something. The jay had been frightened from his perch. Marsh would drive in on the back road. He wouldn't walk in from the forest below.

So who or what had Kyle heard?

CHAPTER 55

Jack crept forward taking it very slow now. He left the stream bank and moved to the cover of the trees. Theresa stuck close to him and moved noiselessly. He was almost glad she was there.

Almost.

He still wished she'd stayed back in the rocks and waited for him. He didn't want to see her shot—couldn't imagine what he'd do. But he couldn't let himself worry about that now. The people with the guns were up ahead somewhere. He could feel it in his gut.

Theresa touched his arm, yanking him from thought.

He froze, then slowly turned to look at her.

She motioned at the trees and pointed at her ear.

He knew what bothered her. The woods around them remained eerily quiet except for the burble of water in the creek. Even the mournful moan of wind in the tops of the pines had stopped. He caught a glimpse of birds sitting on limbs, their heads cocked. But none sang. It was as if nature herself watched and waited.

"You two outta turn around and head on out of here," a man said.

Jack jerked his head and faced in the direction of the voice. The guy was close. Too close. And he obviously had a clear view of them.

Jack ducked behind a cluster of saplings and pulled Theresa with him. Not much cover against flying bullets, but a fair amount of concealment. They crouched there a moment, listening.

Only the burble of the brook.

Peering through gaps in the foliage, he made a quick scan of the trees and brush ahead.

No one.

He could hear himself breathe. Full breaths only slightly quickened. Even his pounding heart slowed to near normal. The surprise of hearing the man call out to them in the eerie quiet was already wearing off.

Good.

He needed to be calm.

Keeping his eyes alert to any movement, he slid the .357 magnum Colt from its holster. He tightened his grip on the butt and held the gun close to him, ready, with the barrel pointed forward. He didn't need anyone to tell him this was one of the men holding his brother.

"Can't do that," Jack hollered back.

"Sure ya can," the man said. "Just stand up and walk on outta here."

"Not without my brother," Jack answered.

"I won't tell you again."

Before Jack could say more, a shot boomed and pellets shredded the saplings above them. A fraction of a second later, another shot and more pellets. Several passed through dangerously close to Theresa's head.

Too close.

Jack fired three times in the direction of the still unseen shooter. Almost at the same time, he dove onto Theresa to shield her with his body. No way would he let her get shot.

More pellets ripped through the brush.

"Don't . . ." she protested.

Jack didn't listen. He held Theresa down with his left hand and raised himself up to return fire.

"Drop it," a man said.

Jack didn't need to turn and look. There were two men.

And the second guy was standing right behind them.

He silently cursed. His concern for Theresa's safety had given the man the opportunity to get the drop on them.

He had little choice but to toss his gun in the dirt.

CHAPTER 56

Jack let his Colt drop onto the dirt and stood up. When he turned and faced the man behind him, he was glad he had done what he was told. Double-barreled shotguns did that to him.

Especially when the barrels are cut short and pointed at his gut.

Theresa hurried to her feet and stood next to Jack.

He eased a step to the side adding another foot between them. A sawed-off at close range was deadly. He didn't want the spread of buckshot to get them both if the guy decided to pull the trigger. He wouldn't even have to aim.

"I only came for my brother," Jack said, holding his hands out from his sides so as to not make the young man holding the shotgun nervous. "Whatever else is going on up here is none of my concern."

"Hector," the man yelled. "You hear that? Says he come for his brother."

"Bring 'em on up," Hector hollered back. "We can have us a regular family get-together."

"You heard him." The man prodded them with a jab of the barrels. "We got no time to play games with you so get moving."

Jack nodded at Theresa and began plodding up the canyon. "Look, mister. I just—"

"Kyle," the man cut in. "Hector up there's my brother."

Jesus, Jack thought.

The dumbshit told me their names.

266

Speaking over his shoulder at the man as they walked he said, "Sure, Kyle. Understand we're not here to make trouble. Like I told you, we only want my brother. His name's Deacon."

"Man back at the cabin named Deacon. Course he's not really at the cabin. He's in his hole."

"That's him." Jack couldn't contain his excitement. He turned to Kyle and said, "Tell me he's alright."

Kyle stopped where they had been standing a half minute before. Jack watched him bend down and pick up the Colt.

"He's all right," Kyle said. "We put him in this deep hole at night and times when we can't keep an eye on him. Don't hurt him none, though."

"Screw that," Jack said.

Kyle eyed the revolver. "Mighty pretty gun you brought for not wantin' to cause no trouble."

"Honest," Theresa said. "Let Deacon go and the three of us will walk out of here as though nothing happened."

"Well now, that would be up to my brother there." He pointed the shotgun. "He makes the decisions. Can't say he'll agree to that, though."

Jack turned and saw Hector step from the brush. Another carrot-top. He gave both of them a quick look. Twins at that. Right down to the sawed-off double-barreled 12-gauge shotguns they carried.

"Times wastin'," Hector called out. "Stop jacking your jaw and get a move on."

"Hector says move your ass." Kyle jammed the revolver under his belt and took a firm grip on his shotgun. "Now get going."

Jack fell in line ten feet behind Hector. He glanced over his shoulder at Theresa. She walked a step behind him. Behind her, Kyle walked with his sawed-off aimed and ready.

Jack clenched his jaw.

No one liked being paraded at gunpoint. Him least of all.

He caught a thin smile from Theresa, and nodded. If having a scattergun pointed at her back was more than she could handle, she didn't show it.

After a couple of minutes of walking, he saw the brush and trees in front of them open up. But when he stepped into the clearing, he discovered he wasn't looking at a broad field of lush green grass and brightly-colored wildflowers. He gazed at a field of marijuana.

Marsh's dope for sure.

Hector led them over to the stream, along its bank, and past the six-foot-tall plants. Jack could only guess how many grew there, a thousand, maybe more. When they marched past another field almost as large, he noticed nearly half that field had been cut and the plants hauled away. But it wasn't until he saw the third field with every stock of dope harvested, that he realized just how big the dope growing operation was.

The redheads had been busy.

From there he could also see a shack that looked like it was barely standing. In front of the hovel, where the yard and white picket fence would have been, sat a table and several stacks of plastic storage bins. And not far away, lay pile after pile of tattered marijuana stocks wilting in the sun.

Probably the cabin Kyle mentioned.

He anxiously scanned the area for Deacon.

Nowhere in sight.

He peered over his shoulder at Kyle and hollered, "You told me my brother was here. Now where is he?"

Jack saw Kyle's fat lips curl and separate into an Alfred E. Newman grin. Different time, different circumstances, he might have found the dumb look amusing.

Not now.

"You jerking me off, or what?" he said.

"I told you, he's in his hole." Kyle chuckled as if it was all some sort of joke.

"Yeah, you mentioned a hole. What hole?" Jack wasn't smiling.

Kyle's chuckle turned to a belly laugh. He stifled a snort and said, "You'll find out in a minute."

CHAPTER 57

Deacon scurried to his feet in the bottom of the pit and craned his neck to listen. Jack's voice, he was sure he'd heard his brother talking. And Kyle's stupid laugh. They were a ways off, though; maybe as far away as the marijuana field.

Was that what Hector and Kyle went to investigate?

Had Jack gotten there?

Did he hike into the valley, and was he being held at gunpoint by those two redheads?

He didn't want to think Jack had been taken captive by them but that was the only explanation. Hector and Kyle would not just let him step into the middle of their dope operation without holding a gun on him.

Unless . . .

That had to be it. Jack got the drop on them first.

"Jack, you there?" he called out. "Jack, in here."

He waited. No answer.

He wedged the toe of his shoe in a gouge in the rock wall and raised himself up. He clawed to reach the rim of the pit and fell back.

"Jack," he yelled as loud as he could. "I'm down here." And again, he clawed and groped, desperate to reach the rim of the pit. And again the toe of his shoe lost its grip on the rock and he slid to the bottom of the hole.

He stood, catching his breath, and listened.

When he didn't hear Jack holler back to him, he slumped against the wall of the pit, slid onto his ass, and closed his eyes. It struck him that he might be finally going crazy. That exhaustion had taken its toll and clouded his mind. But then he couldn't believe that was the case. Not now.

It must have been wishful thinking.

He could accept that.

Jack had been on his mind a lot.

We're brothers. Brothers stick together.

That might not have been Jack he heard talking, or anyone else. But Jack was out there searching. He knew that. Jack would never abandon him.

And he'd give his life to save Jack.

* * * *

Jack marched up the hill. Deacon's whereabouts was all he could think about. Deacon was right there, someplace. In a hole, Kyle had said.

A stinking hole!

But was he alive?

Nothing was funny about throwing someone in a hole. Yet Kyle had laughed when he said that's what they had done. Jack wanted to strangle the worthless shithead. He wanted to hammer his fists into the dimwit and his brother Hector, break their damned necks.

He'd see them both in hell for what they had done to Deacon.

"Do you see him? I don't see him anywhere?" He heard Theresa say from a few feet behind.

He pivoted and glared at Kyle. "All right dammit, where in hell is this hole you're talking about? Where's Deacon?"

"Right over there." He pointed the scattergun. "And that's where you're headed."

Jack didn't wait to be lead there. He took off at a trot, and they let him go. When he reached the pit, he slowed to a stop and peered over the edge.

Jesus.

"Deacon," he hollered down.

Tattered, filthy, and ten pounds lighter than he was when Jack last saw him, Deacon looked half dead.

But he was alive!

He watched Deacon slowly look up at him. Saw his eyes widen.

"Jack." Deacon's voice was scratchy and horse.

Jack watched him struggle to his feet. It ripped at his gut. Deacon had held on, but barely by the looks of him. All he could do was thank God for sending a guardian angel to look after his little brother, and kick himself in the ass for not finding him that first day on the mountain.

Thrown into a fucking hole.

Thought sickened him. He extended his hand even though there was no way he could reach far enough to help him up.

"You all right?" he said.

"Tired," Deacon sighed. "Sure am glad you're here."

Jack smiled. "Took some time, but I made it."

"One big happy family," Hector said from behind Jack. "Seems the hole's filling up."

Jack turned and glanced from one twin to the other. He'd found Deacon; always believed he would. But he hadn't figured on ending up in a rock pit with him. Theresa, too. Now he just had to figure out how the three of them were going to get away from there.

"You're not going to throw us in that hole?' Theresa directed her question at Hector.

"Not going to leave you standing out here," Hector said. "Are we Kyle?"

"Sure ain't," Kyle agreed. "You'd run off for sure. And we can't let you do that, can we Hector?"

"Nope, can't do that."

"Is there some other way we can do this, boys?" Jack asked. Talk might not get it done, but it kept them out of that pit.

Hector grinned and said, "Not unless you have a million dollars stuffed in your pocket."

"Not likely," Jack huffed. "Let's be realistic."

Hector pointed the barrels of his shotgun in the direction of the storage bins stacked in front of the cabin. Then he swept the muzzles toward the field of marijuana.

"You want real," he said. "That dope you see is our last big score. We intend to buy us a tomato farm. We let you go now and you'd spoil everything."

"Is a hundred acres of tomatoes good enough?" Theresa asked. "I know of a farm for sale. Let us go and I'll buy it for you."

Hector and Kyle looked at each other.

"A hundred acres, boys" Jack said. "Just think about it."

Hector turned his gaze on Theresa. "You're—"

The high RPM roar of a big-block V-8 motor stopped Hector in mid sentence. The four of them stared in the direction of the top of the hill.

CHAPTER 58

Jack took a step toward Hector, paused, and listened to the drone of the engine grow louder. A back road in. He hadn't figured on that. But it made sense, given the cabin and dope growing operation.

From the low-growl of gears and raw horsepower, he knew a truck headed in their direction. There was no reason for him to wonder, he knew who was behind the wheel. Their only chance to come out of the situation alive was for him to get close enough to Hector to get his hands on that scattergun.

He steeled himself to take another step and froze. Kyle held him there with a hard gaze and a point of his sawed-off.

Shit.

Jack didn't dare make a move closer.

From just a few feet away, the buckshot from that scattergun would cut him in half.

Movement drew his gaze to the top of the hill as the red F-350 pickup roared into view over the rise and skidded to a stop.

He drew in a breath and held it.

He heard Theresa gasp, turned his head, and saw her glance in his direction. Her wide-eyed expression told him what she was thinking. He exhaled. Exactly what they both feared.

He focused his gaze on the truck, his arms at his side, hands tightened into fists.

The driver's door popped open and Marsh climbed out,

slamming the door behind him as he stepped around it. His nephew Roy slid from the passenger's side with the deadly fluid grace of a cobra.

It figured—Jack thought—they would be together.

Neither man appeared to be in a hurry as they walked. Jack guessed that was because of the two sawed-off shotguns pointed at him.

He studied both men.

Marsh was trouble enough by himself. Having that back-stabber with him turned the tables even more. And that wasn't counting Hector and Kyle with their double-barrels.

Jack's blood froze. No way were they going to get out of this alive.

Not now.

With Hector and Kyle, they stood a chance. Marsh and his piece-of-shit nephew were a different story.

But he would go down fighting. They could count on that.

"Well Jackie Boy," Marsh said with a smug grin. "Couldn't stay away, could you?"

"Came for my brother," Jack said. He straightened. "And nothing you, that chicken-shit back-stabbing nephew of yours, or that whore Sheriff did was going to stop me."

"Jackie Boy, do you see your brother anywhere?" Marsh's smug expression hardened. "All you did was stick your nose into something that was none of your business."

"Wrong, asshole." Jack pointed at the pit. "My brother's down there. In that stinking hole where your two friends here put him."

Roy stepped to the edge and peered down at Deacon. "Someone's in here alright." He glanced at Marsh and flicked open his switchblade.

The blade appeared so quickly, Jack hadn't seen him pull the thing.

He raised his fists, ready.

The knife-happy sonofabitch.

Marsh shot a hot glare at Hector and Kyle.

"How long?" he asked.

The twins looked at each other, but didn't answer.

"I asked how long?" he said again, his voice loud with irritation.

"He weren't going nowhere," Kyle finally said.

Jack saw the muscles in Marsh's neck bulge. The man was clearly losing control.

"Let me cut 'em," Roy said.

Marsh pointed at Jack. His eyes narrowed. "Him first."

Roy took a step toward Jack.

Jack tensed, prepared to dodge the blade.

At that exact moment, a rock the size of a baseball flew from inside the pit and hit Roy in the side of the head.

"To hell with you," Jack heard Deacon say.

Roy's legs sagged.

Jack forgot about the shotguns. He hit Marsh's nephew with a body-block that put Roy over the edge of the pit. Regaining his feet, he kicked hard at the side of Marsh's knee.

Marsh staggered.

Jack knew at once the kick had been too high to put the big man down. He scrambled to add a few feet between them, but a huge right hand clipped his temple just enough to make him see stars.

He shook his head and brought his arms up to block the next blow. Marsh smiled as though he planned to enjoy himself.

Cat and mouse.

Jack could read Marsh's mind.

The big man taunted him with a wave of his fingers.

Jack's head cleared.

He blinked to clear his vision. He was ready to give back what he got and more.

To his right, Hector and Kyle watched, gun barrels lowered. They seemed content to be looking on. Theresa was standing there, too. Watching.

* * * *

Deacon jumped back a step just in time to get out of the way. Roy hit the stone floor on his left side, a sack-of-flour-thump of flesh and bone against solid rock. To Deacon's amazement, the man managed to hold onto the knife.

275

And the guy wasn't out.

The man's right hand came up.

The shiny blade slashed the air and sliced Deacon's thigh.

Deacon's eyes widened with surprise, then narrowed with anger.

The skinny ass wipe had cut him.

He pressed his palm over the wound. Blood seeped through his fingers. The shithead wouldn't do it again.

With his hand pressed to his leg, Deacon took a step back and watched knife-man roll onto his butt and clutch his left arm; his left wrist hung at an odd angle. His left leg didn't appear to work, either.

"I'm going to gut you," the man waving the knife said. "And piss on your intestines."

Deacon could see the guy's left side had been ruined in the fall. He allowed himself a calming breath, but stayed ready. Even busted up, the asshole talked shit. And he'd had enough left in him to use the knife.

Even crippled, he wasn't to be underestimated.

Their gazes met and held. The feral look in the killer's black eyes suggested drugs. Cocaine—Deacon figured—or methamphetamine. Probably where Hector and Kyle got theirs.

Asshole.

"Piss on yourself," Deacon said.

He watched the animal hold the knife in front of him and peer lovingly at it. And cringed in disgust when he saw the crazy fuck lick the blood from the flat sides of the blade.

"I'm going to enjoy cutting you," the man swore as he brought the blade down from his tongue.

You sick sonofabitch, Deacon thought.

Enough of this shit.

Injured or not, the jerk off wasn't getting a second chance to cut him.

He cocked his leg and kicked the asshole solidly in the chin.

He felt as much as he saw the man's head snap back amid a spray of blood and broken teeth. He heard the spine crack, watched the body fall back in a slack heap, saw the head flop grotesquely to the side. At once, he knew he'd broken the weasel's neck.

Dead.

He said, "Not today, fucker."

CHAPTER 59

Jack backed away from the granite shaft, his muscles taught, his fists balled hard. He wanted room to move when the big man came at him.

Marsh had his arms up like a great huge bear.

And that was exactly how Jack saw him.

Jack's first thought was where best to hit the man. Marsh was a giant mass of rock-hard flesh and bone. His next thought was that the Neanderthal belonged in a cage, or dead.

"I'm going to enjoy breaking you," Marsh snarled.

"What makes you think you're going to get the chance," Jack said. He kept his fists up, ready.

The sharp *thwack* of a small caliber gun stopped them both.

Jack glanced at Theresa and the small chrome semi-automatic pistol in her hand. She held the gun steady. He turned his gaze on Marsh.

In obvious shock that he'd been shot, Marsh peered at the bloody tear in the shirtsleeve covering his right bicep. Jack could see it was little more than a flesh wound. But the bullet did get his attention.

"Shoot 'em," Marsh growled at Hector and Kyle.

Jack turned his head and saw the twins take a couple of steps back. The barrels of their shotguns remained pointed at the ground. Neither of them appeared eager to shoot anyone.

278

Another sharp crack from the handgun brought all their gazes to bear on Theresa.

She kept the gun in front of her, raised and pointed.

Jack glanced back and forth at her and the big man.

"You can't hit shit," Marsh said. "I should have put you in your place months ago."

"You should have tried," Theresa said.

She pulled the trigger twice more.

One of the bullets grazed Marsh's ear. Jack saw him furrow his brow in the direction of the twins. They made no move to help.

Theresa kept the gun pointed at Marsh.

Marsh glanced toward his truck. Hector and Kyle stood in the way.

He glanced at Jack, then the gun.

He peered into the pit.

Jack could see the wheels turning inside Marsh's head. Too much was against him.

"I'm not done with you," he swore to Theresa. He glanced at Jack, Kyle, and Hector. "Any of you."

Before anyone could stop him, Marsh bounded off in the direction of the north slope of the canyon.

Jack saw Theresa lower her gun. She had tears in her eyes.

She said, "The pig tried to rape me."

Now Jack understood. He looked at Marsh and saw him pound up and over the side of the canyon and disappear into the brush and trees. He was surprised at how fast the big man moved.

He stepped to the pit and glanced at Deacon.

"I'm fine," Deacon said. "Get the asshole."

Jack looked at Hector and Kyle. Hector tossed him his shotgun and said, "He's all yours. Me and Kyle's out of here."

Jack caught the sawed-off by the barrels and shifted his grip to the stock.

Kyle broke open his scattergun, removed the two shells, and tossed them one at a time to Jack.

Jack plucked the extra ammunition out of the air and shoved them into the front pocket of his jeans.

He hadn't forgotten about Theresa.

She stepped into view and nodded.

No further urging was needed. He took off in a dead run after Marsh.

He was sure he could catch him.

Jack topped the rise no more than a minute behind the big man. He stopped and looked and listened. Marsh was nowhere in sight. Most likely, he had dodged right or left before disappearing from view in the brush and trees. An obvious abrupt change in direction meant to cause confusion.

In the dirt, a pointed-toe boot print gouged deep into the bare soil showed the way. He'd veered left, downhill through the forest. Possibly, with plans to circle back.

Then Jack heard him crashing through undergrowth, moving away.

The next hundred yards took Jack through a thicket of Manzanita a rabbit would have trouble negotiating. But broken branches and shreds of cloth told Jack that's the direction Marsh had gone.

Twenty-five yards farther in, the brush opened onto a small clearing. On the far side and to his left grew a wall of Manzanita more dense than the thicket he just busted through. To his right a pine tree had fallen and all but rotted away. It held the way open to the north.

Jack eyeballed what remained of the log. He could see scuffmarks in the pulpy remains suggesting Marsh had walked the length of it.

That was all Jack needed to see. He took off at a fast walk. At the other end of the fallen tree, Marsh's boot tracks led north. It was open forest here and the length of his stride suggested he was moving fast.

Jack remained confident he could run the big man down. But he had to keep in mind Marsh was probably armed—a handgun he'd kept hidden.

He followed the boot impressions, moving fast and cautious at the same time. The big man was not making it easy.

And Jack didn't expect him to.

He continued after him.

The sun was low on the horizon when Jack finally heard Marsh's labored breathing. He too was sucking wind.

The man was an animal, but Jack had to give him credit for keeping up the pace he'd set hours before. Throughout the day, he'd followed game trail after game trail—a wise man always holds to paths he finds in the mountains. And always he worked his way in a northerly direction—higher into the hills—and always far enough ahead to remain hidden from view.

But the big man had finally slowed.

The chase had gone on for so long, it took a moment for Jack to realize he'd caught up with him. But it only took a second for Jack to know there were a lot of places for Marsh to hide and wait, to double back without being seen.

The trail led into a small clearing. In the middle of the open ground lay the strewn logs and stone foundation of what had once been a log cabin. The east wall was virtually intact. A square hole in the center of the stacked logs—grayed and cracked from age—held the broken remnants of a pane of glass. Beyond the window, rose the high peaks of the Sierras. A rock fireplace stood where the north wall would have been.

For a moment, he was taken aback by the scene.

Whose cabin was this?

Who had built it so long ago?

Without warning, a voice boomed behind him, a voice he hadn't wanted to hear.

"It's just you and me now, Jackie Boy," Marsh said.

He heard the hammer being cocked back on a pistol and knew Marsh meant to see him dead. He sure wasn't there to talk.

And Jack did not intend to stand still and discuss the weather.

He tightened his grip on the stock of scattergun, slid his index finger onto the triggers, turned, and cut loose with both barrels.

Marsh was ready to kill, but his aim was off. Jack felt the bullet from the big man's gun graze his ribs even before he pulled both triggers. The sawed-off did its work. The double load of buckshot from the short-barreled 12-gauge took the big man right in the middle, folded him over, picked him up, and slammed him onto his back.

Jack broke open the shotgun, plucked out the empty shells, shoved in the two extras from his pocket, and snapped the breech closed.

But it wasn't necessary.

Marsh was clearly dead.

Jack gripped his left side where the pain from the wound had begun to settle in. He could feel where the bullet had broken a rib, and where it had entered and exited his skin. He was lucky to be alive.

And he was lucky Marsh wasn't. He stepped to the body, peered down at the two-inch barreled .38 still clutched in Marsh's right hand, and the death mask of the man who wanted him dead.

Money and power.

The thought made Jack's stomach churn.

He glanced at the deep shadows in the trees around him and gazed to the west. The sun had died too. Darkness was coming quick to the mountain. It would be a long, dark, cold night.

CHAPTER 60

Jack propped himself up on his right elbow and shivered against the morning chill. He reached to his pile of wood, tossed a couple of sticks onto the dying embers aglow in the tumbled-down fireplace, turned, and stared at the golden rays streaming through the window in the east wall. The sun was only just now rising above the high peaks of the Sierras and it shined through the opening like a beacon onto the stone floor.

He could picture a grizzled miner doing this same thing. Only the man would have had a bed. And a cup of coffee. And some beans.

All at once, Jack's mind clicked.

Gripping his injured side, he rolled onto his butt, sat there, and studied the granite floor where the sun shining through the small window lit up a flattened rock maybe eighteen inches square. The entire floor was a masterwork of stones of different sizes and shapes fitted tightly together. The sun's rays hit solidly on that one rock.

The morning sun shining through the window of my resting place points the way to the glory I've sought my whole life.

Joaquin Murrieta's last words.

For the moment, Jack forgot about the wound in his side and pawed through the remaining sticks of firewood. Spying a shard of pine that looked strong enough to do the job, he grabbed it up, crawled on his hands and knees to that rock, and went to work prying up the chunk of granite.

The heavy stone did not give way easily. He broke that stick and had to find a replacement. After another five minutes of gouging and prying, he managed to raise the stone enough so that he could get his hands under the edges and lift the rock from its place in the floor.

A spasm of pain took his breath away. He sat a moment holding his side and stared at the dirt where the stone had lain. It looked and felt right; a voice in his head told him this was the spot. Theresa should be there with him to share the moment.

But then he was glad it had only been him and Elliot Marsh alone on that trail.

Working with his hands and a section of the broken stick, he began to scratch and dig and scoop away the packed earth. Ten inches down his fingers scraped on something hard.

Another stone.

He pawed the dirt away and found the pale, yellowed bone of a human skull, its empty eye sockets staring lifelessly back at him. Murrieta died in old Mexico. There was only one person he could think of that could be buried here.

Snake-Eye Carlos Sanchez.

Jack didn't like the thought of desecrating a person's final resting place. But the man buried here *was* a murderous bandit. He'd killed people for money and horses.

Did he truly deserve the respect due a more saintly person?

It took Jack another fifteen minutes of carful digging around and between bones and rotted cloth and leather to find what so many people had sought. He could hardly contain his excitement as he brushed the dirt away. But he took a deep breath and spent several long seconds just looking at the brick of yellow metal. Then he slowly lifted the two-pound gold bar from the dirt and cradled it in his hand.

Good and bad men had died for this gold.

Murrieta gold.

He nervously glanced around for those unseen eyes. Maybe their spirits did wander these mountains. He'd felt a presence. So had Theresa.

Perhaps they watched even now.

Or maybe it was just the lonely, lonely wind blowing mournfully in the tall pines.

He slowly worked his way to his feet and tested his legs. Then he tested his ability to walk. It only took a few steps back and forth for him to know it was going to be a long painful hike out of the mountains.

He turned a hardened gaze on Marsh's body where it lay at the edge of the woods. A hike the big man wouldn't be making. Not on his own, anyway. Like Snake-Eye Carlos Sanchez, he would lie in the dirt and wait to be carried away from this place.

Jack brought his gaze back to the hole and peered in at the bandit's bones. He focused on the skull and found it impossible to not stare into the empty eye sockets staring back at him. For a moment, he wondered how the killer looked in life. He recalled Al's description of the bandit and pictured several he'd seen in old westerns.

Had Snake-Eye Carlos Sanchez looked anything like them?

Probably, he thought. But then after a hundred and fifty years of lying buried in the ground we all look the same. It's what a person does in life that sets them apart.

Snake-Eye Carlos Sanchez was a thief and a killer. So was Marsh. They were the same . . . in life, and in death.

Jack hefted the gold bar in his hand. It would be hard enough to hike out of there with a broken rib and a hole in his side. There was no way he could lug three hundred pounds of gold on his back.

Every ounce was buried there, he was sure. Under the bones of Murrieta's right-hand man.

He lowered himself onto his knees, returned the dirt to the hole, and reset the stones. Snake-Eye Carlos Sanchez and the gold would be safe until the bandit's remains and those beautiful heavy yellow bars were properly unearthed by the appropriate authorities.

Marsh would lie where he had fallen.

Jack stood and scoffed at the man's body. Buzzard and coyote bait for all he cared.

He picked up the one gold bar grabbed the sawed-off, took one more glance around, and stepped off the foundation and into the clearing.

From overhead came the familiar *wop, wop, wop* of helicopter's rotor blades beating the air. The sound drew his gaze skyward. The chopper hovered a couple hundred feet above him, then descended.

He watched it come down.

The green and white Notar 520 settled onto its skids in the open ground next to the broken-down cabin. A second later the co-pilot's door popped open and a uniformed state narcotics officer climbed out.

Jack dropped the shotgun to the ground and stood with his hands away from his sides. Marsh had fired first. And that's the story he would tell. He didn't feel he had anything to worry about as long as Sheriff Doug Bell wasn't involved.

And Bell would be.

These were state cops.

He stood still, waiting to be ordered to lie on the ground. Instead, he saw Robert climb out of the rear door of the chopper and flash him a thumbs-up signal.

Jack smiled.

His friend had come to help after all. And he'd brought the cavalry.

CHAPTER 61

At seven thirty the next morning, Jack lay wide awake in a hospital bed—a small private room, with a narrow window overlooking the tarred roof of the adjoining wing. For the past hour, he'd watched the sky beyond his window brighten along with his mood. None of what happened soured his disposition, not even killing Marsh.

A clear-cut case of self defense.

He'd given his statement to the BNE officer onboard the chopper during the flight to the ER in Sacramento. There would be more questions—there always were. For now, state authorities had the information they needed.

Zero regrets.

Except that it had taken him four days to find and rescue Deacon. And that he had to spend a few days in the hospital recovering from surgery.

Lucky, that's what the doctor called him.

He agreed.

Another inch to the right and the .38 caliber slug would have ripped through bowel and possibly a kidney. He most likely would not have survived the night. And he certainly wouldn't have found the gold and solved the enigma behind the death of Joaquin Murrieta and Snake-Eye Carlos Sanchez.

He hadn't stopped thinking about that.

Counting his lucky stars, it seemed, was becoming a habit.

"How are you feeling?" Robert asked from the doorway.

Jack pulled aside his gown, exposing his heavily bandaged left side. Then he raised his left arm so that Robert could see the antibiotic drip flowing into an IV catheter inserted in a vein in his wrist.

He said, "Like I've been stomped on and kicked."

Robert chuckled and stepped into the room.

"You've been through worse," he said

"So."

"So BNE is up on that mountain right now putting the case together. They're bringing in a forensic archeologist to excavate the grave under the floor of that shack."

"The gold?"

"That's up to the court."

"And Deacon?"

"You know he broke that guy's neck?"

"Good. The punk-ass backstabber had it coming."

"He cut Deacon."

"But Deacon's all right?"

"Self defense, same as you," Robert said.

"No problem, then?"

"None. In fact he's been chomping at the bit to see you."

"He's here?"

"In a room two doors down."

"For observation?"

"Malnutrition and dehydration. Not to mention a dozen or so stitches. He has more tubes in him than you do."

"Lucky me. How goes it with Theresa?"

"That's quite a lady you hooked up with."

Jack furrowed his brow. "I'm talking about the shooting. That was her bullet in Marsh's shoulder. And you know how the law can be at times."

"No charges have been filed. And I really doubt there will be. Seems she has a good attorney."

"Someone we know?"

"I made a suggestion. She told me not to worry."

"Did I hear my name," Theresa asked from the doorway.

"Rooms filling up," Robert said. "I'll grab a cup of crappy cafeteria coffee and let you two talk by yourselves a few."

She smiled at Robert as he steeped past her on his way out of the room, and took a seat in the chair next to the bed.

"It's good to see you in one piece," she said. "Well, mostly in one piece. I was worried."

"You heard I found the gold? My guess is it's all there, every last bar."

"And Snake-Eye Carlos Sanchez, it appears."

"His bones, anyway."

"So Captain Harry Love lied."

"And Governor John Bigler. Or at the very least they got it wrong."

"Aren't you going to ask about Marsh or his nephew?"

Jack shook his head. "Marsh is dead. And I couldn't care less about his nephew. I heard he's dead too. But I am curious about Hector and Kyle."

She chuckled and said, "Remember those plastic storage containers of dope stacked by that table, and that U-haul trailer? Well, they threw those containers in the back of Marsh's truck, hooked up that U-haul, and drove out of there. Took them all of five minutes."

"A big score."

She smiled. "I think they'll have that tomato farm after all."

"It wouldn't surprise me. Probably read about it in the paper." He reached for her hand and squeezed her fingers. "I want to thank you for everything you did out there."

She peered pensively out the window. "I didn't even realize I'd fired the gun until the second shot."

Jack grinned. "And the third and the forth and the fifth."

She returned his smile. "Got his attention, didn't I?"

"Saved our lives."

"Mine and Deacon's, maybe. You took off after Marsh, remember? He easily could've killed you." Once again, she turned her gaze to the window. "I worried he had."

He thought he saw her blink back a tear. "Thanks for looking after my little brother for me."

She arched a manicured brow, questioningly. "Looking after him?"

"You got him out of that hole, didn't you?"

"He's not so little, you know."

"Is to me."

A broad grin creased her face. "Has he told you yet?"

"Told me what?"

"That I hit the mother lode," Deacon said from the doorway.

He stepped into the room dragging his IV pole along with him. "In that pit," he continued. "Struck a rich vein when I started chipping foot holds in the rock so that I could climb out of there."

"Glory be," Jack cheered.

"I think glory hole is the term," Deacon corrected.

"So now you're a miner," Jack said. "You going to be able to keep all that wonderful gold?"

"According to Robert and his attorney, I will. It's all US Forest Service land up there, and with no claim on record, all I have to do is file one, which—with the help of Robert's attorney—is being done."

Deacon tossed Jack a nugget the size of a Robin's egg and said, "Smuggled that sucker in here for luck."

Jack hefted the nugget in his palm. "Big sucker."

"There's bigger locked in a safety deposit box at my bank, one really huge one. But you found the gold I was looking for."

"In a way, you did," Jack said. "If you hadn't gone looking for those gold bars in the first place, they'd still be buried up there, along with Snake-Eye Carlos Sanchez."

"Speaking of those gold bars," Theresa said to Jack. "What are your plans?"

"Robert says it's up to the courts."

"And if they release them to you?"

"We're partners," he told her. "Nothing's changed."

Theresa's expression sobered. "You know what that means?"

Jack held her in his gaze. "I'm not sure we can even find out for certain who all those gold bars belong too."

"Perhaps I can help with that," Robert said. He stepped into the room with his cup of coffee in hand.

Jack said, "You were holding out on me."

"Only that I called in a few IOU's in an effort to answer that very question. According to Wells Fargo historical archives, the company suffered three hundred and thirteen stagecoach holdups during the 1860's, with losses totaling $415,000. Black Bart, along with Rattlesnake Dick, got credited for the biggest payoff of $80,000 in a single holdup. But there was no record of a stagecoach robbery north of Angels Camp in 1862. How exact Wells Fargo's records are, I don't know. There was a fire in their San Francisco office around that time. It's quite possible the documentation was lost."

"What about the smelter's mark?" Jack asked. "The assay office surely had records of the gold shipment."

"Winters and Clark," Robert pointed out. "They operated from 1850 to 1863. It seems fires were a problem in the mining towns in those days."

Jack shook his head. "You're saying that company's records went up in smoke as well?"

"A few survived the blaze. But they're a dead end."

"What you're saying," Theresa said, "is there's no record of who the gold belonged to?"

"The bottom line is you own it now," Robert pointed out. "Or I should say Jack does since he found it."

Jack smiled at Theresa. "Hers as much as mine."

Robert nodded in understanding. "There'll be legal expenses of course . . . and a ton of taxes if and when the court releases the gold. It'll take time to pull everything together, but I think it's safe for me to say you're both going to be very rich."

"I'm already rich," Theresa scoffed.

"A person can never have too much money," Jack shot back. "It's what they do with their dough that counts."

"And just what is it you plan to do with yours?" she asked.

Jack grinned. "I prefer not to count my chickens until they've hatched."

"Right." She gave him a good long look and asked, "So where do we go from here?"

"*Ho`oponopono*," Jack told her.

She cocked her head. "What's that?"

"The name of my boat, remember? *Pono*, it's Hawaiian.

Ho`oponopono—correctness—making things right."

"Of course." She nibbled the nail of her index finger a moment and then smiled. "And I believe you mentioned something about a cruise around the islands."

EPILOGUE

Maui, Hawaii
Six Months Later

Dressed in faded swim trunks, Jack stood square-footed on the grass in front of the guest cottage at the rear of Robert's estate on Kaneohe Bay. Arms extended above his head, he arched his back from side to side and silently called out each repetition. One, two, three—at ten, he stopped counting and lowered his arms in front of him chest-high. Again, he mentally counted off the reps as he twisted his body at the waist—first to the right, then to the left. He repeated the stretching exercise until he counted ten. His last set. Sweat dripped from his forehead and soaked the hair on his chest and legs.

From now on, he'd stick to mornings.

He scooped a towel off the grass next to him and quickly wiped the sweat from his face, neck, arms, and chest. His gaze settled on the gunshot wound navel-high on his left side. He gingerly fingered the nickel-sized pink pockmark where the .38 caliber hollow-point bullet entered. Lucky, that's what the doctor had called him. Another inch farther to the right and he most likely would not have survived the night.

He hadn't stopped thinking about that.

Counting his lucky stars, he feared, was becoming a habit. The wound had healed without complications. No pain. No lasting effects. Just the scar; and a matching star-shaped purplish scar the size of a fifty-cent piece on his back where the mushroomed slug exited. Two freshly healed wounds that stood out in stark contrast against his deeply tanned hide.

He draped the towel around his neck and walked toward the covered lanai where Theresa and Robert lounged in the shade.

The sight of her sprawled on the padded chaise made him smile.

"You could have joined me," he said.

"What?" she scoffed. "And spoil the glow from this wonderful Mai tai."

"You take this vacation stuff seriously," he said. "And did I tell you that swimsuit looks wonderful on you?"

"What can I say, you have great taste." She threw her legs over the side of the chaise, rose to her feet, poured him a drink, garnished it with an orange slice and a tiny umbrella, and handed it to him. "And since we're talking vacation, yours started a couple hours ago when you picked me up at the airport."

He took his drink, raised it, and said, "To sunshine and salt water."

"And don't forget you're meeting me in Monterey in August for Car Week and the Pebble Beach *Tour d'Elegance.*"

He laughed. "Seeing your Cobra up close was enough for me. I'm not sure I'll be able to handle being around so many classic automobiles in one place at one time."

"Just try not to drool," she said.

Again, he lifted his glass.

"Here's a human-interest article you two might like," Robert said looking up from the newspaper spread open in front of him.

Jack nodded at the periodical. "The *San Francisco Chronicle*— really? I thought you were strictly a Wall Street Journal man."

"Theresa brought it." Robert folded the pages back and flattened them. "And it's good to broaden one's horizons."

"I picked it up at the airport," Theresa offered.

"So what's this article he's talking about?" Jack asked.

"Beats me," she said. "I didn't get past the front page."

"Please," Robert said. He read:

Hector and Kyle Stamper ended a San Joaquin Valley family legacy today when they closed escrow on the hundred-twenty-year-old Modesto tomato farm previously owned by Alvin Henderson. Henderson—third generation to George Harris Henderson—sold the five hundred acre family farm citing poor health and increasing financial problems as the reason for the sale. The Stamper brothers remain confident they can turn around the farm's failing crops and become a major tomato producer in the valley.

"There's a picture as well." Robert held the paper so Theresa and Jack could see the article.

"I'll be damned," Jack said.

He exchanged glances with Theresa and they both laughed.

"Those goofy shits did it," he said. "They got their farm."

ABOUT THE AUTHOR

William Nikkel is the author of four *Jack Ferrell* novels and a steampunk, zombie western featuring his latest hero Max Traver. A former homicide detective and S.W.A.T. team member for the Kern County Sheriff's Department in Bakersfield, California, William is an amateur scuba enthusiast, gold prospector, and artist who can be found just about anywhere. He and his wife Karen divide their time between California and Maui, Hawaii.

Made in the USA
Columbia, SC
23 May 2018